by Charlotte Keppel in Piatkus Books:

Villains

The Ghos
Fonten

Also

The

The Ghosts of Fontenoy

Charlotte Keppel

PIATKUS

First published in Great Britain in 1981 by Judy Piatkus (Publishers) Limited of Loughton, Essex

ISBN 0 86188 107 9

Photoset, printed and bound
in Great Britain by
REDWOOD BURN LIMITED
Trowbridge & Esher

Prologue

1750

When Miss Juliet Smith married Sir Richard Vierville in St Matthew's Church, Matley Bishop, the entire town was bewildered and astonished. Apart from the fact that the bride was seventeen and the groom forty, it was in every way an extraordinary match. Mrs Purefoy, who lived at the end of the town above her husband's shop, prophesied disaster from the very beginning. "They are not even the same class," she said. She added darkly, "He has a reputation." All this was true enough, and she indicated without actually putting it into words that Miss Juliet had a reputation too, and not of the kind to make a suitable wife for a lord of the manor, a baronet with years of history behind him. She was the schoolmaster's daughter and pretty as a picture: she had romped through all the eligible males of Matley Bishop and a great many more beside; no man could look at her without instantly falling in love. She might not technically lack virtue – this no-one knew and everyone surmised – but shc certainly was fast, and for one so young had been affianced an amazing number of times, though the betrothal seldom lasted more than six weeks. The local curate had been her beau, as had two of the better-off farmers. Assistant schoolmasters fell helplessly at her feet, and there was a visiting gentleman from

London who had been so taken with her that he wished to set her up as his mistress in a wicked London place called Park Lane.

Juliet attended church and secretly laughed at the curate behind her prayer-book, accepted rings from the schoolmasters and broke the engagement a week later (without returning the ring). She made pretty faces at the farmers, giving them the impression that she would be up at five each morning to make the hands' breakfast, and managed not to let them know that she scarcely knew one end of a cow from the other. She distracted the teachers from their work so badly that parents began complaining, nearly got herself into bad trouble with the head boy who was one year younger than herself, and kept the London gentleman dangling until he at last lost patience, swore at her and departed for Park Lane, never to return to Matley Bishop again, one diamond brooch, two silk gowns and an ivory fan to the bad.

Sir Richard Vierville lived a comparatively solitary life at Fontenoy. He was not a local man though he had been born in the district. The house, which was ten miles out of the town, was originally called the Hall, but he never forgot his French origins, his family having come over with the fleeing Huguenots in the seventeenth century, and when the English were beaten hollow in the War of the Austrian Succession, obliterated the former name and defiantly made the victory his. Matley Bishop was in no way offended for it took little interest in the war, but visitors were sometimes astonished that Fontenoy's windows remained unbroken as well as Sir Richard's head.

It would perhaps have been difficult to break Sir Richard's head. He was big and dark and formidable, with the significant family motto of *L'épée dans l'ombre*; the local children were terrified of him, and the fond mamas who longed passionately to marry their daughters to him were stunned into stammering silence by his presence, and decided to settle for someone less handsome and wealthy, who did occasionally smile and who was not so forbidding in manner. He was however a good employer, and the men who worked his land for him – he owned a vast number of acres, sheep and cattle – spoke well of him and told tales of his kindness and generosity.

There were a number of women in his life. "Hanky-panky!" said Mrs Purefoy, who always knew everything about everyone, and Matley Bishop, catching occasional glimpses of them, whispered that they were beautiful and well-born, but there was never the slightest rumour of marriage until Sir Richard Vierville danced with Miss Juliet Smith at the local hunt ball.

This meeting was as odd as everything else, for Sir Richard had little taste for social life. Indeed, he had quarrelled with almost everybody and once horse-whipped an insolent but minor lordling who dared to make fun of him: he seemed only too willing to use the sword that was his family emblem. He seldom appeared at any local function, spent a great deal of his time in a vast library that contained more books than Matley Bishop had seen in a century, and when he was not in London, which he visited three or four times a year, rode out into the countryside on his favourite horse, Aramis, visiting his workers who lived in tied cottages a couple of miles out and inspecting his land and live-stock. Why he went to the hunt ball, no one knew, but – this was Mrs Purefoy again – it was rumoured that he had already met Miss Juliet Smith and chose this means of furthering the acquaintance.

She was, of course, surrounded by young men, and dressed in an extraordinarily pretty gown of white and silver that made her instantly noticeable. Her card was already full ten minutes after her arrival: no-one could imagine Juliet as a wallflower. When Sir Richard appeared in the doorway, there was a dead silence. He paid no attention to anyone else, simply came straight up to her. He brushed aside the adoring gentlemen as if they were flies, made the most perfunctory of bows and demanded – one could hardly put it otherwise – the first dance.

Juliet looked down at her card, then up at Sir Richard. She really was an extraordinarily lovely girl with a figure to dream of, huge, dark, flashing eyes and chestnut-brown, curly hair. The delicate colour in her cheeks owed nothing to rouge. She did not say one word, but a tremor of a smile accompanied by the ravishing dimples that had been the undoing of half Matley Bishop's male population, caught at her lips.

"Give me that card," said Sir Richard.

She handed it to him, always in silence. The young men who encircled her began to back away in affright. He tore the card into three pieces then dropped them onto the floor. He held out his hands to her and she at once moved into his arms.

They danced together for the whole evening. Six weeks later he married her.

The marriage lasted for five years. There were no children. There were several scandals, including one major one, and Sir Richard, involved in a dreadful riding accident that no-one could explain, spent the last year of his life totally disabled and helplessly dependent on his wife. He died at the age of forty-five.

I

1980

When Julia Brown married Rick Burton in a register office in 1965, their friends could not believe it. It was not so much the matter of age, though she was nineteen and he was thirty-five; it was simply sheer incompatability. Rich was a gentle, shy man, almost an eighteenth century eccentric, intended plainly to be a bachelor for life. He was good-looking in a quiet, intellectual way with an imposing dome of iron-grey hair, he enjoyed the company of women and was attractive to them, but his main interest lay in his detective novels which had an amiable, steady sale, backing agreeably a small but steady private income. He would never be a best-seller, but connoisseurs knew about his Marcus Tremayne the anthropologist-don, reviews were always good and library sales were excellent. Everyone liked him, he was invited out, was godfather to a dozen children, and could be depended on for dry, amusing speeches on ceremonial occasions. He was certainly odd, he worried a great deal about everything, and liked to take solitary evening walks, whether he was staying with friends or simply at home. Nobody knew where he went; he would be out for two or three hours, then he would return and go to bed. It was accepted as part of his character: it came to the point where friends were surprised if he chose to stay at home. A charming man, well-informed and mildly left-wing, he would live this kind of life to the day he died. The idea of his marrying and settling down with a family was absurd.

Julia bounced into his life – it was the only way of describing it – and to the amazement of his entire circle of friends he fell headlong in love with this pretty, bright, bustling little girl who instantly took charge of him, laughed him out of his worries, accepted his evening perambulations, and within six months married him.

"It will never work," they said. "Julia is too young. Julia is too bossy. Julia will drive him mad in a few months, she'll organise him out of his mind, she goes in for social work and she'll make Rick part of it, she talks too much, she'll upset his writing, he'll never be able to stand her."

Rick stood her very well and grew younger. Julia stood him, even the solitary walks which at the beginning disturbed her, and grew up. It seemed a remarkably solid marriage, and three years later Alan was born, which astonished everyone more than ever: it was just possible to think of Rick as a husband but certainly not as a father. Julia, however, made an excellent mother, as might have been expected. If she organised Rick she did so with sense and discretion. His writing flourished, his waist expanded under her good cooking, and the little parties that she gave for publishers and journalists became quite celebrated. It was all very happy, and Julia ran part-time social work as well as a husband and son. Alan was a delightful, very bright boy, now at boarding school, and it was at this point, when he was twelve years old, that after a great deal of discussion they decided to give up their London flat and move into the country.

The decision took a long time. Rick did not worry as much as he used to, for Julia skilfully removed the worries before he had time to take them in, but this was something cataclysmic, and for a while he became what he was before she married him: an anxious man for whom the disadvantages and difficulties were so vast as to be insuperable.

He sat there with Grendel on his knee – they had acquired a snow-white cat as well as a son; Rick loved cats – and the arguments poured from him.

"We cannot afford it. Houses are a terrible price these days. No doubt the whole place will need doing over. The journeys up to London will cost the earth in petrol. I shall no longer meet people. They say that if you live in the country you become dull and lethargic; I'll probably dry up and not be able to write any more. Besides, all our friends live in town. Alan will be bored to death. In the winter we'll probably be snowed in . . ."

Julia fielded every ball with the adroitness of fifteen years of married life. She was no longer nineteen, and she knew her Rick. They would not, after all, choose a house that was falling down. The books were doing well, there was the small private income, they would take out a mortgage, and the London flat would bring them in quite a large sum of money. People would be invited down, in the summer friends would come so often that they might be quite a nuisance, the quiet and peace of the country would inspire more books than Rick would be able to write.

"And think," she said, "of your lovely evening walks."

At last the decision was made, and Rick, as was his

way, stopped worrying. Every weekend they drove out to take a look at possible houses, and it was in October that they first saw Fontenoy.

It had not been a good day. Even Julia, incurably optimistic, remained silent when Rick said in an explosion of irritation, "Oh, my God! We'd better hang on to that London flat after all."

They had seen three other houses, and each was more hopeless than the last. There was the vast manor with three acres of garden, at a price of eighty thousand pounds. Under no circumstances could they afford such money, besides, the house was far too large and the garden would need professional attention. However, they dutifully went over it, noting the five bedrooms and the enormous drawing and dining rooms. "Our furniture would swim in it," Julia whispered when the agent was out of earshot. It was quite a relief to see that the walls were flaking, the ceiling coming down and the garden windows broken.

"There's a lift," said the agent, trying to revive their interest. "The last owner was very old and couldn't manage the stairs." He added to Julia, "Why don't you try it?" and opened the door for her.

He was not to know that she suffered from claustrophobia. It was the one neurotic element in her character, and she was very ashamed of it. It was chiefly because of this that she stepped defiantly inside, despite Rick's efforts to stop her. It was a very small lift, of the coffin kind. It went smoothly up to the top floor, then the door would not open. The agent, it seemed, had no key and would have to go back to the office to collect it. Julia, silently screaming with panic, struggled to control herself, then suddenly Rick, who was as frightened as she was, shouted through the door that she should try going down again. She did so, and this time the door opened. Julia, white and shaking, simply ran outside and collapsed in the car. She did not speak one word to the agent who stared after her, bewildered.

Her first words as they drove off, were, "For God's sake, get me a drink." Then both she and Rick began to laugh in an hysterical fashion: he was not claustrophobic himself but had enough imagination to know what she had endured. "I don't think," she said, "that's quite our house. I'd rather have a ghost."

It only struck her a long time afterwards that this, in the circumstances, was a strange thing to say.

After the drink she recovered enough to look at two more houses, one dull and too remote, and the third belonging to two dotty old ladies who had six cats and who had done no repairs for the past twenty years. The house had a certain whimsical charm, and the dotty ladies were delightful, plying them with elderberry wine and home-made plum cake, but Rick shook his head emphatically over their white hair, and muttered once in Julia's ear, "You be careful. That elderberry's the purest hooch."

They were slightly drunk by the time they left. The old ladies had tried to persuade them to have a third glass. "It's not really wine," they said, "it's just fruit. We make it ourselves. It couldn't harm a child." And they beamed as they said this, nodding their trembling heads. Julia said afterwards they must be pickled in it; it was like swallowing dynamite.

"Anyway," she added as she waved goodbye, "they don't really want to sell. I'm sure this was just entertainment for them. Poor old souls, they must be about eighty apiece."

"They may be poor old souls," said Rick, "but their

poor old heads are remarkably well screwed on. Did you hear what they were asking for that ruin? Poor old souls, indeed!"

They had lunch and decided to call it a day. They were both tired, disappointed and out of temper: they even bickered in a desultory way, which was unusual for them. Rick brought up again the arguments about petrol and being isolated, while Julia said she would not have much chance of a job in the country; she really could not bear to stay at home all day and be a housewife.

Then they both laughed and made it up. "It was that beastly lift," said Julia. She looked around her as she spoke. They were driving through a small, bustling town, and she noticed a hardware shop called Purefoy, which amused her, it was such an extraordinary name.

"Where are we now?" she asked, and Rick answered, "It's called Matley Bishop. There's an estate agent on the corner. Do you want to try him?"

"Oh no, I've had enough. I don't suppose he's got anything."

They drove through Matley Bishop in a companionable silence. Then suddenly, as they came to the countryside again, some ten miles out of the town, she exclaimed, "Oh, stop, stop! Look, Rick. You must look. It's absolutely gorgeous."

The house was small and precise and seventeenth century, enclosed in a wild garden full of fruit trees that were already laden. Jutting out of one corner was a small outhouse that was presumably a lavatory, and on the other side in the middle of the garden and to the right so that it was visible, was what seemed to be a summer-house, a little strange in a mock-oriental style with two cupolas, as if built on a century later. The path winding to the beautifully carved front door was overgrown with weeds, but the building itself, with creeper-covered grey walls was unsullied. The windows were bright and welcoming; the whole place had an inhabited air.

The only incongruity was the agent's notice, just inside the garden gate.

Julia whispered, so excited that she could hardly bring the words out, "It's for sale."

Rick answered mechanically, "It probably costs a fortune." Then, as if he had not spoken, he opened the car door and swung his long legs out. He said in a strange, deep voice, quite unlike his own, "I think – I do believe – this is ours."

Julia stared at him in silence. He strode up to the garden gate and pushed at it: it swung open. She followed him. It was a beautiful October day, crisp and cool. There was a blackbird singing its heart out on one of the apple trees. She stooped to gather up a fallen apple and, munching it, came up to the front door. The moss and weeds were springy beneath her feet. She felt very strange, as if she were in a foreign land. She was reminded of last Christmas when they had taken Alan to *Hansel and Gretel*: she half expected the witch to come out to greet them.

Rick tried the front door. It was unlocked. He turned to look at her. His breath was coming fast in excitement. Then he said in an assertive voice, as if somehow she were arguing with him, "Well, the door is open, after all."

She was surprised and amused. It was utterly unlike Rick to take the initiative. He was a very law-abiding man: she would have expected him to retreat, saying they had no right to go in, they could be arrested for trespassing, there might be people still living there. Instead he turned the handle and opened the door wide.

They stepped inside.

Julia said, "Oh God! It's just not possible."

For indeed the house was everything they desired. If they had designed it, it could not have been more perfect. They wandered through it in a daze, holding hands like children. It was light and airy with a long corridor leading to a magnificent circular staircase with wrought-iron balustrades. There were three bedrooms on the top floor, all overlooking the garden. The little summer-house was now plain to see, grotesque in the surroundings but with a certain charm; how Alan would adore it. Perhaps Rick could work there in the summer months. A small stream meandered at the end of the garden, making a soft, chuckling sound. The wildness of it all was so beautiful that it would be a blasphemy to tame it: remove some of the weeds but otherwise leave it as nature had intended. It must be an enchantment in the summer, foxgloves entwined with roses, borders overflowing onto the tangled lawn, sweet peas on the trellis and a long strawberry bed on one side. It was autumn now, yet the air was filled with summer: it was like another world.

Yet when Rick exclaimed, "We must buy this, we must, we must!" a sudden protest stirred within her and she did not answer.

He exclaimed half angrily, "You can't pretend you don't like it."

"Yes, yes, of course I do."

"You don't sound very enthusiastic, I must say."

"Of course I am. It's marvellous. Only . . ."

"Only what?" He sounded quite angry. She could hardly believe it was Rick speaking. This was the moment for him to start about dry rot and mice and old wiring; she had once told him that even if they found the ideal house, he would raise so many objections that they would never take it. And here he was, his mind made up while it was she who was doubtful. She was cross with herself for not responding to his enthusiasm, and said again, "It's marvellous. But let's have a look at the rest of it before making up our minds. That's probably an earth closet, that thing in the corner – we don't want to be lumbered with just that and a seventeenth century kitchen."

He gave her a look that was positively hostile and did not answer. But he followed her over the rest of the house, and everything was perfect: the kitchen had been modernised and the large, bright bathroom, complete with shower, had obviously been built on. There were electric plugs everywhere and radiators for central heating. They came down the stairs again to the main living-room that led off the hall: it was high-ceilinged with French windows onto the garden, and there was a large open hearth with a settle on either side.

Rick sat down on the settle, stretching out his legs.

"You look as if you already own the place," said Julia.

He answered simply, "I do."

And indeed he looked so proprietary, so entirely at home that she made him a mock-curtsey, exclaiming, "My lord!"

He turned his head sharply. He said, "Why do you call me that?"

"You look so very eighteenth century," said Julia. "There ought to be two large dogs here instead of our one poor little cat, and you should have a large tankard in your hand." She broke off. She had the feeling that this absurd conversation was getting out of control. She said quickly, "I'm going to have another look at the hall. I was so taken with the staircase that I didn't really bother to examine it. But I think there are some pictures there. I must see them."

There were indeed pictures, two full-length portraits facing each other. Julia leaned forward to examine them, then called out, "Rick! Rick, come here a moment."

He came reluctantly as if he had been dragged away. He said, "There's a room leading off the drawing-room. I suppose it would have been a parlour or something, but it would make a perfect study for me, there are even book-shelves. Perhaps it was part of the library. Why are you so excited? What's the matter?"

"It's the portraits. You must look at them. I suppose they owned the place. It seems rather odd finding them still here anyway, but the peculiar thing is they're nailed to the wall."

And so they were, unframed, immovable. Rick tried to shift one but could not do so. The gentleman, about forty, with powdered hair, cravat and high-collared coat, faced the lady who seemed much younger, a white lace cap on her chestnut hair, a low-cut silk dress revealing a rounded bosom, and holding in one soft, beringed hand a red rose.

There was no inscription, no signature, only at the corner of the male portrait a shadowy shield with a sword on it, and underneath, still plainly legible, the one word, *Reveniam*.

"Which means?" asked Julia.

"'I will return.'"

"Our landlords," said Julia, then fell silent. They stood there, staring at the pictures, Julia in slacks and sweater, Rick in his country tweeds, tie askew; he always wore a tie.

For Julia it was as if the house stirred about her, tugging at her, claiming her. She was possessed of an extraordinary fear, the stranger because there was no conceivable reason for it. She said below her breath, "I don't want to come here."

"But just now you . . ."

"I know. It's lovely. It's perfect. And I want to go away – Now."

"Darling, are you out of your mind?"

Then she smiled at him. "Of course I am. I don't mean a word of it. Besides, it's too late."

"I suppose," said Rick, "you do know what you're talking about."

"No," said Julia, "I don't, but it doesn't really matter. How nice of you not to shout at your crazy wife. Most husbands would by this time."

And indeed Rick seldom raised his voice: Alan, accustomed to the more impatient fathers of his friends once remarked on this, and it was true that Rick when angry usually retreated into silence.

He was silent now for a while, but more in meditation than in anger. He said at last, "That child looks like a whore."

"Rick! She's lovely."

"Yes," he said, "she's very lovely."

"Well," said Julia in sudden irritation, "I don't think much of him either. If he's her husband, he must have given her quite a time. I've seldom seen a worse-tempered or more overbearing face. Besides, he looks old enough to be her father."

"You could say the same of me," said Rick a little bitterly, and at this Julia, who hardly ever cried, burst into tears and flung herself into his arms, sobbing, "Oh Rick, Rick, I don't know what's happened to us, and I feel so odd about everything, but I do love you, truly, truly, and we'll buy this house and be happy for ever and ever, amen, so you might break your vow and give me a nice kiss to celebrate, and please lend me your handkerchief because I can't find my own."

He gave her the handkerchief. Then he said in a bewildered voice, "Don't I ever kiss you?"

"Not very often," said Julia. She had recovered herself. She mopped her face, blew her nose then looked up at him.

He stooped his head to kiss her. He said remorsefully, "I've not been much of a husband to you. I'm too old. I'm sorry, Julia. I do love you, you know."

She answered in her normal, cheerful manner, "You've been a marvellous husband. Don't be silly. After all, I did the pursuing, didn't I? The only thing wrong with us just now is we're tired. Four houses in one day is a bit much. I suggest we go back to London and ring the agent tomorrow morning. It's the only one we saw in Matley Bishop. I remember the name. Anyway, we can easily find it in the telephone directory."

"No," he said. He moved away from her. "We'll go to the agent now. There's still time. It's not very late. Something as wonderful as this could be snapped up in a moment. Come on, love, it'll take up quarter of an hour at the most."

Julia made no attempt to argue with him. In her heart she agreed with him. It would be terrible to miss what was plainly the chance of a lifetime. As Rick walked towards the front door she looked about her. There was nothing there but beauty. It was their dream house. Only as she turned to follow Rick, her eyes met those of the gentleman in the portait. He was certainly very handsome, but formidable: broad, jetty eyebrows, square forehead, hair that was black beneath the powder, decisive nose with distended nostrils that signified temper, grim mouth, jaw and chin . . .

"Where have I heard that before?"

"Julia, do come on. It's nearly five o'clock."

"Okay, okay." And she thought, I'm afraid, it's absurd, I have no reason to be afraid, I do not really want to come here and if I do not, I believe I shall die.

She said as she climbed into the car, "So we're already the blooming owners, are we? I think we're jumping the gun a bit. We've still got to pay for it, you know, and it hardly looks cheap. What do you think? Seventy thousand? Eighty? A hundred, perhaps . . ."

"Nonsense!"

"It's not nonsense at all. For one thing it's in perfect condition. And it's just the right size too. Nobody really wants one of those National Trust places: the upkeep must be appalling unless of course you open them up to tourists. An extra fifty pence for seeing the author at work. Even this place will be quite a job to keep clean, especially if I find myself some part-time work. I wonder if there's someone in Matley Bishop who would do for us."

Then he smiled at her, the old Rick, good-tempered, pleasant, understanding. He patted her hand. "You see," he said, "you're already the chatelaine. Come on, Julia, admit it. Jumping the gun, indeed! You've already organised everything to the hilt. You've got the settee here, the chairs there, and Alan's photo of the school games on the mantelpiece. You don't really care if it costs the earth. I'm right, aren't I? Come on now."

"I suppose in a way you are," said Julia with a sigh,

and lit herself a cigarette. "But," she said, "it's no good crippling ourselves. We must have a ceiling price. There's Alan's school fees and you said we needed a new car, and then there'll be redecorating and buying things; one always has to buy things for a new house."

"I don't think we need worry."

It struck Julia once again that their roles seemed to have been reversed: it was she who was doing the worrying and Rick taking everything in his stride. She said crossly, "Of course we need worry. I want the house as much as you do, but not if it means dining on bread and cheese for the rest of our lives."

"I tell you it will be all right."

"How do you know?"

"I just do know."

Julia opened her mouth to protest, then gave it up. She said instead, pointing to a beautiful church in the centre of Matley Bishop, "Lovely old graveyard. We must have a look at it."

Only as they came up to the agent's, which was still open, she cried out, "I knew I'd seen him before. I just couldn't think of the name."

"I don't know what you're talking about," said Rick, parking carefully by the kerb.

"Rochester!"

He said, "Oh yes?" as if he were not listening, and opened the car door: it was plain that his mind was entirely concentrated on the house.

"He looked just like Rochester. Oh Rick, you've read *Jane Eyre* . . ."

But he only said, "Oh, never mind Rochester. Just turn on the charm, and look appealing, worthwhile and poor."

The agent, whose name was Thomas, summed them

up well enough: a professional couple, reasonably well-off but not in the top bracket. He thought Mrs Burton looked a little like Julie Andrews, with her fashionably boyish hair: he did not know that this had been said before much to Julia's irritation. "It must be the jaw," she said, "and I can't sing a note in tune. Besides, you only say that because of the name." But all the same she examined herself closely in the mirror, running her hand over her admittedly determined chin, and for some days afterwards could be heard singing tunelessly, "What ho the sound of music," because she did not know the words.

As for Mr Burton – Mr Thomas prided himself on his ability to sum up his clients – he was obviously much older than his wife and looked like an absent-minded professor. It was easy to see who wore the trousers, for he left most of the talking to his wife. But she seemed a nice girl, if a trifle bossy, and mainly because he was rather tired and had been about to go home, he asked his girl to bring them in some coffee.

He said, "I gather you want a house in this district. There's a nice property about three miles from here. Four bedrooms, two baths, one en suite, one lounge, kitchen . . ."

"We've seen what we want," said Julia in the rough, husky little voice that went so oddly with her personality.

"Ah yes," said Mr Thomas. "That must be the house on the hill. Very nice too, though it needs doing up."

"Oh no. Ours is about ten miles out of the town. We only saw it by chance. I'm afraid it was naughty of us but the door was open and we walked in; we just couldn't resist it. I hope," said Julia, smiling prettily, "you're not annoyed with us. We didn't pinch anything except for one apple. But we both thought it absolutely lovely. And it has such a wonderful garden. It's seventeenth century. You must know the place I mean. There are two portraits in the hall. They're nailed on, which is a bit odd. I suppose they once owned the place."

"You mean Fontenoy," said Mr Thomas. His voice had perceptibly flattened. Julia, surprised, stared at him but could not see his expression for he was looking down and fiddling with his pen.

She said, "I've no idea what it's called. What an odd name. Wasn't that a battle or something? I hope you're not going to tell us it's sold."

"No, Mrs Burton, it's not sold."

"Oh thank God for that. We've set our hearts on it, haven't we, Rick? What battle was it?"

"War of the Austrian Succession," said Mr Thomas. "1743 to 1748. The French defeated us under Marshal Saxe." Then seeing her awed expression, he laughed. "I just mugged that up to impress the clients. I got it from my boy's cramming book. It doesn't matter. So you're interested in Fontenoy. It's certainly a beautiful house, and in top-hole condition too. Originally, there was a terrible kitchen and of course no bathroom. They didn't wash in those days."

"Why does it have a French name?"

"It was owned by a Frenchman. Originally it was called The Hall, but he decided to change it. I think he was born in this country but his ancestors came over with the Huguenots. He was Sir Richard Vierville. Bart." He added, "Old Norman family, I believe. The family motto was *L'épée dans l'ombre*. If you look closely at his portrait you'll see a black shield with a golden sword, and the word *Reveniam* underneath."

"I did notice it. So his name was Richard." She gave

her husband a sudden smile. "How funny. Next you'll be telling me his wife was called Julia."

"Not quite," said Mr Thomas. "She was called Juliet. It's almost the same thing."

This provoked a silence. He could see that Julia looked startled, almost disturbed. When she spoke again, she did not refer to the matter of the names. She said, "Isn't it a bit dangerous to leave the house open like that? There are so many vandals and squatters around, and anyone could just walk in. We did, after all. Do forgive me, but I really think you should lock that front door. In London you'd have it taken over in a couple of hours."

Mr Thomas thought that if vandals burnt Fontenoy to the ground, he would heave a sigh of relief. It really was, as he had several times remarked to his wife, more trouble than it was worth. He suspected that now it was going to spell trouble again. He said a little savagely, "I doubt if anyone would walk into Fontenoy if the front wall was down."

The husband spoke for the first time. He raised his head to say, "Why not?"

Mr Thomas hesitated. But then if he kept quiet, nobody else would. The locals from Matley Bishop would be roped in to get the place in order, and they would all gossip like mad. Especially Mrs Purefoy. Mrs Purefoy would never miss such an opportunity, and Arthur, her husband, would have to see to the keys, if nothing else.

He said at last, "It has a reputation. You know what these country places are like. I don't pay any attention to it myself."

"What kind of reputation?" Mr Burton looked quite excited.

Mr Thomas did not answer this directly. He said in a resigned voice, "It's going for thirty thousand."

"What!"

This was Julia. The amazement pealed through her voice before she could stop herself. She even added, "Our flat will fetch far more than that."

At this point Rick leaned forward and demanded, "What's wrong with it? Is it drains or something?"

"Certainly not," said Mr Thomas. "It's haunted."

They both burst out laughing. He remembered that the three former owners of Fontenoy had laughed too. They had not laughed at the last meeting.

Julia said at last, "Oh, come on now. You can't mean it. What is it? A walled-up nun – I wonder why it's always nuns – or a headless cavalier? You don't expect us to believe nonsense like that. I hope the ghost isn't homicidal. We have a twelve-year-old son who comes home for holidays: if he hears about this he'll be bringing the whole school with him."

Mr Thomas did not laugh at all. He looked so worried that they became serious too. Julia had sometimes used the cliché about someone walking over her grave. It was just a silly phrase, it meant nothing. At that moment, though she was not a superstitious girl, it did mean something, and her spoon, as she laid it down in the saucer, rattled against the cup.

Mr Thomas said, "All right. I suppose you'd better hear the story. It's probably all nonsense, but when three different lots of people who don't know each other all say the same thing, I can't just ignore it. Of course I don't really believe in ghosts, and anyway there aren't any actual ghosts, I mean, there's nothing to see. Nobody walks or moans or makes things fall from the wall. It's – I don't quite know how to put it – it's as if the house takes possession. The people who live there change. Mrs Hepplethwaite – she was the last but one – said her husband became a completely different man. Not, I gather, a very nice one."

Julia, who had recovered herself, tapped Rick on the wrist. "I hope you're listening," she said.

Mr Thomas was irritated by her frivolity. He felt that now he had decided to talk she might at least take him seriously. He found himself thinking that a few weeks in Fontenoy might teach her a lesson. But he only said, "I daresay she was exaggerating. She was that kind of woman. All I know is that nobody seems to stay more than six months. Whatever it is, they can't stand it. That's why the place is in such good nick. The Fosters, who were the last owners, did it up completely. Of course the garden's gone a bit wild, but the house is perfect, everything repainted and modernised and central heating put in."

"There's a nice modern kitchen," said Julia. She loved cooking.

"That's the Fosters too. They must have spent thousands. The place really is a splendid bargain. If you manage to stay the course."

"Do you know," said Julia, "I think we might do just that. What do you think, Rick?"

"I think," he answered, "it sounds completely irresistible. Perhaps the house will take my novels over and turn me into a best-seller."

"My husband's a writer," Julia told Mr Thomas who replied, untruthfully, that he knew he had heard the name before.

Rick said, "Do you know the story of our namesakes? It seems to me that if they're taking us over we ought to know more about them."

"It's not much of a story. It's rather nasty. I expect you'll hear several versions of it. Mrs Purefoy is bound to tell you the worst one."

"Purefoy? I saw the name," said Julia. "It's a shop in the town. Hardware, I think."

"That's right. Arthur, her husband, cuts keys and does odd jobs. She'll probably offer to come and clean for you. She always does for Fontenoy. She's a peculiar soul with funny religious ideas, but she's utterly reliable. Only you mustn't be surprised if she crosses herself every time she comes in."

"Good heavens!"

"She's like that. You'll get used to her."

"Well," demanded Julia, "what's the story then?"

"It's all rather gothic stuff. Sir Richard Vierville was one of those lords of the manor type, very autocratic and domineering, and she was the local schoolmaster's daughter with the reputation of being an all-out flirt. Anyway, he married her, and it didn't work out. I don't know the details except that she was years younger than him and remarkably pretty. There were other men and fights and duels and endless quarrelling, and then he had a frightful accident that everyone believed she engineered: he broke his back and was a cripple to the end of his days. After that she apparently became a reformed character and nursed him devotedly, but I don't know, it sounds unlikely, and anyway he didn't last long; he died a year later. I don't know what happened to her, except that she didn't get Fontenoy. She went to live somewhere else."

"What a depressing story," said Julia. "I was expecting something much more romantic. It doesn't seem much of a haunting."

Mr Thomas did not answer this. He was not a man of

much imagination and before Fontenoy came on his list thought ghosts were rubbish, but he would never forget Mrs Foster arriving white and frantic on his doorstep, saying she would not stay in the house one more day, he had to sell it for her, and she didn't care tuppence for the price as long as he got rid of it.

This he kept from the Burtons. They were going to buy Fontenoy, and that was good enough for him. He said, "There's one more thing I should tell you. The lighting's a bit odd. It's a local supply, a dynamo or something, and sometimes the light goes down. It doesn't last long. The Electricity Board keep on saying they'll do something about it, but you know what they're like."

"It sounds like *Gaslight*," said Julia, not very impressed, and laughed when Mr Thomas, who did not know what she was talking about, said, "No, it's electricity."

She said suddenly as they were going, "I'm surprised you haven't had the Psychical Research people down. I should have thought this was just their cup of tea."

"They came," said Mr Thomas.

"And didn't conquer, I gather?"

"No. They stayed for a night, then they just left. I don't know what happened exactly, but they said the vibrations were terrible."

Then he cursed himself, thinking he had done it and the Burtons would instantly retract. But everything he said seemed to make them more enthusiastic; they really were rather odd people. When they had gone, after a brief business discussion and an exchange of telephone numbers, he sat at his desk for a long time until his girl came in to say it was very late and Mrs Thomas would be wondering what had happened to him.

"I've sold Fontenoy again," he told his wife at dinner. Then he said savagely, "They won't stay. They never do. The next time I'm going to burn the bloody place down."

Julia and Rick drove off through Matley Bishop. "There are nice shops here," said Julia, noting the new supermarket with satisfaction and privately registering the name of what seemed to be an excellent greengrocer.

Rick was very quiet as was his custom, and for a while she was silent too, her eyes moving over his intent face. He was a careful and conscientious driver, his only fault being that he was a trifle slow.

He was a handsome and distinguished-looking man. She had fallen in love with him at first sight. She had led a wild and happy life before she met him, flirting outrageously though, in defiance of modernity, never actually having an affair, but Rick seemed to her everything she had ever really wanted, and it was only nowadays, and occasionally at that, that she felt she could do with a little more excitement. She was not a prim girl nor was she mealy-mouthed – one of Rick's reforms was to stop her from swearing, which he found detestable in a woman – but a natural loyalty and genuine affection prevented her from enlarging on the word "excitement": she never spoke one word about this side of her marriage to her friends or family.

It was just possible that if it had not been for Alan the marriage would not have lasted. Julia's looks had improved with age, she was only thirty-four, and she lived now in a world where men made passes whether one wore glasses or not: Julia did not wear glasses and had large, beautiful eyes. Sometimes it strained her temper to have a husband who worked in his study from morning to dusk then three or four times a week took himself out for lonely, nocturnal walks, returning sometimes at midnight or later. It was, he said, how he found inspiration for his books. Sometimes Julia grumbled, even lost her temper, and Rick was at once conscience-stricken, reproached himself bitterly – and behaved in exactly the same way again. He must have known, however, that he had nothing to reproach her with; she ran his home as efficiently as she did everything else, revised his manuscripts, did most of the final typing, and was a delightful hostess to publishers, agents and anyone else who might be of help to him. It was perhaps a pity that there were other attractive men around who, for all that they also wrote books, seemed to have time for amusement and distraction, and once or twice Julia, who was human after all, hesitated, but then common sense prevailed, and the wry smile she sometimes gave her husband was probably not even noticed.

And then there was Alan.

They both adored Alan, and fortunately the adoration in no way affected him: he was from every point of view a delightful boy, and in some ways, Julia suspected, more adult than his father and certainly more observant.

He was of course very much the only child. Julia wanted more children, at least two, and Rick did not. There were no more children, only the cat; a charming cat but no substitute. Alan, with a father of fifty, was old for his years: he looked like Rick and was quiet, very, very bright and sometimes, even to Julia, startlingly self-possessed. But he was in no way a prig or a show-off, and it took Julia a long time to make up her mind to send him to a boarding-school: she felt he was leading too adult a life, that he would benefit by a contemporary atmosphere, away from an eccentric father and a mother who, what with her social work and her preoccupation with Rick, was always dashing about and seldom at home.

Rick was entirely against it. They argued into the small hours. "Why," he said, "should one produce a son, an exceptional and gifted boy, then be without him for three quarters of the year? He'll probably be bullied. He's different, and you know what swine little boys can be. He'll be unhappy and homesick, and we shall live without him. In the end we may become almost strangers."

But on the subject of Alan Julia was adamant. "I think," she said over and over again, "it would be better for him." She added, "If he's in any way unhappy, I'll take him away at once."

Alan was not unhappy. He enjoyed school life enormously. He was quiet and scholarly, with a passion for music, and he was not much good at cricket or football, but he possessed one enormous advantage; he was a wonderful boxer. This baffled both of his parents; it somehow seemed out of character. But certainly nobody bullied Alan. If they did they were laid flat on the floor. He was popular with his schoolmates as eccentrics often are, the headmaster spoke lyrically of him, an Oxbridge career was certain, and Alan wrote calm, agreeable letters home with never one hint of complaint.

"I don't understand it," said Rick, positively affronted by this enthusiasm. He was disappointed and frustrated.

"He's lovely," said Julia, who was neither.

If ever in her worst moods Julia considered leaving Rick, she knew at once that she could never leave Alan.

Indeed she still loved Rick, and it was only occasionally that she felt deprived by the lack of warmth and the lonely evenings when she was left alone with nothing much to do but watch the television. And even then there were moments: Rick hard at work all day, then suddenly booking seats for a theatre, taking her out to dinner and afterwards making love to her.

Julia looked at him now, thought she had married the oddest man in Christendom, then leaned over and kissed his cheek.

He said crossly, "Don't do that. You could cause an accident."

"That was what I was hoping," said Julia.

This was daring of her, for nowadays they never referred to the prospect of more children. Julia was not of the temperament to cheat, though sometimes she was sorely tempted, and she tried to make herself see that she was lucky to have one wonderful son. But Rick, instead of looking angry as she expected, suddenly smiled, the slow, half-sly smile that was the thing she first remembered about him. They were coming up to the old church. It was called St Matthew's. "You're a lovely girl," he said. "I'm a great deal luckier than I deserve. Didn't you want to have a look at this graveyard? It's the biggest church in Matley Bishop. Sir Richard will almost certainly be buried here; perhaps there's a family vault. As we are apparently to be taken over by him we ought to put flowers on his grave."

"I'd like to have a look at it. Rick . . ."

"What is it?" He parked carefully by the kerb.

"You'd never really been in love before me, had you?"

He turned to stare at her.

"I mean, love with a capital 'L'. I suppose you'd have

married her if you had."

"Good God!" he said. "What a question to ask me, and just outside a church too."

"Well, had you?"

His lashes moved down. They were long for a man, longer than Julia's as she once complained. "Ah," he said, "that sinister encounter in Whitechapel. Those advertisements in our local newsagent. Massage. Ring Patsy. They never really found out who Jack the Ripper was, did they?"

Julia said without thinking, "Why don't you put that in your books?"

For Marcus Tremayne led a sex life so pure as to be non-existent, and these strange remarks of Rick – she had never heard him speak like this before, it was almost like swearing – would certainly liven up the novels no end, even perhaps produce the best-seller he joked about a little bitterly.

The withdrawal was so plain as to be almost physical. He said coldly, "I don't write that kind of book." Then, opening the car door for her and speaking in his normal tones, "Sometimes I think you'd really like me to be tough guy, a sort of Bogart."

"Oh no," said Julia, "not really. I think tough guys in real life must be awfully boring. I've never cared much for being knocked about."

"I didn't mean as tough as all that." He was still sitting in the car. His eyes moved over St Matthew's Church, grey and a little sinister in the half-light. "I'm not talking about Bogart-tough. I know I mentioned him, but that kind of toughness is childish and silly. I was thinking more of Rochester. I haven't read *Jane Eyre* for longer than I care to remember, but he was one of these rough, tough-talking men, wasn't he? I wonder what he'd have been like to live with. I daresay it's pretty boring to be married to an author who sits there writing all day, but Rochester striding about the house and ordering you around might be a little wearing too. What happened to him, or doesn't the book say?"

"Of course the book says. He was lamed and blinded, wasn't he, when the house burnt down. She had to look after him. She was apparently utterly devoted."

"Is that the kind of situation you want?"

She stared at him. She thought how strange he was, she had never known him behave or talk in such a fashion. It was as if something had happened to him. She said, "Oh God, no! What a terrifying idea."

"If it did happen, Julia, would you look after me?"

"What a question to ask me!" Her voice was shaking a little: she found this new Rick frightening. "Of course I would."

He repeated, "Of course you would. You are a dutiful girl. But would you still love me? You might have to do everything for me. In the eighteenth century there were servants, but we could never afford anything like that, especially if I couldn't work. I know that women are supposed to like looking after people, but I wonder if love could stand the strain. I'd never forgive you if you walked out on me, but I couldn't really blame you, however bitter I felt."

Julia, after a pause, spoke in her most bracing voice, the voice she sometimes employed in her social work when clients became impossible. "Well, darling," she said, "you seem to me in perfect health, and I gather you can still walk for all that you're just sitting in the car. I suggest we meet this awful problem when it comes, and in the meantime we'll see if we can find Sir Richard's grave, and then go to that pub across the way for a celebratory drink." Her voice shook into a laugh. "Shall I help you out, old man?"

Then, at last, he smiled. There was a sudden flicker of excitement between them. This delighted and astonished her: it did not happen so often. But she held out her hand to him as if he really needed her help and he, as he swung his legs to the ground, leaned so heavily on her that she all but collapsed under the weight of him.

"A fat lot of use you'd be," he said, then he took her arm and they walked into the graveyard.

Sir Richard Vierville's grave was there, but it took some minutes to find. There appeared to be no family vault. The grave was at the far end in the shadows under the wall. It was untended and overgrown with grass and weeds, but the inscription on the tombstone was still clear: *Here lies Sir Richard Vierville, Bart., born 1710, died 1757. God rest his Soul.*

That was all. There was no verse, no eulogistic description such as the century loved. There was no mention of his wife. There was only the family coat-of-arms, now hardly decipherable: a drawn sword with the outline of the shield blurred. The words could not be read any longer, but Julia knew them: *L'épée dans l'ombre*. Only the one word was startlingly clear: *Reveniam*.

Julia shivered. It was, after all, October. "I think," she said, "we need that drink." Then as they turned to go, "He was quite young. He was younger than you."

"Well," said Rick in a practical voice, "he broke his back. In those days there was no Stoke Mandeville or anything like that. They wouldn't be able to do anything for him."

"I wonder what happened to his wife," said Julia. They stepped inside the pub. It was light and bright and modern and garish and she heaved a sigh of relief. She felt that for the moment she had had enough of ancient remains. She took a gulp of the scotch that Rick brought over to her; it seemed to her she had never needed a drink more.

He answered a little grimly, "I have no doubt she continued with her whoring."

Julia said crossly, "Why do you always use that word? We don't really know anything about her, and there's no proof that she was in any way responsible for his accident. We only know she was much younger than he was and had the reputation of being a flirt. After all," she said, "that applies to me too. I flirted like mad before I met you, in fact at that time I was wildly in love with someone else and contemplating an affair with him. I don't see how that makes me a whore."

Her voice rose a little as it always did when she was excited. The man at the next table looked at her with interest, and she went a little pink. She had warned Rick from the very beginning that her conversation in pubs and restaurants tended to be uninhibited: she was easily carried away, and on one occasion the people near her actually laid down their knives and forks so as to listen.

Rick did not answer this, and forgetting about the eavesdropper, she persisted, "What would you do if I did go whoring?"

Then he did look at her. He answered in a rough deep voice such as she had never heard from him. "I'd break your bloody back," he said.

Julia, not easily quenched, was stunned into silence. Not only was the voice strange, not only were the words totally out of character in so quiet and gentle a man, but the epithet from Rick was unbelievable: in the whole course of their marriage she had never heard him swear.

Then he grinned at her as if somehow he had not heard his own words. He became once more dear old Rick, who wrote gentle thrillers with an academic background, who seldom lost his temper, who lived in a quiet world of his own. "Let's find somewhere to eat," he said, "then we'll go home and gloat over our new acquisition."

The man at the next table remarked as Julia walked past him, "Don't you put up with it, love. If he talks to you like that again, you just come to me."

Rick said to him, "I can't help it. You see, my name is Rochester."

They were both laughing as they came out into Matley Bishop's main street.

They moved into Fontenoy five months later, in the miserable month of February, one of the coldest Februaries on record. Julia coped with everything: solicitors, surveyors, builders, carpenters, the packing of some five thousand books, and of course Mrs Purefoy, who turned up the first day she came down from London.

"She really is the oddest little woman," she told Rick when she came home. She was very exhausted but was enjoying the drama. Life at Fontenoy was certainly not dull. "Arthur – that's the husband – is seeing to shelves and keys and cat-doors and everything else; and he seems to have planned the garden for us. I don't know about the house taking us over, but Arthur certainly has. He never seems to stop working, and he's as cheerful as she's gloomy. He must have told her about our arrival. She absolutely takes it for granted that she's doing the cleaning: she even brought rubber gloves and a duster with her."

"Well, it's very convenient, isn't it?" said Rick. He was immersed in the new book. He made no attempt whatsoever to help with anything, but Julia was used to this and took it for granted that everything should be left to her. Sometimes she felt exasperated that there was no nice, hot dinner waiting for her when she came back, but Rick was incapable of boiling a potato, and she made him take her out to the little restaurant across the way, only cooking at weekends. It was the way he was; if he had tried to help he would have made a hopeless mess of everything. Sometimes she grumbled, mostly she laughed.

"I don't suppose Rochester would have been much better," she said.

Rochester had become a family joke. If there was a burst pipe, it was Rochester's doing; when the Fontenoy kitchen window got stuck up with paint, Rochester had done the painting. "The Rochester syndrome," Rick called it. It was as if he had become part of the household. Only Alan, down for Christmas and very excited about the new house which he declared was absolutely super – "Why do you use these jargon phrases?" his father asked – was a little bewildered by what seemed to be the fourth member of the family.

"Surely you've read *Jane Eyre*?" said Julia.

But he had not. He read insatiably; indeed, he had read since he was four years old, but he was mad on history and seldom bothered about fiction except for thrillers which he devoured like sweets, good and bad. There was not a detective or policeman whose name he did not know, and in strange methods of death-dealing he was such an expert that Julia once suggested he planned for himself a career as murderer. Poisoned darts, bizarre potions, hermetically sealed rooms, outrageous medical and surgical deviations – all this was part of Alan's life; but he had never heard of Charlotte Brontë, and Julia at once pushed the book into his hands, saying firmly, "You will read that at once, and never mind *Dewy Death* or whatever nonsense you're carrying around with you."

"It's a love story!" said Alan, turning over the pages.

"Well, so what? Most great novels are."

"It's soppy." He grinned at her as he spoke, for he was having her on. He had no objection to love stories, but he enjoyed arguing with his mother who excited easily and screamed at him in an amusing way.

"It is nothing of the kind. Don't be silly. You liked that portrait, didn't you? That's Rochester to the life."

He looked at her gravely. The book was under his arm. It would be read by tomorrow if he had to sit up all night. He said, "You always go on about him, but you hardly ever mention her, do you?"

Julia had of course taken him down to Fontenoy the day after his return from school. The house was as always beautiful, for it could not be anything else, but it was hardly cosy: the furniture would arrive later, and at present there was one bed, and in the drawing room a couch and a chair. The kitchen was a little better stocked, with a new fridge and gas cooker, a few bits of crockery and cutlery and a kettle for Mrs Purefoy's interminable cups of tea. The effect, as always in an empty house, was a little eerie, but it made no difference to Alan who instantly fell in love with it. After that first day he always accompanied her. Despite his resemblance to Rick he was far handier than his father, good with fuses, liked making things and enjoying himself enormously as Arthur's handyman, banging in nails, fitting up shelves and laying down lino.

"I'll take you on when you're older," Arthur told him, "only you'll have to stop all that reading. I can't have you wasting my time."

Alan obediently put the book of the moment down, but sometimes he wandered away on his own, studying the lay-out of the house. He was particularly fascinated by the summer-house, the one thing Julia did not like, finding its mock-oriental air vulgar, out of place and occasionally even sinister, though she would have found it hard to explain why.

But it was the two portraits that absorbed Alan, and Julia, rushing to and fro with little Mrs Purefoy bustling beside her, was always finding him standing there, gazing at them.

He did not talk much about them, though Julia knew that by now he would have memorised every detail from Sir Richard's coat-of-arms to the lace cap on the lady's hair. When he said that his parents hardly ever mentioned Lady Juliet, she was a little disconcerted for it was perfectly true.

She said thoughtfully, "No, we don't, do we? I wonder why."

"Don't you like her?"

"I don't know. There are very ugly stories about her, but of course I've no idea if they're true."

"She's very pretty," said Alan. "Whatever she did, I think she must have had quite a tough time. It couldn't be all that fun in those days marrying out of your class and being so young too." He had by now finished *Jane Eyre*. "Anyway, I don't care much for your precious Rochester."

"Most women wouldn't agree with you," said Julia.

He made a face, one of his father's faces when he disapproved. He could look disconcertingly like Rick, though he had Julia's thick, dark hair. "You're a bit hard on her," he said. "I don't suppose she was an angel, but he must have been a hard man to live with. As for that accident, of course nobody really knows. Didn't the girth slip or something? I wouldn't have thought a girl could fix that. But you've been listening to Mrs Purefoy. She hasn't a good word to say for her."

Julia saw dimly that her household of three was now a household of five, even, if Mrs Purefoy was included, of six. She sighed, then laughed. She knew she was enormously lucky to have such a wonderful domestic help, one moreover who would not have touched a matchstick that did not belong to her, but she found Mrs Purefoy a little alarming, if only because she sometimes spoke of Sir Richard as if he were still alive, and addressed Julia as Mrs Foster or Mrs Hepplethwaite, two of the former owners.

She appeared with Arthur on the first day. She was a small, pale woman in her fifties, with an enormous mountain of yellow-brown hair piled high, in which sometimes her face almost seemed to vanish, and very light blue eyes. She had five children, all girls, aged from eighteen to twelve. It was difficult to imagine her doing anything so improper, but she seemed devoted to Arthur who was a jolly, carefree man, tending to sing nautical ditties while he worked, interspersed with Gilbert and Sullivan. Arthur seemed equally devoted to her, and sometimes when they left together they held hands.

Julia, remembering Mr Thomas's remarks about Mrs Purefoy crossing herself, watched in a kind of apprehension, and certainly the moment she crossed the threshold she made an extraordinary, furtive gesture, a snap of the fingers with her hand stretched out in front of her. It was done so quickly that if she had not been looking out for it, she might not have known it had happened. Alan, warned and fascinated, swore it was not the sign of the cross at all but a warding off of the evil eye. But it happened every time, and Julia could never quite accustom herself to it: she was always aware of a vast relief when it was over, as if somehow evil had been exorcised. She knew to her shame that if ever the day came when Mrs Purefoy neglected to sign herself in, as it were, she would be terrified.

Mrs Purefoy belonged, it seemed, to some strange sect. Julia never discovered what it really was. It was not Jehovah's Witnesses, but similar in that it was exclusive: anyone who did not belong was automatically damned. Her first remark to Julia, after the preliminary introductions, was to ask her if she was safe. Not "saved", simply "safe": it was somhow more sinister. Julia did not immediately understand her. As her husband cut keys, she presumed it was an inquiry about Chubb locks; it was only a moment later that she realised it was a question of salvation.

Once the misunderstanding was over she answered a little sadly that no, she was not safe, and waited for a flood of leaflets and papers, none of which came. Mrs Purefoy did not frankly seem to give a damn whether she was saved or not. She simply said, "Pity, pity," and went on with her work. At this rate it looked as if hell would be grossly overcrowded, and heaven sparsely dotted about with the Purefoy family and friends: it would be so boring that hell would obviously be preferable.

The strange thing was that Mrs Purefoy, for all that she sometimes behaved as if she had worked for Sir Richard Vierville, could not by her married status be in any way related to her namesake of two centuries ago. Perhaps the Purefoys intermarried. Whatever it was, she worked like a slave, and talked all the time as she did so: it did not seem to matter whether an audience was there or not. Alan, who discreetly followed her round, swore that she held a conversation all by herself in the bathroom. She was full of odd phrases of which the favourite, invariably a prelude to condemnation, was, "Don't get me wrong," and she had a curious way of emphasising every comparative: it would be "more easier" to fit the cat-door lower down, and "more prettier" to have nylon curtains on the kitchen windows.

Her main topic was doom. Alan, being young enough not to take it seriously, encouraged her. "War," said Mrs Purefoy, "is more nearer than we wot of," and Alan found this gorgeous, quoting it interminably until Julia screamed at him to stop. "Don't get me wrong," she added. "I don't hold no truck with them thieving Iraniums, but war is the only thing that will get rid of them."

She always finished her work by two. She refused lunch and Julia never dared offer her a drink, but she made endless cups of tea, drinking them as she worked, cup in one hand and duster in the other. When Julia begged her to sit down and relax for a few minutes, she only said, "I have to be gone in half-an-hour, there's no time."

"Oh," said Julia, "the children, I suppose."

"At their age?" said Mrs Purefoy scornfully. "If they're not old enough to look after themselves now, they never will be. I never stay here when it gets dark, I wouldn't if you paid me a hundred pounds."

"Why not?" asked Julia. She knew the question was unwise, but she was too tired to be cautious, having worked quite as hard as Mrs Purefoy and resolved to go on working after she was gone.

Mrs Purefoy looked at her. Julia up to now had found her funny, but at this moment she was unaccountably chilled, though the central heating was working beautifully and the house warm.

Mrs Purefoy said at last, "This is not a good house, ma'am. There's been too much hanky-panky here. I believe in my God and Saviour, Mrs Burton, but I believe in the devil too, and I wouldn't set foot here in the night-time, however much you begged and begged me. It's my duty to tell you you'd be better off in your London flat than coming down here. You won't stay, I can tell you that. None of 'em does; it's a waste of time and money."

Julia said weakly, "But it's only two o'clock. It's not dark till four, and in the summer – I had hoped you could help me occasionally in the evening, when we have a dinner party."

"No," said Mrs Purefoy. She did not embroider on this. Somehow the bleak monosyllable was more alarming than her usual spate of words. And she said no more on the subject, only dropped to her knees – not to pray, as Julia for one awful moment believed, but to wash under the fridge where the mop could not reach. Then, as she rose to her feet again, she said, "There's no-one here as will come at night-time."

"Well," said Julia, "I do think that's rather silly. I mean, we've got the electricity on now, and I know it's a bit funny, but it doesn't last long, and it's only something to do with the dynamo; it's not really sinister."

Mrs Purefoy did not bother to answer this at all. By five to two she had tied a scarf round the mountain of hair, and put on her coat. When the clock struck two she was already out on the front path.

Alan, later in the week, suddenly asked her, "What happened to Lady Juliet? I know he had that accident and died, and I went to St Matthew's to have a look at his grave, but nobody ever mentions her. Did she stay on here? It must have been pretty dreary for her. Did she get married again? After all, she was still very young, and she was awfully pretty."

Mrs Purefoy replied stonily, "She did what she should have done from the first."

"What does that mean?" asked Alan, astonished.

"I wouldn't like to say."

Alan brooded on this for a long time. It sounded extraordinarily sinister, but then Mrs Purefoy could achieve this effect simply by discussing the weather. Julia, when he repeated this to her, begged him to leave the subject of Lady Juliet alone, but Alan's next remark brought her spinning round, her face alight with interest.

"Mrs Purefoy," he said, "says there's a colony of Iraniums just outside Matley Bishop."

"What are you talking about? Iraniums! It sounds like the Chelsea Flower Show. What on earth are they doing here anyway? We don't seem to have much in the way of diplomatic relations."

"'Iraniums'," said Alan, savouring the word, "just stands for any kind of bloody foreigner."

"I hope you don't use that word in front of Mrs Purefoy."

"She doesn't mind. We're damned anyway. I did say 'bugger' yesterday when I dropped that hammer on my foot, and I said I was sorry, but she only said, 'I've heard them all before,' and went on working. I think actually they're boat-people."

"Boat-people, here! You must be joking."

"No, I'm not. Mrs Purefoy says they're Iraniums who've left their country in little boats and someone has opened a hostel for them. There are twenty of them, mostly children. They eat horrid foreign food and have yellow faces and slitty eyes. She thinks it's a great pity bringing them here, why didn't they stay in their own country? When I said they'd just starve, she said she didn't see why we should waste our food on them Iraniums who're no better than they should be. I don't know what her religion is, Mummy, but it doesn't seem very full of Christian charity."

"I suppose it's a kind of closed shop," said Julia reasonably. "Perhaps their heaven has Christian pickets about."

She did not comment again on the hostel but a sudden delighted hope filled her, for the only disadvantage of moving to Fontenoy was that she had to give up her job, and work of the kind she liked to do would be difficult to find in Matley Bishop. A Vietnamese hostel, if that was what it was, would suit her down to the ground. In London she had spent three hours a day in a playschool, and done so well with both parents and children that she was sometimes sent out visiting families with problems. Presumably people in market towns had children and problems too, but it would be difficult to find something that suited her so well, especially as she was such a new arrival. Julia was efficient in the home, but too much domesticity bored her. It was one of the few things she and Rick quarrelled about, for though he worked all day and sometimes walked all night, he liked to feel she was there: she knew perfectly well that he hoped no job would turn up in Matley Bishop.

However, all this had to be postponed until the house

was in order, though she did find out where the hostel was, noted that it was run by a Mr Mark Rossiter and wrote down the phone number.

Christmas came, celebrated in London for the last time, and Alan went back to school, and Mrs Purefoy turned up regularly, still making her strange sign of the cross every time she came in at the front door. The telephone was installed, the central heating continued to work perfectly, and the Electricity Board explained to Julia why the light sometimes dimmed about five o'clock – it was not a regular daily occurrence, which made it somehow more irritating, for one never knew when to expect it – to be restored half an hour later.

"But surely you can do something about it," she said crossly, for though she had laughed at it with Mrs Purefoy, the laughter was a little forced: it very much got on her nerves.

"We are doing something about it, madam."

"Well, it doesn't seem to make much difference."

The electrician became extremely technical, and Julia did not understand one word of it. The light still dimmed as the fancy took it, and she could only be thankful that she cooked by gas.

She had no time to think about ghosts. She would, indeed, have forgotten all about them if Mrs Purefoy had not reminded her so insistently. The house seemed to her in no way haunted; indeed, it was welcoming, friendly and warm.

"I'd think it was all nonsense," she told Rick three weeks before the move, "only everyone does go on so about it. Even the local shopkeepers. You don't really believe we're haunted, do you?"

He said, "Of course not." He was entirely his old self these days, speaking in his normal voice, gentle, warm, as he always had been; she had almost forgotten his extraordinary behaviour that day in Matley Bishop. He looked at her as she sat there in the armchair, her feet tucked beneath her. "You've lost weight."

"I've been working myself to death! I don't think I've ever worked so hard in my life. Oh well. In a little while it'll all be over. I'll tell you one thing, your study looks absolutely lovely."

And she described to him the room, once a parlour, leading off the drawing-room, which she had carefully and lovingly arranged. But she did not tell him that she had actually rung the Vietnamese hostel and that the next day a young man called Mark Rossiter was calling in for a drink before she drove home.

It was a nasty day, spitting snow and bitterly cold. The roads leading to Matley Bishop were slippery and dangerous, and Julia drove down with care, thinking that if the weather became worse she might have to stay the night at Fontenoy. The heating, thank God, worked, and there was the one bed which she had made up for emergencies. For the first time she felt depressed and exhausted. The work had been non-stop. A great many things, including most of the books, had already been moved, and it seemed to her that in some strange way she was living between two lives and two homes, settled in neither. She hoped she did not have to stay the night: for some reason the prospect quite alarmed her. The London flat, half-stripped now, was hideous, with great gaps everywhere, dirty squares on the walls where bookcases had stood and pictures hung, and the kitchen, once the pride of Julia's heart, looked, as she said, like a works canteen that had been vandalised by discontented staff.

But it was still home, Rick was there, and Fontenoy

seemed like alien territory, despite the fact that in London one could not move without tripping over trunks, suitcases and carrier bags.

They would have moved much sooner only there was a writers' conference that Rick had to attend: it seemed silly, especially in such weather, to go to Matley Bishop at a time when he would have to drive to London every day.

She arrived at Fontenoy, shivering with cold, having picked up bottles of sherry and whisky for Mr Rossiter and, as an afterthought, some frozen food in case she had to cook herself a meal.

Mrs Purefoy was already there. Mrs Purefoy would turn up in a hurricane or an earthquake. She greeted Julia in her usual non-smiling way. Julia had never seen her smile, but the odd thing was that she had produced charming and cheerful children: the youngest, who was called Donna, called in one day with a message, and Julia thought her pretty and delightful, in no way affected by her mother's aura of doom.

Mrs Purefoy remarked grimly, "The roads are terrible. I thought you had had an accident."

Julia was quite sorry to disappoint her, but said she had driven with the utmost care and nothing had happened.

"I had a neighbour," said Mrs Purefoy, filling the kettle as she spoke, "who was killed on a day like this. The car skidded into a wall. They had to get the fire brigade to cut him out. I daresay you'd like a cup of tea, Mrs Burton."

Her eyes moved to the two bottles that Julia had set down on the kitchen table. Julia saw this. She said defiantly, "I'm frozen stiff. I'm going to have a whisky. Wouldn't you like one, Mrs Purefoy?"

"I don't mind if I do," said Mrs Purefoy, which astonished Julia so much that she nearly knocked the bottle over. She added, "Don't get me wrong. It's just medicinal. The Bible recommends it."

"Of course," said Julia, doing a slightly frantic run-back over the parts of the Bible that she knew. Wine, she believed, was permitted, but not even the most minor of prophets had ever advocated scotch. However, this was the first time she had seen Mrs Purefoy so human, and she poured her out a generous half-cupful – she could not remember where she had put the glasses – which Mrs Purefoy downed in one waterless gulp, continuing immediately with her hoovering as if nothing had happened.

"Mrs Purefoy," said Julia, leaning back in her chair, her coat still round her shoulders.

"Yes, madam?"

"You worked for the other people here, didn't you?"

"Yes, madam."

"I gather from Mr Thomas they only stayed for six months. Why was that? What happened to make them leave?"

She saw the mask, which had disintegrated slightly under the influence of whisky, tighten again. Mrs Purefoy simply said, "I've no idea, madam."

"Oh but you must have – You're one of the most observant people I've ever met. Something must have happened. Did they see something?"

"I couldn't say, I'm sure." Then Mrs Purefoy, looking quite distraught, cried out, "Don't get me wrong! I'd help you if I could."

"Help me?"

"I just don't know. The only thing I do know is that it would be more better for you to go back to London this very instant, and stay there. And now," said Mrs Purefoy, breathing a little heavily, "I'll take another sip of that whisky of yours and go on with my work, because I can never stay after two o'clock, and there's still a great deal to be done."

Julia thought, "Well!" She meekly poured some more whisky into the cup, reflecting that if she drank so much and so quickly as Mrs Purefoy she would end up flat on the floor. She made no attempt to start work again. There was not, after all, so much left to do, and she felt unaccountably tired. She continued to sit there with Mrs Purefoy working round her. She reflected on Mr Thomas's visit last week: he had not called, she suspected, out of kindness, but simply to find out how things were going.

"No ghosts?" he had said in a jolly voice, his eyes studying her as if he hoped to see some dramatic indication of a haunting.

"No ghosts," said Julia.

"I'm delighted. You've made the place look very nice, quite homey."

"Well, it will when the furniture arrives. But I do feel at home here. It's a welcoming kind of house. We are all looking forward to the great day."

Mr Thomas did not tell her that the other occupants had said virtually the same thing, nor did he mention how six months later they had been hysterical to depart. He accepted a cup of coffee, exchanged a few words with Mrs Purefoy, then asked Julia if there were any difficulties.

"Not really. Just the electricity. I can't understand why from time to time it dims at five o'clock. It's always on the hour. The electricity man tried to explain it to me, but I don't honestly believe he understands it himself. I suppose it doesn't really matter, but it's a bit disconcerting, and it'll be awfully annoying if you're watching the telly. Besides, my husband uses an electric typewriter. He's bound to be in the middle of a vital chapter . . ."

"I don't think it would affect typewriter or television," said Mr Thomas. "It doesn't go off. It's just that the lighting is temporarily reduced." He hesitated. Then he said "They say – useful phrase, that for old wives' tales! – they say Sir Richard was brought home after his accident at five o'clock. Nonsense, of course. But that's the story."

"Well, of course it's nonsense!" cried Julia. "They didn't even have electricity then. How absurd can one get."

"Oh, I agree, I agree," said Mr Thomas. "I'll ring the electricity people tomorrow and see if I can galvanise them into doing something."

Then he talked of other things, and the matter of ghosts and electricity was not mentioned again, though Julia could not rid herself of the picture of the stretcher-bearers with the motionless, ashen-faced man who would never walk again.

Mark Rossiter was due at six. Julia did not mention this to Mrs Purefoy. Apart from her views on Iraniums she would certainly put the most sinister interpretation on her employer inviting a strange man in for a drink, with her husband tucked away in London. Lady Juliet had obviously been a naughty girl: Julia Burton had always been respectable and did not propose to court a scandalous reputation before she had even moved in.

Mrs Purefoy left as always sharp on two. "It's a terrible night," she told Julia: for Mrs Purefoy night began the moment she left Fontenoy.

"It isn't snowing quite so heavily," said Julia, looking out of the window. Her voice was uncertain. It was not a blizzard, but the snow had not stopped once and the sky was grey and leaden with it.

"The forecast says it will become more worse," said Mrs Purefoy.

"Oh, I daresay I'll manage to get back."

"The roads round here are very treacherous," said Mrs Purefoy. "I shouldn't be surprised if we wasn't snowed up for days and days."

Julia thought that in any moment of national disaster she would keep well out of Mrs Purefoy's way: she would be one of the enemy's most potent weapons. She did not bother to answer, only lit herself a cigarette.

"I hope the pipes are lagged," said Mrs Purefoy.

"They are, yes."

She saw out of the corner of her eye Mrs Purefoy glancing around, presumably to see if the ceiling was falling down, the snow creeping under the door or the windows broken. She was relieved when, scarf tightly wrapped round her hair, another round her neck, and wellingtons pulled on, Mrs Purefoy at last left. Not even the urge to prophesy doom would keep her here after the appointed hour.

Julia found herself bored. There really was nothing left to do. There was no television, which would have helped, no record-player – only a transistor broadcasting sport. She thought of ringing Rick, but he would be in the middle of the new novel; he would dislike being disturbed and really, she had nothing to say to him. She wished she had not asked Mark Rossiter round or had at least fixed an earlier hour. It was maddening to have to hang around till six; she could have been back in London by then and got the dinner on.

She read the newspaper. She looked listlessly at her library book. She made herself a cup of tea and listened to the news. After this she could stand it no longer and decided, in defiance of the weather, which – Mrs Purefoy was perfectly right – was getting worse, to take a walk in the snow round the garden.

It was quite crazy, but gorgeous. Julia, muffled up in her winter coat but bareheaded, liked the feel of the soft flakes that stung her cheeks, and found the still untended garden beautiful beneath its white covering, soft and mysterious in the gathering dusk. The stream at the end was frozen solid.

The lights were on in the drawing room. The gleam of them caught the snow through the French windows which she had left a little open. She stood in the middle of the path – it was high time Arthur got down to the weeding – raised her face to the snow and gazed at the grotesque summer-house which so far she had hardly had the time nor the inclination to visit.

For the first time since she had seen Fontenoy it seemed to Julia that the ghosts stirred. Until now she had never really thought of them, though Alan talked of little else, and the two portraits in the hall followed her with their eyes every time she went upstairs.

What was he like, Sir Richard Vierville – lovely name! – who seemed to spend his time frightening the neighbours, horsewhipping his enemies and who had elected to marry a girl young enough to be his daughter, who was not even of his class and whose reputation seemed remarkably dubious. Rochester, after all, had been fundamentally kind; Sir Richard did not seem to be kind at all. And Juliet – "You never talk about her," Alan said. Alan seemed to have a weakness for her while nobody else had one good word, but then he was always one for the under-dog; she had aroused his protective instincts. Certainly it could not have been much of a life for her, married to a man twenty-three years her senior. The glamour of it all would have vanished very soon. There would be plenty of money, and of course there was the title, but the other accompaniments of the *vie en rose* were certainly lacking: no parties, no trips to London, no theatres, no lovely weekends either away or at home with celebrated people spilling out into the garden in their fine clothes, exhilarated by magnificent food and drink.

"How do I know that?" Julia spoke the words aloud. Of course she did not know. No one talked about her except to denigrate her: she was a bad girl, she went in for hanky-panky – what a phrase! – she was the cause of her husband's dreadful accident. Yet when he was crippled for life she had apparently nursed him devotedly until he died.

Until he died. He had died so young, even for a century when no-one seemed to live much beyond sixty. Why had he died? He had broken his back. That did not mean he had no life ahead of him – not much of a life, God knows, but it would not necessarily affect his general health.

Perhaps the little madam had assisted him. Perhaps he had wanted to be assisted.

Julia had scarcely sworn at all since her marriage, and Alan, whatever he did or said at school, never dropped a rude word in his father's company, though he occasionally did so with Julia. Julia herself had become so careful that even in moments of acute crisis she never said more than, "Damn".

She was now so cross and cold and disturbed that she shouted aloud a word that would have horrified Rick, caused him hardly to speak to her for the rest of the evening. Then furious at her lack of self-control, and furious too because she had at last permitted the ghosts to encroach, she ran towards the summer-house.

She stepped inside, kicking away stones and branches that crunched and slithered under her feet. She wished she had brought a torch with her, but then she was out of her senses to be here at all, on a winter's afternoon when it was nearly dark and the snow falling heavily. The place stank of age and dust and decay. It must certainly be cleaned out. One side of it was open to the garden and the snow blew in: there were little drifts of it against the wall. There was a bench inset on the other side, and the ceiling as far as she could see it was raftered like an old church.

She stood there for a minute. She loathed it with a passion. She would certainly have it pulled down. She would get Arthur to build another for Alan, a proper summer-house, neat and bright and light, open all the way round. He might grumble at first, being filled with ghost mania, but she would make the new place so delightful that he would soon be converted.

Then very slowly she grew aware that she was not alone. There was nobody there, and she was not alone. The realisation was not sudden. Someone had been there all the time, watching her, and now whoever it was, was moving towards her.

She peered into the shadows. She could see nothing but the blanket of falling snow. She whispered in a gasp, "Who's there?"

A hand touched her arm. She could have sworn that a hand touched her arm, very gently, moving down from wrist to elbow. She saw nothing but she knew the person was smiling. Then the fear blasted through her. She screamed, and the scream came out in a thin whine, whirled away in the snow which was now descending in a blizzard, blinding her, beating against her open mouth.

The touch on her arm ceased. There was nothing to see, only the snow and the walls of the summer-house and the dark garden outside, but she knew the person was still there, had moved a little away so that he stood behind her.

Her screaming, almost soundless, stopped. She spoke in a strange voice that was not her own; a high, young voice that pronounced words strangely. She said, "Have you no thought for my reputation? For my life? He'd kill us both if he found out. Go away immediately, sir, or I'll set the dogs on you."

Then it was as if something broke inside her head. Julia turned and ran, stumblng over the summer-house step, skidding and sliding on the path and at last, within a few yards of the house, falling her length, bruising the hand with which she tried to stop her fall, tearing her trousers and laddering her tights from thigh to heel.

Gasping and dizzy and struggling for a foothold on the icy path she managed at last to stagger to her feet.

At this moment the lights within the house dimmed.

It was the last straw. Julia had never been one to panic, indeed she secretly prided herself on being able to cope with emergencies. When a friend at whose house she was staying cut herself badly, with the blood spurting out, Julia improvised a tourniquet, made hot, sweet tea and rang for the ambulance. When Alan, at the age of three, was discovered on a balcony four floors up with one leg over the railing, it was Julia who came quietly out, smiling and humming, and lifted him off while Rick, ashen-faced, would have dived at him and sent him over.

"You always cope so well, Julia," he told her frequently, and sometimes repeated this to his friends.

Julia now was not coping at all. She fell through the French window into the half-lit drawing-room, slammed the window shut with such force that she nearly broke it, and made instantly for the whisky bottle which was on the table with glasses beside it, waiting for Mr Mark Rossiter. She poured herself out an enormous dram, slopping half of it onto the table, burst into tears, and gulped the drink down, instantly pouring herself out a second.

When Mark Rossiter arrived an hour later, the lights were on again and Julia at the door, her hair blown about, her slacks torn and her face frantic and drawn.

She said in a tear-choked voice, "I'm terribly sorry but I'm afraid I'm drunk."

She was to say afterwards that Mark was plainly accustomed to arriving at strange houses where the hostess was drunk and in tears. He stamped the snow off his boots, said cheerfully, "That's all right," took her arm, led her back into the drawing-room and settled her on the couch, with himself beside her.

Julia whispered, "Please help yourself to a drink. I daren't have any more." Then she said, "I believe I have just seen a ghost."

He looked at her. He was pleasantly surprised. Voluntary helpers who worked with the Vietnamese children were seldom so pretty, drunk or sober. Worthiness and good looks were not often allied. He thought Julia looked delightful, possibly more so than if she had been dressed up to receive him: the boyish hair was tousled, her face was flushed, and the great rip in her pants somehow added to her charm.

He hesitated very briefly then put an arm round her.

He said, "Tell me about it." He added after a pause, "I've always heard this house was haunted. I'm afraid I didn't take it very seriously. What happened? I'm sure you should talk about it: it'll get it out of your system."

Julia, who was beginning to feel better, gazed at him, then laughed in a shamefaced way. It was really all so silly. He would think her mad. A hand on her arm, the awareness that someone was watching her – and uttering those preposterous words as if she had guard-dogs on the premises instead of one small, white cat.

She said at last, "I think it's just because I'm so damned tired. We're moving in shortly and I've been slaving away to get everything ready. It was partly those lights – We have funny electricity, you know. It dims at five in the evening, but not every evening, which makes it rather more unnerving because you never know when to expect it. I know there's some perfectly rational explanation but no one seems to know what to do about it, and it happened tonight just when I was coming in, full of ghosts. I'm sorry I look so awful. I was frightened, and the lights were the last straw. I slipped on the path. It really is a horrid night."

"What on earth made you go out in such a blizzard?"

"I just wanted some fresh air."

"Fresh air!"

"Well, I rather like snow. Look. I really am in a disgusting state and I've torn my trousers and drunk far too much whisky. Let me go upstairs and tidy up. It won't take a minute. And then . . ."

"Don't be silly," he said.

Then Julia looked at him properly for the first time. Up until now he had simply been the human reassurance she so desperately needed, an amused voice, a kindly arm. She moved a little away from him. She felt that Mrs

Purefoy's ghost might be there as well. She saw a slightly-built young man of about her own age, perhaps a couple of years younger, dressed casually in sweater and slacks, with longish brown hair and a face that was struggling not to laugh. She laughed herself, and so did he.

"What an introduction," she said. "Do you think you'll ever accept me as a social worker after this?"

"I've already accepted you," he said.

He began to talk about the hostel and, as he talked, he changed, became a different person. Julia, who found him attractive, now discovered that she liked him. The slickness, the womanising air, the over-confidence, disappeared. The Mark who worked in the hostel was not the same as the young man who had found her drunkenness and disarray so amusing, who had obviously been only too ready to console and comfort her. There was no doubting his passionate feelings, his love for his charges, his anger that they had been so maltreated. When he said that sometimes he hardly went to bed, yet was up at six in the morning, Julia believed him: he would fight to the death for his children and, as he added bitterly, there was a great deal of fighting to be done. The local authorities were hardly cooperative, Mrs Purefoy was not the only one to speak contemptuously of the yellow-skinned "Iraniums", and the county ladies turned up their noses at the foreign kids who could not speak English and stared at them silently out of huge black eyes.

"Sometimes," said Mark, "I could kill them. But of course I smile and beck and bow and say thank you for sixpence; I have become a wonderful scrounger. I can't pay you, you know."

"I never expected to be paid."

"It will be hard work."

"I don't," said Julia, "spend my days drinking whisky and seeing ghosts. I've done social work before, you know. Besides, I have a son of my own."

"How old is he?"

"Twelve. He's at boarding school. He's a very nice boy, though I suppose I shouldn't say that. I think in the holidays you'll have him down at the hostel. He's good with small children, and there's no side to him, no side at all."

"Has he seen the ghost?"

Julia looked around her before replying. The lights were full on, the central heating was splendid, and the room, despite its half-furnished state, looked cosy and lived-in and safe. She gave a half laugh, and he said, instantly on the defensive, "Have I said something funny? Why are you laughing?"

"Oh," she said, "I'm sorry. You reminded me of something Mrs Purefoy said. She asked me if I was safe. I thought she was talking about burglars but she was referring to salvation. I daresay you know her."

"I do indeed," said Mark rather grimly. "Everybody here knows Mrs Purefoy. She thinks all my children will burn in hell, and me with them. What made you think of that?"

"Ghosts. Just ghosts. I've never really believed in them myself. Now I'm not so sure. Today's the first time I've felt aware of them, not felt entirely safe in this lovely house. It'll pass. As for Alan – that's my son – he's madly interested in the two portraits in the hall, and he's heard all the story and he pries around, but whether he's seen anything or not, I don't know. I hope not. I have a feeling it wouldn't be very good for him. He's a sensitive and imaginative child." Then she said briskly,

"Anyway I feel perfectly safe now. I'm sure it was all imagination. When my husband's down here and we're all settled in, I shall forget all about it."

He persisted, "What did you see? You still haven't told me."

Julia answered him with some irritation. She had said she felt perfectly safe, but there was still a faint unease in her mind which made her feel she never wanted to go near that horrid summer-house again. She said, "I didn't really see anything. It's not that kind of thing. I just felt – Oh, never mind. I'd rather not go into it, if you don't mind. I want to forget all about it. Look, I'm awfully sorry but I've got to get back to London and my poor husband who's waiting for his dinner."

"Won't he get it ready for you?"

Julia sighed then laughed. "Oh good heavens, no. He's not that kind of man. We'll probably go out anyway. There's a nice little trattoria almost opposite the flat. You're not married, are you?"

"I was."

"I'm so sorry. I didn't mean . . ."

"It's all right. It was over three years ago. There are two children."

"Oh no!"

"Oh yes. Don't sound so tragic. These things happen. I daresay it was mostly my fault. I see the children from time to time."

Julia stood up and walked over to the window. She could see nothing in the dark but driving snow. She said over her shoulder, "What I wanted to say was this. I really must go now, but I'd love you to come to dinner with us in a few weeks' time. We'll really be settled in then, and I'll come to the hostel every afternoon if that suits you, except for weekends when Alan is here.

Perhaps I could look in tomorrow? I know where it is and then I can have a look round and see what you want me to do. I'm sorry to cut this short but Rick will be wondering what has happened to me, and the journey's bound to take a long time; it's an absolutely foul night."

"You can't possibly drive back to London tonight!"

"Of course I can . . ."

He rose to his feet too, and came to stand beside her. "Come on," he said, "Take a good look."

She followed him out into the hall. She saw him pause in front of Lady Juliet's portrait. He did not look at Sir Richard. He said, "How pretty she is," then winced as if her beauty hurt him: he suddenly rubbed his hand across his eyes.

"She looks a bitch to me," said Julia.

"Perhaps I like bitches."

Julia did not like the way he said this, nor did she care for the way he was looking at her. She began to wish fervently that she was on her way home. She opened the door, then recoiled.

Mrs Purefoy was perfectly right. The snow was descending in a blinding fall. It was an unmistakable blizzard. Julia could not even see her car parked outside the gate, but knew that it would be covered with snow, with the engine probably frozen up. It was bitterly cold, the smoky, snuffy smell came to her nostrils, and a savage little wind spattered her face and hair. Suddenly she remembered the summer-house. She gave a little angry cry of protest and slammed the door; even the mat was already white.

"You see" he said. What an irritating phrase that was. "You'd be stuck in a couple of miles. I know the roads here and the hostel is only ten miles away, but I'm going to have a devil of a job getting there. I wouldn't dream of attempting London; it would be suicide. Your phone's on, isn't it? If the lines aren't down. You'd better ring your husband and tell him you're going out to dinner with a strange young man who looks after foreign children and has a shocking reputation."

Julia said weakly, "Have you a shocking reputation?"

"I am regarded as a suspect character."

She moved back into the drawing-room. She said with some asperity, "If I can't get back to London, I can hardly go out to dinner."

"There's an excellent hotel half a mile away."

She felt as if she were pushing something away. It was like the summer-house. Everything was going out of control, the pressure was almost more than she could bear. She did not look at Mark, but his presence blocked her view, obscured the world. There were strange words fermenting in her mind, words that did not belong to her, words that were not hers. "*I'll set the dogs on you. My husband will kill you. How dare you, oh please, how dare you, oh please no, please, please . . .*"

She spoke at last. She did not know how long the silence had lasted. Her voice was strained and her mouth very dry. She said, "I couldn't do that. I've been working hard all day and I'm very tired. Besides, I should have to change, I couldn't go anywhere looking like this." She managed at last to look at him. "You're quite right. I couldn't possibly make London in this weather, but I'll stay in and cook myself some supper. I've got some things in the fridge. I'd ask you to join me, but there wouldn't be enough, and anyway it's only fish fingers, it's not very nice. I'll give you a ring tomorrow about the hostel. Thank you for coming. I hope the journey home won't be too awful."

He neither answered nor stirred.

Julia began slowly to move towards him. When he pulled her into his arms she made no protest, only after the first kiss she came to her senses. She cried out at the top of her voice, like a child in a temper, "No!" Then she leapt back, almost losing her balance, her hands reaching out as if for support.

He began to laugh. There was a deep, astonished anger in that laugh. "I didn't know you were so virginal," he said, then, as if his own words shocked him, "Oh, I'm sorry, I'm sorry. I don't know what's the matter with me. I didn't mean to behave like this, only you are rather attractive, you know, and I suppose being cooped up with the kids all day... Will you please forgive me? Please, Juliet. I'm not going until you do."

She said, "How do you know my name is Juliet? It's Julia, actually. Juliet is the lady in the portrait you find so pretty."

A kind of mask came over his face. He was breathing heavily. He said, "I don't know. I don't think I know anything any more. I – I must have heard the name somewhere." Then suddenly he changed, smiled, became the amiable young man she had just met. He said, "We're talking nonsense. It must be the snow. Well anyway, my name is Mark, and there's no formality in the hostel, so we'll be Julia and Mark, shall we, just good friends, and look on this whole episode as a kind of aberration."

She nodded. She did not speak. Her eyes were fixed on him.

He walked back into the hall. He said, "Don't worry. This sort of thing doesn't usually last."

Her voice rose, sharp and shrill. "What sort of thing?"

"The weather, of course. What did you think I meant?" He was standing by the portrait of Lady Juliet, his eyes moved briefly towards it. His mouth twitched into a faint smile. It seemed to her a cunning smile, and she hated him, wanted to hit him, scream abuse at him, but she managed to restrain herself, standing very still, praying he would go.

He said, "May I kiss you good night? Just to show we're friends."

"No," said Julia. "I'm sure we can be friends without that." She opened the door. The snow seemed worse than ever, it was like something out of a film. She laughed in a way that sounded to her own ears artificial and affected. She said, "I hope you don't have too bad a journey home."

He looked out at the snow. He said, "It's pretty grim. I can't remember anything quite like this."

"Oh," said Julia, "you know the roads, and I expect it isn't really as bad as it looks. It's tomorrow when it freezes up that it'll be dangerous."

Then he lost his temper. She really could not blame him. The world was an impenetrable white: one would not throw a stray cat out in such weather. When he turned on her, shouting out, "You bitch! I'll make you pay for that," she jumped back as if he had hit her, and then he rushed past her, slamming the door with such violence that the whole house seemed to shake.

She stood there, trembling from head to foot. She heard the car start up. He obviously had some bother getting the engine going, but she did not open the door again; she dared not. She did not know what she would do if he banged on it, even if he collapsed on the step. When she heard him drive off, she closed her eyes as if some awful crisis had passed.

Then she poured herself out a drink and sat down by the phone.

Rick answered immediately, which meant he was working: there was an extension on his desk. He sounded a little cross, it was after all nearly eight o'clock and she should have been home an hour ago. Then she heard the anxiety flash into his voice.

He exclaimed, "What's happened? You've had an accident. Are you hurt? Where are you? . . ."

"Darling," said Julia, "I'm talking to you, aren't I? I'm not the police telling you I'm dead. There's nothing wrong except this abominable weather. I've decided to stay the night here. I couldn't possibly drive home. It's a real blizzard."

There was a pause and she could picture him rising to his feet and pulling the curtains back to take a look. When he picked up the phone again his voice was more peevish than anxious. He said grudgingly, "It's not as bad as all that . . ."

"Well, it mayn't be in London, but in Matley Bishop it's murder. It's really awful, Rick. I don't think I've ever seen anything like it. I almost certainly would have an accident if I attempted to drive home. I'm terribly sorry, but you can get yourself dinner at Giovanni's. We'd probably have gone there anyway. And you can think of me with fish fingers."

"Fish fingers!"

"They're quite nice, actually. Alan adores them. Fish fingers, potatoes and frozen spinach. It's a good thing I laid a store in. How's the book going?"

Rick now sounded a little subdued. Perhaps it was the awfulness of fish fingers. He detested all frozen food, believing it to be totally devoid of nourishment, and had not the faintest idea how often little packages were inserted into his dinner, deliciously camouflaged with herbs and spices and sauces. He said, "It's going all right. I've been worrying about you. Why didn't you ring me before?"

"Because," said Julia, "I was having a drink with a handsome young man."

She heard him laugh. For some unaccountable reason that laugh enraged her. It seemed to imply that the idea of herself with a young man was a joke: she was now a middle-aged matron incapable of attracting anyone.

"*He kissed me. I enjoyed it. I enjoyed it very much. He wanted to stay the night and I do not believe he meant just sitting there and listening to the radio. He liked me, he found me attractive. I found him attractive too. I'm not quite past it yet, you know.*"

She said, "It's quite true. I suppose he wasn't as handsome as all that, but he was young and charming and rather nice. He runs a hostel for Vietnamese children. I thought perhaps I could help him there for a few hours a day."

Rick said in a resigned voice, "So you've got yourself a job after all."

"Only part-time. You know how bored I get if I'm at home all day. I thought we might ask him to dinner when we're settled in."

"Why not?" She knew he was not in the least interested. He was not a jealous husband, but then she had never so far given him the least cause. She found the irritation surging within her again. He had not even asked the young man's name or whether he was married, or indeed any details about him. He only said, "All right, my dear. If the weather's as bad as all that, you're much better off in Fontenoy. I'll stand myself an Italian dinner when I've finished this chapter." Then he said, knocking away her irritation and arousing her conscience, "I'll miss you, Julia. I think this is the very first time we've spent a night away from each other."

"Oh Rick!"

"Never mind. We'll both survive. Sleep well, my darling. I do love you, you know, even if we have been married for fifteen years. You'll be back tomorrow morning, won't you?"

"I'll be back if I have to hire a helicopter," said Julia. She wished him good night and put the receiver down. She felt dreadful. At that moment she hated Mark, was resolved never to speak to him again and knew that the idea of working at the hostel was impossible. How could she have behaved in such a fashion! Of course she was a little drunk, but really, that was no excuse, in fact it made it worse; it implied that under the influence of alcohol one behaved according to one's nature, and her nature was plainly that of a whore.

She disliked the sound of that word. Rick had used it. It was the kind of thing that was out of character. She rose to her feet and went into the kitchen to prepare her supper.

As she put the fish fingers under the grill – it was not quite up to escalope milanese and lasagne, but it was not so bad – she found herself reflecting for no known reason on Marcus Tremayne.

Marcus Tremayne was, she once said to Rick, the other man in her life. Marcus Tremayne had bought Fontenoy, the car and a number of other civilised luxuries, the anthropologist-detective who was an Oxbridge don and who in his spare time explored the criminal world, solving problems by his knowledge of tribal customs, initiation ceremonies and racial peculiarities. The last book concerned head-hunters and had a jacket portraying a stockade of skulls: it was called *Danse Macabre* and had sold well on both sides of the Atlantic.

The books were civilised. In Rick's books people did not gouge each other's eyes out or beat each other up in alleyways. The background was faultless, and the readers were largely educated, professional people, dons, doctors, lawyers and of course anthropologists. Marcus would never be a best-seller, but his readership was faithful and permanent. He had only one great disadvantage. He was no good with women. Indeed, Rick's women were something of a disaster: either they were sugary and coy (good women) or vampish and nineteen-twenties (bad). He introduced them as little as possible. Marcus was not married and never likely to be, he was completely asexual and before him lewd insinuations withered and died. The odd female who cropped up seldom spoke more than a few words, and on the rare occasions when characters fell in love, the whole business was glossed over as soon as possible.

"Why don't you put me in?" Julia asked him once after reading a really rather ghastly chapter in which a female anthropologist used a native aphrodisiac to achieve her evil ends.

He stared at her as if she had blasphemed, then to her surprise went very red. The colour flared upon his fine skin like rouge. He said, "I could never do that under any circumstances."

"Why on earth not? I thought all authors used real people."

He said gravely, "It would be totally impossible." Then trying to explain to her so that she would not feel hurt or snubbed, he said, "It is a different world. I couldn't write any other way. Oh, it's a real world too, otherwise I fancy I would not sell, but it bears no resemblance to the terrible world we all live in. I love you very much, Julia, and it would be entirely wrong, even wicked, to put you in a book; you are far too precious to me. It would be a kind of insult. It might even turn you into a fantasy, which would be unbearable. I believe that if ever I confused my two worlds, I should become a different person, a person you might not be able to like, much less love."

Julia did not understand this at all, but hoped that one day Rick would elucidate: she had seldom seen him so moved. On her way back to the drawing-room, with her dinner on a trolley, she paused between the two portraits.

They were both painted on wood. She had not noticed this before. And they were screwed into the wall, not nailed. It would be almost impossible to take them down: half the panelled wall would come with them and even the beautiful staircase might be damaged. Sir Richard, who was presumably responsible for this, was resolved for some reason of his own to stay there. *Reveniam.* He had no need to return, he was there for ever. The thought made her edgy, and for a guilty second she wondered if somehow they could be removed, and what the effect would be. She had a sudden curious conviction that Fontenoy would become a completely different place, and Mr Thomas would be able to sell it without any qualms. The pictures must, of course, be very valuable, but somehow at that moment she did not care for these landlords who were eternally on the premises. They were not even very attractive, they were after all stereotyped eighteenth century portraits, dressed up for the grand occasion, wearing the pompous air of landed gentry doing some impoverished artist a favour. There was no signature to indicate who the artist had been.

Julia, forgetting her cooling fish fingers – what on earth would the eighteenth century think of such a thing? – turned her eyes to the lady who was virtually her namesake. Alan was perfectly right. She had so far looked mainly at Sir Richard, ignoring the pretty girl who faced him.

The eighteenth century style was not the modern one. Lady Juliet in 1980 would be running to a health farm to shed at least a couple of stone. Julia herself was on the plump side but, compared with this young girl, was almost a sylph. She must have weighed all of twelve stone. Julia looked at the round, delicately curved arm, the prominent bosom surging from its silk and lace. There was a suggestion of a double chin, the cheeks were round like a child's, the wide mouth sensual, a little petulant. It was a slut's face rather than a whore's, what this century would call an easy lay. Lady Juliet was plainly sexy, liked men and men must have liked her. Lady Juliet must have been enchanted to be asked in marriage by a wealthy baronet, but this would in no way have hindered a cuddle on the sly. Julia thought she really did look a slut, but perhaps it was not entirely her fault: Sir Richard could not have been an easy husband, and this pretty, soft little girl who had romped through all Matley Bishop's eligible males, must have raged at the dull life she was now leading, with none of the wonderful excitements she had imagined in her dream.

Julia suddenly swung the trolley round. This was ridiculous. She was at it again. She knew absolutely nothing of the married life of Sir Richard Vierville and his lady. They might, for all she knew, have been idyllically happy. Life at Fontenoy might have been a round of parties and dances, or else this plump little girl might have quieter tastes than she imagined and settled down to domesticity as to the manner born.

After all, when he had that dreadful accident, she looked after him devotedly: no one denied her that. Not all wives would behave in such a fashion, not all wives would surrender their youth to coping with a complete invalid.

Julia ate her fish fingers – on the cool side – and enjoyed them very much. She thought they were a much maligned food, and decided she would eat them more often, perhaps for lunch when Rick was out of the way. She curled up in the one armchair, thought it was a pity there was no television, then decided it was not such a pity after all. This was her first night in Fontenoy, and it was more beautiful than she had ever imagined. The heating was on full-blast, the lamplight softened the bare corners that would soon be filled, and the driving snow outside heightened the warmth and comfort within.

She pushed the trolley to one side. The washing-up could wait. She snuggled back in the chair and closed her eyes. Then she said aloud, her voice soft and slurred, "Come on, ghosts. Tell me all about it. This is my house now. I have the right to know."

The house stirred about her. There were sounds. There were people. A rustle of silk. The patter of high heels. The touch of a hand. And through the sound of weeping, a childish sniffling and sobbing, a high, young voice.

"*I'm so bored. Why cannot I go to London? Why don't your friends ever come down here to see us? I'd like to go to the play. I'd like to have a ball here, a big, wonderful, grand ball, with music and people and laughter, wine to drink, rich food to eat, the dancing to go on and on till the small hours of the morning.*

"I do not like you. He amuses me. He flatters me, makes a fuss of me. When do you ever tell me I'm beautiful? You don't even see me. You're an old man, you're too old to notice me. You'd best be careful. I am not putting up with this kind of treatment much longer. Why should I? I'm young. I'm alive. You treat me like some kind of ornament, pretty, useful to show off to your friends. But I am not. I am a human being. If I choose to take a lover, you cannot prevent me.

"No! I didn't mean that, I swear I didn't. Oh don't be so angry, please don't, don't, don't! Can't you see I'm so unhappy I don't know what I am saying? Be kind to me. Please be kind to me. I'm so miserable I could die, and you never even smile at me, you never jest with me, you don't even love me any more . . ."

The phone rang.

Julia leapt from her chair. Her face was flushed, bewildered, afraid. She took off the receiver with a hand that shook badly.

"Mrs Burton? I daren't call you Julia. Are you still very angry with me? I'm very sorry. I'm a bastard. A silly bastard. A very cold bastard – more frozen than your fish fingers. It took me nearly an hour to get back to the hostel, and I called you the most dreadful names all the way. You'd never have got to London. It's frightful but they say the thaw is already setting in. When are you coming to work for me? Please don't say you're not. I really will behave myself, I swear it. I don't know what got into me. I don't usually behave like that, though I don't suppose you'll believe me."

Julia said, "I was aslccp."

"It's all that whisky."

"But I really am glad you got back safely."

"Are you?"

"Well, of course. I don't know about the hostel. I don't think my husband cares much for the idea. Could I let you know later? Naturally, if you hear of anyone else . . ."

"Naturally."

Julia said, "Oh God," then burst out laughing.

He said, "That's better."

She said in her normal, brisk voice, "I think it's this house. I do truly believe it's haunted. I've just had the strangest dream. I've never really believed in ghosts, but everyone talks about them so much, and what with Mrs Purefoy crossing herself every time she steps over the threshold, it's beginning to get me down. There definitely is something here that seems to affect everyone, in the oddest way. I don't think what happened is your fault. But it'll be all right when the family is here, I shan't have time to brood about anything. Perhaps we'll do a kind of exorcism. I'm sorry about this evening too. I should never have turned you out into that frightful weather. I told my husband about you . . ."

"Did you now!"

"With reservations," said Julia austerely. She was beginning to recover herself. "He said I was to invite you to dinner once we were settled in. We'll just forget about this ridiculous evening, and I'll give you a lovely dinner. Not fish fingers."

"I like fish fingers."

"Well, my husband doesn't. And I'll be sober, which will make a nice change, and – and – Look," said Julia, her voice tight and rough, "I was very silly. I really owe you an apology."

"I thought it was I who owed the apology."

"Well, I think I do too. Let's not ever mention it again. I'm ashamed of myself. I don't know what got into me."

"I won't say a word."

Julia did not like this any more than she liked the hint of laughter in his voice. But after all, this was a great deal of fuss to make about one kiss, so she said stiffly, "Well, I'm glad you got home all right. And I'll let you know about the hostel when I've discussed the matter with my husband."

"You do that." Then he said, "Good night."

The phone clicked off.

Julia could not feel she had in any way distinguished herself. The young voice still sounded in her ears, but the memory of the words it had uttered were blurring with her own words. There was unhappiness, fear and excitement warring within her. The house was exquisitely beautiful, soon when it was properly furnished it would be cosy and friendly, it would be hers, but at this moment she was for the first time afraid of it, and even more afraid of herself.

"Please be kind to me."

Rick had always been kind. She thought he was incapable of being anything else. When she first met him she was in the throes of a violent love affair and was struggling to make up her mind: whether to sleep with her man, which was against all her principles, or break it off altogether, which seemed to be the only alternative.

"You're absurdly old-fashioned," her best friend told her. "What's the matter with you, Julia? I didn't know you were such a prig. It's the done thing these days. I'm not surprised that Jack is growing fed up with you. You're behaving like a Victorian miss. I suppose you expect him to marry you."

"Yes," said Julia, red with defiance and embarrassment.

"He's just not the marrying kind."

"But I am!" Then Julia burst out, "I don't care. I know you think I'm idiotic, but I'm not a prig, I'm not, I'm not. It doesn't matter to me what other people do. I don't lay down moral laws for them. They can have it off with – with their dogs if they want to. It's their business. But I don't feel like that, and if it's old-fashioned, well, I'm old-fashioned and that's how it is. It's become a kind of convention nowadays to sleep around, but it's not mine. I want to get married, and what's more I believe that marriage should last. You don't just wear your husband like a pair of tights that can be chucked away when you've had enough of them."

The friend was too staggered even to laugh. She could only stare in bewilderment, especially as Julia by no means wore an old-fashioned air and was indeed extremely attractive: men turned their heads to gaze at her. And then of course Rick came along, who was as old-fashioned as she was, who would never have dreamed of suggesting an affair. They became engaged, ring and all, had a white wedding a few months later and slept together for the first time on their wedding night.

It might have been disastrous, with the pair of them such innocents, and Julia, now alone in bed in Fontenoy, was the first to admit it, but it was not disastrous at all: perhaps Julia's vitality and optimism helped or perhaps it was because they were so much in love.

"How strange," she once remarked a long time later – they were in bed at the time and Alan was then three years old – "how strange that virginity should have become something almost shameful. One could begin to imagine an irate father throwing his daughter out into the snow because she was still a virgin. Perhaps in another few years – isn't seven the fatal number – I shall go all modern and rush out on the rampage."

"I trust not," said Rick, and the tone of his voice disconcerted her so that she raised herself up to stare at him.

She said after a pause, "And what about you? Perhaps in a little while you'll decide to make up for all the wild oats you've never sown. What will happen then? After all, we neither of us know each other."

He said harshly, "What do you mean?"

"Well, we don't, Rick. You and I are married. I think we're rather happily married. But we're away from each other quite a lot. I do my social work, you do your writing, you go out for long, solitary walks. You don't know what I do. I work in a play-school. Perhaps I'm like the girl in that French film, I really work in a brothel . . ."

He said in a low, fierce voice, "Don't ever talk like that again. Promise, Julia. You must promise."

She was amazed by the urgency, even savagery of his voice. She said, "All right. I don't know why you're so excited about this, but okay, I promise."

And Julia never did mention it, but naturally reflected on it a great deal, and sometimes when Rick came back late from one of his walks, looked sideways at him, wondering if Marcus Tremayne was entirely responsible.

Now, tossing and turning – there was something unattractive about an empty house at night, and a great deal had happened – she brooded on her own inconceivable behaviour, decided that it was out of the question for her and Mark to work together and at the same time thought she would take a look at the hostel on her way back home.

She said aloud, "I think I must have been mad." And, "If drink has this effect on me, I'd better lay off the whisky altogether."

She fell asleep at last, and no strange voices whispered through her dreams, but Sir Richard's face was oddly imprinted on her vision, and when, with a headache and rather bad-tempered, she stumbled down in the morning to make herself some tea, she decided she would pay him the courtesy she had accorded his wife, and paused in front of his portrait.

He certainly was handsome, even allowing for flattery on the part of the painter. *L'épée dans l'ombre*. The sword in the shadow. It suited that dark, forbidding face, with the flash of steel beneath its courtly veneer. Yet for the first time it struck her that under the fierceness there was a certain vulnerability, even – God help us, what was the matter with her? – a certain innocence. She had a sudden picture of a man who was remote, even shy, who frightened people, who perhaps wanted to be loved, who could, despite his appearance, be gentle. She had begun, like Alan, to feel sorry for poor, silly little Lady Juliet who had expected so much and apparently got nothing, but now pity stirred within her for this man who had sought tenderness in a soft, young, tender little wife, and perhaps children too, and found himself tied to a tough, ambitious little creature with sharp claws and no loyalty, who wanted everything that was anathema to him.

"*We neither of us know each other*." Did Rick perhaps want a less pushing wife, did she herself want someone younger and more passionate? "Oh, this is ridiculous!" said Julia. It was a word she was beginning to use too frequently: in any case this habit of talking aloud to herself must be stopped immediately.

She thought again, "Those portraits have a horrid effect on us all; somehow we have got to have them removed." Then she straightened herself as if for some kind of moral effect, made her tea and greeted Mrs Purefoy in her normal manner, wishing secretly that she would for once stop that absurd ceremonial of crossing herself: it never failed to jar her.

"The thaw has set in," said Mrs Purefoy, making it sound inevitably like the end of the world. She added, "There will certainly be floods. It is always more worse after a thaw." She looked at Julia out of her pale blue eyes. Her hair today seemed piled higher than ever, so that her face looked like a tiny cottage exaggeratedly thatched. "You couldn't get back to London yesterday. I never thought you would. We have bad snowfalls in Matley Bishop."

Julia found herself flushing. It was almost as if Mrs Purefoy had been present when she kissed Mark. The only thing to be said about it was that Mrs Purefoy would not have been surprised: she had a permanent belief in the depravity of anyone who did not belong to her sect.

She left Mrs Purefoy to her work and set out for the hostel before returning to London. The roads were appalling with slush and melted snow, and twice she nearly skidded into another car, but she felt she could not endure another whole day in Fontenoy by herself before the final move. She felt tired and depressed, but her spirits rose at the thought of seeing Rick again, and in a little while this division of homes would be over, Alan would be coming down for the weekend to celebrate, and the new life would have begun.

The hostel was ten miles out. She asked the way at

Matley's Post Office, and could see that the question shot her down immediately: the town, as Mark had implied, did not care for these intruding foreigners. And certainly the hostel, when she got there, was not attractive: a broken-down old farmhouse, with stables and outhouses turned into impromptu rooms, all set in a barren field where some of the children were listlessly playing, wrapped up in second-hand woollies, stumping through the heaps of dirty snow that had not yet been cleared away.

Julia looked at them with a rush of pity and love. She knew then that despite Mark she must work with them, they looked so cold and lost and wretched, and this weather must be entirely alien to them. The little almond faces were drawn with the cold, the coal-black eyes stared up at her, then they seemed to sense her feelings for, when she smiled, one of them ran to her and caught at her hand.

Mark's voice said, "You're sunk, Mrs Burton," and at this Julia sighed and laughed, turning towards him, the cold, damp little hand still clutching hers.

"I suppose I am," she said, then, "They do look so lost."

"Well, wouldn't you? Vietnam isn't much cop at the moment, but at least it's warm, and they've been cooped up on wretched little boats on stormy seas that made them sick. Half of them have lost their parents, and even now when we try to feed them properly, they are faced with a kind of food they've never seen before. We do our best with the cooking, and of course their mothers try to produce the right kind of thing, but it does tend to become English stew with rice on the side. Won't you come in and have a coffee?"

"I'd love to," said Julia, releasing herself gently from

the little girl who still leaned against her, and followed Mark into the house.

She found to her relief that the violent physical attraction seemed to have vanished. She hoped it was so for him, though she was not entirely sure. He was polite, friendly and amiable: they were instantly back on Christian name terms, for it would have been silly to be otherwise. She glanced at him covertly once or twice, and wondered what had made her behave in such a crazy and uncharacteristic fashion. He was not particularly good-looking, with slightly receding hair worn to his shoulders, and very untidy. He was slight in build with nondescript features, and one arm was shorter than the other.

"Polio when I was a kid," he told her, noting her swift glance, then bestowed on her a perceptibly malicious smile as she flushed and looked away. "It doesn't worry me," he said. "It could be far worse."

She thought that malice was definitely part of his character, especially when he spoke of the good ladies of Matley Bishop – "they stink of the Victorian soup kitchen," he said – and of Mrs Purefoy who lived nearby and who flatly refused to have anything to do with the "Iraniums", even when the town organised a welcoming tea for them. "She wouldn't even bake us a cake," said Mark, a ring of fierce anger in his voice, "and she came round to tell me so. When she's angry her face almost vanishes, have you noticed? She looked like a big yellow bun, and she frightened the kids so much that they huddled away from her. The old bitch! I don't know how you put up with her."

"She's a marvellous worker," said Julia, "and as she vanishes on the stroke of two I don't have to put up with her for very long."

She explained about this and the furtive crossing, and Mark laughed, saying, "Any more ghosts?"

"Oh no, of course not. There is something, I suppose, but I think, I hope, it's worn itself out. Perhaps," said Julia, "when something really dreadful happens, it leaves a kind of atmosphere. I mean, you must have had the experience of going into a house where there's been some fearful row. Your host and hostess are perfectly delightful, but you just know they've been screaming at each other and loathe each other's guts, never mind the bright smiles and affectionate glances. Well, I gather there were all sorts of goings-on at Fontenoy, to put it mildly. Sir Richard from the look of him was hardly an amiable character, and as for my namesake she seems to have been a little toughie, what my husband likes to call a whore. So what with all this and that frightful accident that no one can explain, there's bound to be something left, and I suppose when one is tired one might pick it up." She added a little defiantly, "And of course I was drunk. Perhaps spirits attract spirits. But I don't think it will happen again. Not when we're properly settled in and all together. My husband sits at his writing all day and usually takes an evening walk after dinner to work out his plots; he's a quiet, calm, reassuring kind of person, and frankly for the first few months I shall have far too much to do, to go brooding on ghosts."

He asked quietly, "Does that mean you're not coming?"

Julia answered without hesitation, "Of course I'm coming. I think the children are gorgeous and you don't seem to have many helpers.

"We have a cook," said Mark, "who comes in every day from the town. And there are a few mothers and they help, but they get rather lost over the strange food, and they couldn't begin to do the shopping, they still speak hardly any English and they've no idea of money whatsoever – not that there's much to have ideas of. They do the cleaning, of course, and we have a handyman cum electrician cum plumber – oh God, the plumbing! – and that's about all. There are some voluntary helpers, but they're not what I'd call dependable. Are you dependable?"

"Entirely," said Julia. She smiled at him. "How conceited that sounds. But then you must remember that apart from doing social work for several years, I have a twelve-year-old son, and a writer husband who's incapable of mending a fuse or boiling a potato. So I've had to be efficient whether I like it or not. What do you want me to do? I can only come in the afternoons but I'll turn up the moment Mrs Purefoy goes. I could probably run her home at the same time."

"As long as you don't run her here! What do I want you to do? Oh, it'll evolve. English lessons for one thing. And nursery school for the kids. One thing I can promise you is you won't have time to breathe. Come. I'll take you over the place."

It was ugly, cold and bare. Julia's mind at once ran to pretty curtains, rugs, comfortable chairs and toys – she had still kept some of Alan's toys: there was a lovely rocking-horse that would be ideal, and a couple of delightful cuddlies – and of course clothes. The children were all lamentably dressed, but there was a sewing machine at home and one could pick up remnants.

Mark, who was watching her face, said dryly, "I see you've got us all organised."

She answered with a simplicity that knocked the mockery out of him. "They need help so badly. It seems so unfair. We're not rich people but we're comfortable, and I don't supppse Alan's ever lacked for anything in his life. I'd just like to do everything I can. I really like children, you know. It's not just being dotty and sentimental. They like me too."

"I've noticed that." And it was true: children who had almost forgotten how to smile were smiling at Julia. Even the mothers came up to greet her and looked sad and disappointed when she said she had to go.

"You love them too, don't you?" she said to Mark as he walked beside her to the car.

"I don't think," he said, "I could work here for five minutes if I didn't. Our pipes are frozen, the roof leaks, the lavatories, of which we have two, are unmentionable – we've twenty children, remember – there are mice, and in one of the outhouses rats, and several children have ringworm and various other unpleasant complaints of the kind you pick up on crowded boats when you haven't eaten enough for most of your life. It could all be appallingly depressing, and there are moments when I wonder what the hell I'm doing here anyway, and then – oh, I don't know – Piak comes running to you to tell you a wonderful story he's just made up, and Wan-dee assures you she loves you and climbs onto your knee, and there you are, sunk and damned and committed, and you sit down to eat that bloody rice as if it were cordon bleu."

"I'll cook for you," said Julia. She climbed into the car. "And don't forget you're having dinner with us as soon as we're organised. No rice, I promise you. And my husband has an excellent taste in wine."

As she switched on the engine she turned to wave goodbye.

He said, "You always talk about 'my husband'. Why do you never call him by his name?"

Julia stared at him. She thought this a stupid question. The engine was running. She did not trouble to answer only drove off. She did not see the derisive smile that crossed his lips.

It was at this point as she drove down slushy, slippery roads on her way to London that she wondered if she were doing the right thing. But these doubts soon passed. The memory of those sad, wasted little faces was too strong. Besides, it was all ridiculous. It was perfectly true that she had behaved badly last night, but these things happened, they were momentary, unimportant. She had never been unfaithful to Rick, and she had not the least intention of being so, but there had been odd kissss, pinches and cuddles here and there, at New Year's Eve parties, and once – of all unlikely places – in the play-school when an inspector had come up to her, said, "You're very attractive, you know," and calmly enfolded her in his arms.

She usually told Rick, who did not seem even interested. But she had no intention of telling Rick about Mark. Perhaps this was a little sinister. Perhaps because it had meant something she had to emphasise the fact that she was married, that Rick was her husband. It was probably just Fontenoy: Fontenoy had a way of exaggerating everything.

"Oh never mind," said Julia aloud, and was thankful to find that the roads, as she came nearer London, improved. She began to think of the toy cupboard in Alan's room, and this, when she arrived back at the flat, was the first place she went to. Rick, coming out of his study to greet her, stared in surprise at the sight of his wife with a teddy-bear in her arms and a rocking-horse at her feet.

He gazed at her, then said, "Oh my God!"

"No, no," said Julia, interpreting this at once. "I'm not pregnant." She was standing on a chair, for Alan had put everything childish at the top of the cupboard. She looked down at her husband who wore the bemused air that indicated he had been working. She said, "Would you really mind so much if I were?"

He said, turning his head aside, "We've already discussed this."

"But would you mind?"

"Yes."

"Why?" She stepped down from the chair, slipped and clutched at his shoulder. She said suddenly, "Give me a kiss, Rick."

He said in a bewildered voice, "You're always talking about kissing these days."

"It's an agreeable pastime," said Julia, "and I feel in the mood. Ah, come on. Give me a kiss." Then as he stooped to brush her lips with his, she exclaimed, "Oh, Rick! Anyone would think you'd expect it to make me pregnant. That's not a kiss. I want a proper kiss. Like this . . ."

And she pushed her mouth against his, forcing his lips open with her tongue, holding him firmly so that he could not back away. His astonished reluctance roused her temper, and she said a little bitterly, "It's almost like rape, isn't it? All right, Rick. It won't happen again."

He said, "You don't understand," and reached out for her but she backed away, saying, "Anyway, these toys are not for our unborn child. They're for some poor little Vietnamese brats who have never seen such things in their lives and probably won't know what to do with them."

He still looked bewildered. It was perhaps unusual for a wife of fifteen years' standing to insist so vehemently on passion at twelve o'clock in the morning. He said stiffly, "Alan won't like this at all."

Julia stared at him. "What do you mean? That's nonsense. He's twelve and unusually mature for his age. Surely you don't imagine he still takes his teddy to bed with him."

"You don't know your own son. Of course he doesn't take it to bed with him, but it's his, and you've no right to dispose of his possessions without even asking him. He'll be furious. I would be, myself. You mustn't boss people about so much, Julia."

Julia flushed up. It was seldom that Rick spoke to her in such a fashion. She looked at the toys she had scattered round her feet. Apart from the rocking-horse – it really was a lovely affair, they did not make things like that nowadays – and the teddy-bear, there was a Lego bought when Alan was five, a big box of bricks and a handful of dinky-cars. It was impossible to think of Alan at his age playing with any of them, but it was quite true, they belonged to him and she should at least ask his permission before taking them. She grimaced, gathered them all together and put them on the nearest table. She said penitently, "All right. I'll write out ten times, I mustn't pinch my son's toys and I mustn't kiss my husband in a provocative manner." She turned to face Rick who still looked angry. "I suppose I mustn't get prengnant either."

He said, "You're thirty-four."

"Thank you, darling, for reminding me. But it's not the end of the world, you know, and I haven't reached the menopause yet." Then she said, "I'm awfully cold. It was one hell of a drive down, and I came specially for you, and you greet me as if I'm something out of Shepherd's Market. I think you should pour us out a nice large drink, and then you can tell me all about Marcus. He's your child really, isn't he? Perhaps we should give him that rocking-horse – Rick!"

For Rick had caught her in his arms, his hands digging into her, and was kissing her with a brutal violence that she had never met in him, not only once but a dozen times, hurting and bruising her. When at last he released her she was too breathless and shaken to utter a word, only stare at him, her hair wild and her sweater torn.

"Is that what you want?" he said. Then he laughed. He said, "Now we'll have that drink."

Julia whispered when she could force the words out, "Have you gone mad?"

"No," he said. "I'm just asserting my marital rights." He looked at her. There was an expression on his face she had never seen. It was as if he were no longer Rick, her husband, but a stranger. He said, "Isn't that what women want? You and your Rochester – I thought you were different. But you're just the same, you're just the same."

"You didn't have to hurt me so much," said Julia.

"Why not? I was playing the handsome, wicked hero. Like Sir Richard – You have always admired Sir Richard."

It seemed to Julia as if for that one second she was no longer in her London flat but in Fontenoy. In that second she wanted to cry out, "Let's not go. Let's cancel it all. Let's stay here". But she did not; then she began to laugh hysterically, and Rick joined her. Presently they were sitting side by side, slopping large whiskies into glasses, their arms round each other.

He said at last, "Did I really hurt you?"

"No," said Julia. "What is a handful of bruises for a

respectably married couple?"

"I'm sorry."

It was the old Rick, gentle, ashamed, so much himself that Julia could hardly believe this had all happened. She said, "I rather enjoyed it."

He gave her an odd, sharp look, but made no further comment, only removed his arm from her shoulders. He said after a pause, "Do you really want another baby so much?"

"I'd love one. You must know that. I'm one of those depraved women," said Julia, "who actually enjoy being pregnant, big belly, morning sickness and all. But you don't want all the yelling, the being wakened in the middle of the night, that dreadful stage where fingers go into light plugs and dear little hands reach for pans of boiling water. I know that. I understand it, I really do. I suppose I'm just being selfish. Perhaps I'm too old after all, I mightn't enjoy it as much as I think I will. Anyway we've got to get this beastly move over before we think of anything. Now tell me the latest about Marcus. I can see you've been working. Did you have your Italian meal? I'm sorry about last night, but it really was terrible, I'd never have made it. Oh, what a wonderful drink! Another move and I swear I'll be an alcoholic. By the way, you'll have to buy me a new sweater. I think I'd like a cashmere. To celebrate."

He looked at her silently for so long that she began to flush again. But he only said, touching gently the neck of her jumper which was split at the seam where his hand had wrenched at it, "I think, my dearest Julia, you underestimate me. I have my moments too. You shall have your cashmere. Yes, I had my Italian meal which you would have cooked much better, and no, I have not been working."

"Oh Rick! What's happened? I thought the new book was going so well."

He moved away, leaning against the back of the couch, his hands behind his head. "I've no right to deny you another baby. I think I could say I'm about to have one myself."

"What on earth do you mean?"

He took a gulp of his drink as if to give himself courage. "I went for a walk last night. In the snow."

"That must have been fun," said Julia, still staring at him.

"And I decided that I'm going to start a new kind of book."

"You mean," said Julia, amazed at something so unprecedented, "that you're dropping Marcus Tremayne. But you can't . . ."

"Look," he said, speaking with more determination than she had ever heard from him, "one can't go on doing the same thing for ever and ever."

"But . . ."

"Now just let me finish. I've been toying with the idea for some time. I was beginning to find old Marcus rather boring, but oddly enough the last time I was at Fontenoy clinched it. You know how it is with ideas, they suddenly click, you know they're right. Do you remember? I was arranging the books in my study . . ."

"I remember."

It was one of the few times Rick had been down. He was only too willing to leave everything to Julia, but the arranging of his library could only be done by himself. He and Alan had shut themselves up in the study, there had been a great deal of clattering and banging and hammering, and neither of them had reappeared until some seven hours later, dusty, happy and ravenously hungry.

"And then," said Rick, "I made up my mind."

"So that's the end of poor old Marcus."

"Oh, he's a dried-up stick anyway. Besides, anthropology has its limitations. I was running out of ideas. There's only so much you can do with one subject."

"And who is the new detective going to be? Not a ghost, I hope."

For the first time he looked a little self-conscious. The fine, betraying skin was growing pink. He said, "There's not going to be a detective at all."

"Oh? What is it then?"

"I'm going to write an historical novel."

Julia was so taken aback that she simply looked at him in silence. Rick had never to her knowledge been interested in history. On anthropology he was, of course, so well-informed that he could have taken a degree: the shelves of his study were filled with Malinowski, Evans Pritchard, Seligman, Rattray and Torday; there were lives of Burton, Stanley and Livingstone, and his greatest pride was a first edition of *The Golden Bough*, which had provided him with one of his most ambitious and esoteric tales. West African statues of a well-equipped nature which Mrs Purefoy refused to dust stood on the mantelpiece, and there were some remarkable portraits from the Congo that certainly made her face disappear into her hair.

It was a professor's library, and Julia regarded it as a part of her life. That it should all go for nothing was unbelievable. She said at last, without enthusiasm, "What kind of historical novel?"

"It will be a love story," said Rick, "set in the eighteenth century."

"But darling, you don't . . ."

"Told in the first person from the woman's angle."

Julia had never until recently been a drinking girl, but she now poured herself out another scotch. She thought of Rick's women. The critics were kind about them because the rest of the book was so good, though occasionally one of them inserted a brief sniping remark, but really as characters they were monstrously bad, almost caricatures, and Julia, who had little writing ability, sometimes wondered wildly if she could take over the brief love scenes: whatever she did with them it would at least be an improvement on Rick.

Oh well, she could probably get herself a job that would pay for the lack of royalties, and no doubt in the end Marcus Tremayne would reemerge. She was so absorbed in this that she did not realise how closely Rick was watching her. When he put his hand on hers, she started and flushed, praying that he could not read her thoughts.

He said, "Go on. Say it."

"I wasn't really going to say anything. I was just so surprised, that's all. Perhaps we should say kaddish for Marcus."

"Kaddish! He's not Jewish."

"It seems somehow appropriate."

"You don't think I can do it. Is that it?"

Julia pulled herself together. Good wives do not discourage their husbands. She said quietly, "I think you could do anything you set out to do."

He said, with a trace of bitterness in his voice, "You are a good and devoted little wife."

"No. I just think you're a good writer, that's all."

But throughout the day she brooded on this. She did think Rick was a good writer, but his range was restricted, and somehow it seemed dreadful to kill off poor Marcus who had done so well for them, especially as what he was planning was, to her way of thinking, totally beyond him; it would make him look ridiculous. She kept on seeing Marcus Tremayne in Georgette Heyer guise, and the vision was alarming. It might not have been so bad if the book were some erudite, philosophical affair, but to write it in the first person and, God help us, from the woman's angle . . .

However, the move from London to Fontenoy was so engulfing that she forgot about everything else. She had not moved for a long time: the horror of it had escaped her memory. Everything naturally went wrong: the removal men were late, valuable pots were broken, doors had to be taken off their hinges to get the bigger pieces of furniture through, and all the electric light bulbs were forgotten until the end when there was not even a chair to stand on, so as to reach them. Once in Fontenoy everything was worse. The furniture was put in the wrong place, the beautiful staircase was scratched, half the crockery seemed to have vanished, pictures were stacked against the wall in the wrong rooms, and only Alan – for it was the weekend and he had come to help – kept his head and his temper. Julia, for all her vaunted self-control, kept neither, and Rick wandered about like a lost soul, getting in everyone's way, falling over the removal men and making inapposite suggestions that were simply ignored.

When at last it was over and the place began to look remotely civilised, they stood there watching the removal vans drive off, then looked at each other.

"Drink?" said Julia.

They took their drinks into Rick's study, a civilised oasis. It was the only part of the house that the removal men had not touched, and there was a lovely familiarity to it that made them all sink down with sighs of relief.

Then Julia noticed a great pile of books from the London Library on the desk: the top title was *English Men and Manners in the Eighteenth Century*.

Alan, picking it up, asked, "What's this, Dad?"

"Turbeville. Very useful," said Rick.

Alan assimilated this. He sipped at his sherry: Julia said if he was adult enough to do so much work he deserved an adult drink. He was sitting on the floor with Grendel on his knee, a distraught and irritated cat who resented the change of habitation and flatly refused to use the cat-door Arthur had so carefully made for him. Alan had read *Beowulf* at school, and Grendel, otherwise a normal white cat, had six toes on each foot, which qualified him for the role of monster.

Alan made no further comment. He had been very quiet during the move, working like a slave, hardly stopping for even a snack, and Julia thought he looked overtired.

She said, "In a minute I'm going to make some supper. I'm sure we can all do with it. It's a nice supper. I thought we deserved a treat. I've got half a cooked salmon in the fridge because I knew I wouldn't feel much like cooking, but we all need something really good, and there's a bottle, Rick, of your favourite Sancerre. Why don't you have a bath, Alan, while I'm getting things ready? There is, thank God, plenty of hot water. You can get into your dressing-gown. You look absolutely exhausted."

He said, "I'm all right, only I'm awfully hungry. I found something interesting. He looked mysterious and mischievous. It obviously was something important. He said, "I put it behind the curtain. Here it is."

He pulled the curtain aside and confronted his startled parents with a sword, which he waved in the air and then made a duelling salute.

Rick said, "Good God!" Julia, who disliked weapons and was frightened of them, simply stared.

The sword was unsheathed. It was rusty with age, but the blade was still thin and sharp. The hilt, when Julia gingerly took it from him, bore the Vierville shield, a sword in shadow with the family name engraved beneath, and the word *Reveniam*.

She instantly laid it down on the table. She felt she could not bear to touch it, it inspired her with such revulsion. She exclaimed, "For God's sake, be careful. With all that rust it must be lethal. I think you should wash your hands after touching it."

"It's still sharp," said Alan, "and I think there's blood on it."

For the first time since their arrival Julia looked at him properly. Up till now she had been too immersed in the general confusion to consider anything except where to hang pictures, where to put furniture, where to place ornaments. Now it seemed to her that she was looking at a stranger.

Alan had always been an easy boy. Sometimes she and Rick were amazed that two such disparate personalities should produce a child so charming and uncomplicated. Their friends complained constantly about their children. They seemed to sleep with their girl friends and sometimes with boys, they smoked pot, they drank, they even indulged in worse things like LSD, and almost always they were out of control, disregarding their parents and in at least two cases disappearing altogether. It seemed to be the modern thing, and Julia who had been brought up in the most conventional manner, was terrified lest something like this should happen with Alan. And there he was, he did not drink, he was not interested in drugs, he liked girls very much but as far as Julia could make our had not yet had an affair, he seemed to have no homosexual inclinations, and his main hobbies were reading, music, stamps and of course boxing, on which he was a fanatic. His manners were excellent, his introverted nature only what could be expected from such parentage. He was, in short, a nice boy, extremely bright but not exceptional enough to create problems, and Julia, waiting always for something outrageous, could only see him as normal, charming, and intelligent.

She looked at him now.

He was still Alan, whom she adored with all her heart and soul, but something had happened to him, he was different. For one thing he had grown thinner, and though this was natural enough at his age, it disturbed his mother who felt she should have noticed sooner. She remembered now that he did not laugh so much, did not crack the silly jokes that sometimes exasperated her but which were a part of his personality. Nor did he discuss the house which was now his home, and throughout the day she had not once heard him refer to the portraits, though she had once caught him staring at them with a kind of passion.

He went on, "I expect it's killed someone."

Rick, who did not seem particularly interested in the weapon now lying across a pile of typing paper, said dryly, "That's rather the point of the exercise."

Alan asked, "Did they really fight to the death?"

"Certainly," said his father. "In France they used to do it for fun. I've forgotten the date of the last fatal duel in this country, but it was late in the eighteenth century and, as I understand, two noble lords killed each other off."

"Crikey!" said Alan. Julia noticed that even in his excitement he remembered to moderate his language. "How on earth did they manage that?"

"Oh, I don't know," said Rick. "It couldn't have been much loss. The lady who caused it all quietly disappeared."

"Did they usually fight over ladies?"

"It's the customary cause, even now. Except, as I said, in France where blowing your nose or clearing your throat was quite sufficient cause. '*Puisque nous sommes ici, battons-nous*.' And away they'd go, usually in the Tuileries. I suppose it passed the time."

"Your French accent is terrible, Dad," said Alan, quite like his old self, and his father laughed. "I don't have the advantage of your education," he said.

"Where did you find it?" asked Julia. She could not take her eyes off it. It must be of great value for all that it was so rusty and tarnished: the hilt was of gold, and the shield was outlined in small stones. There was no sheath. It looked to her older than the eighteenth century. Perhaps it belonged to the first de Vierville who escaped from France three centuries ago. The more she looked at it the more she disliked it. It had a stink of death to it, though of course in the olden days gentlemen wore their swords on state occasions, like white tie and tails.

"In the summer-house," said Alan. His head was bent over Grendel, purring on his knee. Julia tensed, but could not see his face.

Rick said after a pause, "What do you mean? It's just an empty, broken-down old building. And a pretty revolting one too." His voice was unexpectedly angry. "You're making this up. Of course it wasn't in the summer-house."

Alan raised his head. His face was very white. He answered in a voice such as Julia had never heard from him, "If I said I found it there, it means I found it there. It was under the bench against the wall. It was covered with dust and mud and leaves. The point was sticking into the ground. The tiling is uneven. It looks as if someone tried to bury it there." He added defiantly, "I found it just after we arrived this morning. I wanted to have another look at the place. You were all too busy to notice."

Rick said in his usual quiet voice, "I think we'd better all have another drink."

It struck Julia that nowadays this was a remark made rather frequently by both of them. They lived in a world where friends were invariably offered a drink as soon as they arrived, where there was always wine for guests and sometimes just for themselves, but Rick, though he could drink a great deal without any effect, was on the whole an abstemious man, and Julia, though she liked her scotch before dinner, seldom went to the drinks cabinet and usually preferred a cup of tea.

However, she made no comment, only poured out two more drinks, with another small sherry for Alan whose feelings were still plainly sore.

They drank companionably. They seldom quarrelled, and it was almost unprecedented for Rick to speak to his son in such a fashion. Julia could see he was ashamed of himself: he even stooped down to ruffle Alan's hair as he had done when he was young, saying, "Sorry, old son. I think this move's got me down." He looked at Julia. "You've done most of the work. You must be utterly exhausted. I tell you what, Alan and I will get the supper and you put your feet up, swill scotch and relax."

"I'm not arguing with you," said Julia.

They ate their salmon picnic-wise, washed down with Chateau de Sancerre. Julia suspected that Alan did most of the preparation. The salmon was neatly set out on a serving-dish with the salad artistically arranged around it, the mayonnaise was not served from the bottle, and the *baguette* she had bought was sliced and set out in a circle with the butter in the middle. Rick was incapable of thinking of such things, nor would he have bothered with napkins and the best glasses for the wine.

The sword was placed against the wall. It was the only discrepancy, and Julia swivelled her chair round so as not to see it.

Alan said suddenly, "May I hang the sword in my room?"

Julia's immediate reaction was to say, "No". She did not say it. It was, after all, the most natural thing in the world. Alan could behave like a mature gentleman when he chose, indeed, was often far more mature than many gentlemen of Julia's acquaintance, but he was a young boy, he was only twelve, and all boys loved weapons. Rick who shared her dislike of lethal things, had once sworn that he would never give his son pistols and knives and suchlike things, but of course it was no use at all. Little Alan, aged four, howled grievously for the lovely pistol with caps that all his friends had, and refused to be distracted from the two-bladed penknife that was in the local shop window. Not even a Mickey Mouse watch would solace him, and the wonderful toy garages, Starsky and Hutch walkie-talkie outfits and other exotica were played with for a couple of days, then kicked aside.

It was Julia who capitulated, and Rick had emerged from his study to the sound of caps and looked at his wife with angry reproach. "He's a boy," said Julia, "and we're causing a trauma," to which he replied, "I don't think you know what a trauma is, and it's all wrong, you had no right to do it."

But it was done and there was no going back, so Alan shot everyone dead for days on end, cut off half his finger with the penknife and later on demanded a set of tools, most of which seemed to Julia completely lethal and one of which ruined a table which Alan happily sawed through.

She said, "All right," then ignoring Rick's expression, "But for God's sake, make sure it's hung properly, and not on any account over your bed. I'd prefer an undecapitated son, if you don't mind."

He grinned at her. He looked more his usual self. He said, "It'll go on the wall between the two book-cases, and I'll get Arthur to put it up for me."

She said later to Rick, "I wonder how on earth it got there. I think all that snow must have covered it when I was there. It looks pretty old and valuable. I suppose it was under the tiles and just wore through, then when the snow melted it was plain to see. Alan said it must have been buried, but who on earth would bury a sword?"

"Perhaps," said Rick, gazing happily round his study and only half listening to her, "it was used to bury something else. There might be a body under those tiles."

"Honestly, Rick . . ."

"Well, there seem to have been some funny things happening here. Perhaps that's why there's all this talk of haunting. We'll get a priest to do an exorcism for us."

He smiled as he said this, for he was a devout atheist, with a courteous and pitying respect for benighted souls who believed in God.

"Sometimes," said Julia as they came out into the

hall, "I think we'll have no peace until Sir Richard is removed. I don't think it's her. I think whatever there is comes from him." She paused by the portrait. "It's funny. When I first saw him I detested him, and all my sympathy was with her. Now I'm not so sure. She looks a right little piece to me, for all she's so soft and young and pretty. I wonder sometimes about that accident. Perhaps she engineered it. You never know."

"Nonsense!" said Rick. "She was only a child. She must have been less than half his age."

"I don't see what that's got to do with it. There are quite a number of dear little souls who'd cut their granny's throat for sixpence – and have done it too. What about Constance Kent?"

"She never did it."

"You've been watching the telly."

They were walking up the stairs. There was still muddle and confusion, boxes and sawdust and wrappings, but nothing could destroy the beauty of it, and Julia looked about her and sighed with pleasure. "I really think," she said, "that it was the wrought iron that decided me to take this place. It's ours, Rick. Ours! I think we're the luckiest people alive."

They paused on the landing. There was a slit of light under Alan's door. Once Julia would have gone in to tell him to go to sleep, but she had learnt her lesson a long time ago: the light would be obediently put out and switched on again the moment she departed. "I can't sleep without reading," Alan said. "Truly, Mummy. I'll stop the moment I feel sleepy."

"He's probably gloating over his sword," said Rick.

Julia lay awake for a long time. She thought Rick was awake too, but he did not move, nor did he do more than give her his goodnight kiss, putting his arms briefly round her and brushing his lips against hers. She remembered that strange, violent episode back in London and thought it would be nice to celebrate the first night in the new home with a little more love, but even as she opened her mouth to say she loved him, he turned away and lay there on his back like an effigy on a tomb.

I'm becoming a nymphomaniac, thought Julia, startled, even shocked by her own passionate longing. She looked disconsolately at his profile. He had a fine profile. She had admired it enormously when she first saw him. Now in her frustration and resentment she found it a little weak, it was too flawless, it was like a statue.

She said in a loud voice, "Rick!"

"What? What is it?"

"You're not asleep at all."

"Well, I certainly am not now. What's the matter?"

"What's the matter? You're an old man, that's what's the matter. This is our first night together in our new home. This is our new bedroom. And what do we do about it? After all, it's a kind of second honeymoon. Do we make love? Like hell we do. A genteel little kiss . . .

"You weren't always so genteel."

"I think," she said sitting up so abruptly that she shot half the bedclothes to one side, "when people use words like 'fuck', they are not just swearing, they are introducing a kind of reality. If you said things like that a bit more and did them too, we'd make more of a go of our marriage."

And even as she said this she perceived the sad truth in her words: the marriage was serviceable, it would go on, but it was no longer substantial, something had been irretrievably lost, even though she could not have said what it was.

Rick said in an aghast voice, "What did you say?"

"Well," said Julia, "I said a great many things, but the actual word . . ."

"You talk like a harlot!"

She nearly asked him what he knew about harlots, and why he used such an oddly old-fashioned word, but she was nearly in tears for he sounded so angry. She said in a subdued voice, "We're quarrelling. On our first night here. Oh Rick, don't quarrel with me. Not tonight. I promise never to say 'fuck' again. I'll be as refined as Mrs Purefoy, though I have my doubts about her all the same; she informed me last week that she had had sexual relations with Arthur and only hoped she wouldn't fall for another baby, five girls was more than enough."

The sheer absurdity of this brought Rick to his senses. He took her into his arms, cuddling her, saying gently, "You really do say the most extraordinary things."

"That was Mrs Purefoy, not me. I think she and Arthur are utterly devoted. She's probably a wow in bed. It's all that hair. You forget to look at the face underneath it."

"Julia!"

They were, thank God, no longer quarrelling. But that was where it seemed to stay. Julia, snuggling up against him, thinking dimly that Mrs Purefoy probably had more of what they used to call S.A. than she did, said, "Rick, don't be angry again, but do you think we could knock down that old summer-house and build something really charming in its place?"

There was a silence. She thought, "Oh God, I've done it again." But he only said at last, "I don't like it either, but I don't think that would be a good idea."

"Why not? It's hideous."

"You liked it when you first saw it."

"I didn't really take it in. I think I was beglamourised by Fontenoy. But now I've really taken against it. It's so ersatz. It has no charm. Somehow it's out of place, almost sinister."

"Oh come on, darling, you're talking nonsense." Then he said in a strange voice, "In a way I agree with you. But I don't think it would be wise. We might be disinterring more than we expected."

"What do you mean?"

Then he said in a jolly manner, "I tell you what. We'll compromise. We'll get Arthur to paint it and level the flooring. That'll make it look more human. And perhaps some nice rambler roses . . ."

"Oh no!"

"It really would make a difference, you know. I'll talk to him about it in the morning."

He said no more, and this time he really was asleep. It was Julia who lay there and thought of rusty swords and uneven flooring, and suddenly of a hand that stole caressingly from wrist to elbow.

The one word sounded in her ears as she at last fell asleep herself.

Reveniam.

II

1980 and 1750

The next few weeks were such confusion that Julia forgot about ghosts, forgot about everything except kitchen units, light plugs, curtains that did not match, carpets that did not fit, and the hundred other things that accompany all moves, however well planned. Mrs Purefoy, still crossing herself and leaving on the dot of two, was a miracle, apparently inexhaustible, and doing the work of three. She got on excellently with Rick, having the deep respect for writers of one who had never read a book in her life, and he was deeply entertained by her extraordinary conversation in which she combined a startling directness with an almost Victorian refinement. In addition to this she tended to adopt startling new hair-styles that eclipsed her small face even more, dyed it various colours and crimped and curled it: whatever sect it was she belonged to apparently encouraged female vanity. The indispensable Arthur turned up every day – Julia often wondered what happened to his shop – and she spoke to him about the summer-house which he promised to do up for her, and also the outside lavatory which worried her very much and which she refused to use.

"I'm claustrophobic," she told him, and might as well have said she was the Ayatollah Khomeini for all he understood her, but he agreed it was a nasty, dark little place and he would fit up a light and paint the walls white so as to cheer it up. "I don't like the key," Julia said, "It could be shut from outside," and he plainly thought her mad but said he would fit on an inside bolt as well.

Alan went back to school. Julia thought he was still unusually quiet and this worried her for, like Mrs Purefoy, he was a great talker, and this silent, withdrawn manner was new.

"Are you all right?" she asked him as she drove him to the station, then laughed a little shamefacedly, for this was a silly family joke: they had once had a help who asked this question in such a death-knell voice that the person so addressed almost fell down dead on the spot.

He only said as he leaned out of the carriage to kiss her goodbye – he was a demonstrative child and never ashamed to show affection – "Mummy, what's all this about Dad's new book?"

For Rick was working as she had never known him work before. He did not even take his evening walks. The typewriter sounded from morning to night, and Mrs Purefoy, suitably awed, crept past his door: Alan remarked once that he was sure she took her shoes off. Of course it made no difference to Rick who, when absorbed, would have ignored a cavalry charge, but it amused Julia, especially as poor Arthur, unaware of artistic sensibilities, plodded past in his usual way, even sometimes opening the door to shout in some question.

"Marcus is dead," said Julia.

"Oh I know that. I expect he'll come to life again. Probably when the rates arrive," said Alan, who was a down-to-earth boy. "But what's all this about a historical novel?"

"I know as little about it as you do, love," said Julia. "He just doesn't mention it. I suppose I'll be allowed to see it some day. I usually do the final typing, but whenever I mention it he just clams up, so I leave the subject alone."

"Mummy . . ."

"Yes?"

The train was just about to leave.

"That house . . ."

"You do like it, don't you?"

"I love it. I love it more than anything I've ever seen. Only it's not quite real, is it?"

The station-master was blowing his whistle. Matley Bishop was a tiny station and old-fashioned in its ways.

"I don't really feel myself in it," said Alan. The train was slowly steaming out to catch the connection on the main line. "I feel as if somebody else's character is always being superimposed on me. It's as if . . ."

His words were lost. It was typical of Alan to leave something like this to the last. Julia, frantic with frustration, ran after the train. She called out, "As if . . .?"

But it was too late. The train was gone. Rick, when she repeated this to him, did not seem even interested. "You probably misunderstood," he said.

"I did not! You must admit it was an extraordinary thing to say. What do you think he meant?"

But Rick was too absorbed in his book to answer.

The only other thing that happened before Mark at last came to dinner, was the argument over Rochester.

Julia did not at first go regularly to the hostel, but after the first week managed to put in at least two hours a day: by degrees the two hours became three, then four and sometimes five. Rick did not, as she had expected, protest, but then he was so busy with his book that it was possible he did not even notice. Mrs Purefoy prepared his lunch – "She's a marvellous cook," he told Julia with some surprise – and Julia was always back in time to cook the dinner.

The house at last became theirs. It was hard to say when the actual moment arrived, but there was a point when Julia turned the key and stepped into her own domain. "We've done the ghosts," she said. "Even Grendel uses his cat-door, and Alan is bringing a friend home for Easter; he'll have forgotten all this superimposing nonsense. It's those portraits. I wish we could get rid of them. As for that old summer-house, which I hate more every time I look at it, Arthur is going to have a real go at it once the weather's better, so that it doesn't go on looking like what Mrs Purefoy calls 'an Iranium place for hostages'."

"Is that what she says?" asked Rick, amused enough to be temporarily distracted from his book.

"Oh yes. She's got Iraniums on the brain. Everyone's an Iranium. It seems to be another term for devil. My poor little kids are all Iraniums – Rick, when shall we ask Mark for dinner?"

He gave her a look that seemed to her a little hostile. "I thought," he said, "we weren't going to start entertaining until we've got the house in order. After all, I've got to ask my agent down, and there's the new editor – surely they have precedence."

"Well, that's up to you. But the house is in order."

"Is it?"

She could see his mind was away again on this strange book she had never been invited to see. It was a little odd for he had always liked to discuss his plots with her: once they had spent a whole evening discussing the Nuer until Julia felt that she and Evans Pritchard were practically one, and the notepad in front of them was covered with tribal designs. It had even got to the stage where she would say, "But that's not in keeping with Marcus's character," or, "I don't feel he would be so friendly with the Badjok, they were such a savage tribe." But now there was never a word, and though she felt she had at last surmounted the ghosts, it was only when she came into Rick's study that she was not so sure: every time this happened the two portraits outside took on a new, vibrant life.

She said in her most matter of fact voice, "Well, what's wrong with it? The curtains are up. The carpets are down. Arthur made a marvellous job of the one in the drawing room. Alan's room looks gorgeous . . ."

"I see he still has his sword."

"It's his most treasured possession."

"I'm not sure if we're really entitled to keep it."

"Why not? It came with the house."

But she did not pursue the matter, partly because she suspected he might be right – Did the weapon perhaps come under the heading of treasure trove and Crown property? – and partly because of the extraordinary matter of the teddy-bear which she had never mentioned to him.

She asked Alan about his toys when he turned up one weekend. She did not expect the least difficulty. "They would mean a lot to the kids," she said. "I don't suppose they've ever seen anything like them. They'll go mad over the rocking-horse, and I shouldn't be surprised if they didn't look on the teddy as some kind of god."

He interrupted her. He had gone bright red. "Do you mean to say," he said, "you're going to give all those things away?"

"But darling, they're baby things! They've been

stashed away at the top of that cupboard for years. You can't pretend you play with any of them . . ."

"They're mine! You've no right to touch them."

"Alan, what's the matter with you? I'm not touching them. I'm simply asking your permission to give them away. It's like mothers passing on their baby's clothes. They're no use to anyone. They're just gathering dust. And these children have never had any toys."

"I don't give a damn about the children."

"Alan!"

"They're not having them. I want to keep them." Then he lost his temper. In this he was like his father: he seldom lost his temper but when he did, it was in a grand way. Julia suspected that if she were a boy and not his mother, he would knock her down. He was shouting at her, scarlet in the face. He said stammering and stuttering, nearly in tears, "They're me. They're part of me. There's not much that is in this house, it's always as if someone's forcing his personality on me, and I'm not letting it happen, I'm going to keep what I've got. I'm not going to be shunted around by a lot of measly ghosts, and if I want to hang on to a teddy-bear and a rocking-horse, I'm bloody going to do so, so there!"

And with this he stormed away, leaving Julia stunned into silence. She had told Rick about the conversation at the railway station, but this she did not mention, though she realised later that it was exactly the same thing.

"I feel as if somebody else's character is always being superimposed on me."

The first time it had been said quite calmly. Fortunately Alan never lost his temper for long. When, a couple of hours later, they met at lunch, he was in his normal senses, recounting the latest saga of Mrs Purefoy and her Iraniums, and repeating a conversation with the amiable Arthur who was a firm believer in capital punishment and declared that he would willingly pull the rope himself.

Julia knew now that however happy she might be in Fontenoy – and for the most part she was very happy indeed – what Alan had said applied equally to her. It was like being taken over. It was nothing evil. It was not even frightening. It was simply that at times she felt like a clockwork doll with someone, God knows who, turning the key. The moment she stepped outside the house, the feeling disappeared. When she was at the hostel she felt entirely her normal self.

She wondered what would happen when Mark came to dinner. But before she pursued the matter – she suspected Rick was hoping she would forget about it – she went into Alan's room. He had ostensibly come up to collect all the things he had forgotten, and of course had forgotten them again. There would certainly be something she would have to send on to the school: it was an automatic reaction to any departure. It would, according to his own system of priorities, be something supremely unimportant like underpants, a dressing-gown or handkerchiefs: the really important things like cameras, stamp album, boxing gloves and the pile of thrillers he was reading at the time, would be safely packed and away.

Her eyes moved to the sword which hung between the two book-cases, carefully suspended by Arthur who swore that not even an earthquake would bring it down. It looked magnificent, and she hated it with all her heart and soul. Alan had polished away every grain of rust, the emblem of *L'épée dans l'ombre* stood out clearly, surrounded by small, precious stones.

"It's worth a fortune," said Mrs Purefoy, who hated it

as much as she did, adding, "Only no-one will ever steal it."

"Why not?" demanded Julia who had thought several times that Fontenoy must be a thieves' paradise.

"Oh, don't get me wrong, there's plenty as would want it. But there's no-one here as would touch it; it's got blood on it, it'd be more better to cut one's throat."

Julia looked away from it to Alan's bed which he had made after his own fashion: she could see the lumps under the counterpane and one pillow had fallen to the floor. It did not matter, she would be changing the sheets anyway. Then she saw the teddy-bear in the middle of the bed, with the copy of *Jane Eyre* at its side.

It shocked her so much that she had to sit down. It did not help that this should be the moment for the lights to dim. Since their arrival the lights had behaved normally, and Rick had laughed, saying, "It's the Electricity Board after all. All this nonsense about the accident. People always believe these silly stories. I daresay it's Mrs Purefoy with all that crossing herself."

Whether or not it was the Electricity Board, one thing was plain: they had not done their job properly. Julia peered at her watch in the half-light and saw that it was five o'clock. She sat there in the shadows, and the sword gleamed with a strange light of its own, while that abominable teddy-bear that Alan had not played with since he was five, and which she remembered was called Kiki – why in God's name Kiki? – sat there, a small, battered, inoffensive object. And it frightened her more than the sword because she knew exactly why it was there. He was a big boy now, he had never really been one for cuddly toys, the boys at school would laugh the life out of him if they knew, but Julia understood with an intensity that hurt: it was him, it was Alan. He was in this way desperately and defiantly asserting the personality that he somehow felt was being eroded into and destroyed.

She did not get up until the lights came on again, and the first thing she did was to whisk the toy off the bed. As she came towards the door with the teddy-bear under her arm, Rick looked in, cross and ruffled. "It's those confounded lights again," he said, as if this were some personal affront, then, "What on earth are you doing with that thing?"

"It's for the hostel," said Julia.

He accepted this. He seemed to have forgotten his outrage at her cavalier invasion of Alan's privacy. He said, "You know, it is a little odd. I mean, the lights go down, which must mean the power is diminished, but I could still go on typing. I admit I don't know anything about electric typewriters, but after all, they're on the main like everything else, and you'd expect the thing to slow down, go heavy or even not work at all. But it didn't seem to make any difference, in fact, I was writing so well that I didn't really notice until I changed the page, and then of course I couldn't really read what I had written. Have you tried the television?"

"No. After all, this is the first time it's happened since we arrived. Well, if it doesn't affect your typing, it doesn't matter so much. How is the book going?"

But at this he instantly withdrew. He only said, "Oh, very well, very well."

Julia persisted, "When am I going to be allowed to see it?"

"Oh," he said, moving backwards, "I don't know. I don't think you'll like it anyway."

"Oh Rick, come off it. You know I always like what you write."

"Ah," he said, "but this is different." Then more

cheerfully, "Of course you can see it. But let me finish this chapter first. Didn't you say we had to ask that fellow to dinner, forgotten his name . . ."

"Mark. Mark Rossiter."

"When is he coming?"

"I haven't asked him yet. What about the weekend? I don't think the week's much use to him, he's so involved with the children."

Rick sighed. "All right. If you say so. I know we've got to start entertaining some time, but I hoped we could put it off for a little while longer. Do we have to have someone to meet him?"

"I don't know," said Julia. "I hadn't really thought about it. I don't seem to know any pretty girls in Matley Bishop."

"Perhaps," said Rick, "that hardly matters."

There was an edge to his voice that made Julia stare at him. It made her think of that disgraceful first meeting, but then he could not possibly know about it, nor could anyone else, not even Mrs Purefoy. However, she chose to ignore it, saying, "I think we'll just make it informal. You'll like him. He's a nice sort of chap, and my God, he works hard for those kids. I'll have to make a really special dinner. He never seems to have time to eat anything but sandwiches."

"Hasn't he got a wife?"

"He's divorced."

She picked up the copy of *Jane Eyre* as she spoke. She said with sudden bitterness, "Do you know, it's odd, Rochester's supposed to be the woman's ideal hero, rough and tough with a heart of gold and all that, but I think he was a rotten kind of bastard."

"I wish you wouldn't use language like that."

"I can't think of any other way of putting it."

"I don't know what you mean." There was a sudden sharpness to Rick's voice.

Julia found herself thinking, This is a ridiculous kind of conversation, we never used to talk like this, teddy-bears and lights and Rochester, but she answered, "Well, it's all very well his being so much in love with Jane, and I admit it couldn't have been much fun having a raving mad wife on the premises always trying to burn the place down, but she was there, she was his wife, and it was a pretty dirty trick to ask Jane to marry him when he was married already, and not say one word about it. In these days it doesn't matter tuppence if one gets married or not, though I believe bigamy is still a crime, but in the eighteenth century it would be a dreadful thing to do, it would brand her as a whore, she'd be a ruined woman, she'd be completely ostracised. And did he care? Like hell he did. If his wife's brother hadn't intervened, poor Jane would have been sunk for good and all."

Rick exclaimed, "I've never heard such sentimental nonsense in my life. I think you're wrong, anyway. In those days it probably didn't matter."

"A hundred years earlier," said Julia, "she would have been burnt at the stake."

"How do you know that?"

"I read it somewhere. To marry someone else's husband was regarded as a capital crime."

"Of course you would adopt the woman's point of view."

"If I was tied to a stake with the flames round my feet, you could hardly blame me..." Then Julia realised they were both shouting, the argument was totally illogical and absurd, and she burst out laughing. There was not much amusement in the laughter, but really, she and

Rick could not stand there roaring at each other about a character who never existed except in the imagination of a young girl from a Yorkshire parsonage. She came up to Rick. She thought suddenly that both of them had changed. She said, "Oh for God's sake, darling – Anyone would think Rochester was your best friend. We'll put Jane in the bookcase where she belongs, Alan's teddy can go back in the cupboard, and we'll have a nice drink, then I'll see to the dinner."

And she slipped her arm through his. Only as they came into the drawing-room he said in a clear, loud voice, "You're not in love with that fellow, are you?"

"What fellow?"

"That – that Mark Rossiter."

Yes. Fontenoy had something. Fontenoy had something all right. It was not the kind of question Rick had ever put to her in his life, though there had been moments when he might have put it, there had been the rare occasion when he could, if he chose, have been jealous. She looked at him. The heating was on, but she felt suddenly cold. The friendly house with its beautiful panelling, the handsome new carpet so carefully laid by Arthur, the lamps that shed a soft, gracious light – none of this at that particular moment was friendly; it was inquiring, it was nosey, it was gossiping, it was like Mrs Purefoy.

Then she said firmly, "I hope you're not turning into one of those suspicious husbands. The next thing you'll be asking is if I'm having sexual relations with Arthur. Yes, darling. You are as always perfectly right. I am madly in love with Mark, I'm having it off with Arthur in the summer-house, and what goes on between me and the Electricity Board is nobody's business. The Mata Hari of Matley Bishop, that's me. And you're having navarin of lamb for dinner with petits pois, and if you don't shut up, it's going to be bread and cheese. Mouldy cheese at that. Make mine a double. Us harlots we like our drink."

He said grudgingly but with the hint of a smile, "You swear a lot these days,"

"I do, don't I? I drink quite a lot too." She added, "And so do you, sweetheart. That's what going back into the eighteenth century does for you. I'm just waiting for you to call Arthur a son of a whore, and then I'll know we're Fontenoy's slaves for good and all."

Rick did not burst into reproaches as she half expected. He even smiled then stooped to kiss her. He poured out the drinks, generously enough. He said a little apologetically, "It's that book. It's got an extraordinary hold on me. I'm not sure if I like it. I've never felt this way about anything before."

"It'll probably be the best thing you've ever done. I expect Marcus has gone stale on you. I believe that often happens to authors who always use the same central character. I won't ask to see it again, but I hope you will show it to me soon. I'm longing to read it."

The evening passed peacefully enough, with a good thriller on the television, and Mark Rossiter came to dinner the following Saturday.

There were no more quarrels, the lights remained on, and there was a long letter from Alan in which he sounded entirely his normal self. It held forth at great length about a science master whom everyone detested, and a new boy known as Frog who was both disliked and bullied and on whose account Alan landed the school's best cricketer with a large black eye. "Frog," wrote Alan, "is a loathesome twerp, and I am teaching him how to box."

"What a marvellous non sequitur," said Julia to Rick as she read this out at breakfast. "The boy will be a novelist."

Julia took a great deal of trouble over the Saturday dinner. There was to be *caneton à l'orange*, preceded by a cucumber mousse and followed by profiteroles. It would make a nice change from cheese sandwiches, and if it was all a bit fattening it would hardly matter to Mark who was as thin as a rake. Rick, still working but apparently restored in temper, was so impressed by this menu that he went down into the cellar and chose his best St. Julien, even bringing up a bottle of brandy.

The cellar was something of a joke. In the Vierville days it had no doubt been full of precious wines brought over from France, and it was vast enough to take a hundred crates at least. The Burton rack, which held two dozen bottles, looked rather silly, especially as it was surrounded by cans of beer, and the various fizzy drinks fancied by Alan. But Rick had a good taste in wine, even if he could not run to hundreds of bottles, and Julia looked fondly at the claret, hoping that Mark would know enough about it to appreciate it.

But despite all this, the excellent fat duck provided by Matley Bishop's best butcher, and the fact that the mousse for once was beautifully intact, Julia found herself uneasy and disturbed, which was unusual for she had always loved entertaining and the preparing of a grand dinner was something she enjoyed. There was a pretty dress to be worn, not too grand but pretty all the same and a nice change from pants: the table looked attractive with some early daffodils from the garden, and the weather, though still cold, was dry with a hint of spring.

There was even a good play on the television if the

evening unexpectedly dried up.

There was no reason why anything should go wrong. Rick was a good and accomplished host, Mark was easy to talk to, the duck smelt delicious. But two things did go wrong, a couple of hours before Mark's arrival, indeed, as two of them were connected, the number could be given as three.

First, the lights dimmed again. Julia, mixing her sauce, found herself once more in that strange twilight in which one could still see yet which somehow blurred all outline. She sent the glass of brandy, meant for the final touch, spinning to the floor, the glass broke and the brandy went all over her shoes. She swore, and Rick appeared in the doorway with the plaintive expression of one who had suffered some personal insult.

"Oh well," said Julia, trying to sound as if it did not matter, "it might have been the whole bloody saucepan. Sorry, darling, but I think a little swearing is forgiveable under the circumstances. Thank goodness I haven't changed. Pour me out another brandy, there's a love. I'll clear it all up when the lights come on again. They would choose this one evening – What's the matter?"

For despite the dim light she could see that Rick looked very strange. She said crossly, "Oh darling, it's only those old lights. It's happened before. Everything will be back on in a few minutes. We're lucky that they always go out so early."

"It's Grendel," said Rick.

"Grendel? What on earth do you mean?"

Grendel had at last settled down happily and well. He popped in and out of Arthur's cat-door on his feline errands, chased birds, ruined part of Julia's herb garden, and slept on Alan's bed at night as he had done since kittenhood. Mrs Purefoy made a great fuss of him.

He caught one mouse which upset Julia and delighted Arthur, and after the initial difficulties might have been a country cat all his life, the white fur thick and gleaming, and even developed an unexpected talent for opening the fridge on his own.

Julia cried out, "He's been run over!"

"Certainly not," said Rick. "Just come and see. Oh, never mind that sauce, I'll get you some more brandy in a moment. I want you to come into the sitting-room."

She followed him in, wiping her hands on her apron. Grendel was in the middle of the room. He was preening himself, leaning sideways, his eyes slitted with sensual delight. The purring came from him in rumbling content. It was as if someone was stroking him, and he was rubbing himself against his caresser in an ecstasy of pleasure and love.

Only there was no-one there.

Neither Rick nor Julia uttered a word, only she instinctively reached out for his hand.

And at this moment the lights came on again: Grendel ran towards them, his tail waving, and gave Julia the little miaow that signified he expected attention.

Julia did not touch him. She did not move. She said at last, "I think I'm going to faint." And for a second she did lose consciousness. Dimly aware of the glass held against her lips, she swallowed the brandy Rick had hastily poured out for her, then collapsed into the nearest chair. When Grendel jumped onto her knee she pushed him away.

She whispered, "Oh not again – He'll think I'm an alcoholic."

Fortunately Rick did not hear her. She raised her swimming eyes to his. She now saw that far from being shocked he was delighted. He said, "Fascinating.

Absolutely fascinating. I've never seen anything quite like it." Then he became aware of Julia's face which was still ashen pale. He said remorsefully, "Oh my darling, you're thinking of those ghosts again." He reached down to stroke Grendel in a gentle sweep from head to tail. "You're not seeing ghosts, are you, boy? This is just a little cat fantasy. They're like that. Only I've never seen it done so blatantly. Oh, come on, my darling. You've seen cats stalking non-existent birds, playing with cotton reels, chasing their tails. It's all the same kind of thing. I know he's neutered, poor creature, but he has his sexual fantasies like everyone else, and he was just in one of those moods. It was a marvellous display. I only wish I'd had my camera with me."

"I wonder," said Julia in a small, high voice, "what would have come out in the photo."

He said gently, "I can tell you. One small white cat making a fool of himself. You saw that the moment we came in, he made for us."

"That's when the lights went on again. Rick," said Julia, "someone was stroking him."

"Oh nonsense. Dear, you're really upset. What am I to do with you? Why don't you go upstairs and have your bath and change? We can't have this young man thinking us all mad." Then he said, his voice a little slurred, "You don't really believe there was someone there, do you?"

Julia rose to her feet. She was in control of herself again, but her face was still white. "I think," she said, "there was a young girl there, waiting for her lover. She would be the kind of girl who liked cats. She was perhaps a little like a cat herself."

"I see," said Rick after a pause, "we are going to have a jolly evening."

Then Julia laughed. Her natural colour had returned. "Do you know," she said, "I think we are. And I'll tell you something else. Mr Thomas, if he ever hears of this, will be laughing his heart out. Only I'm not leaving, I'm not, I'm not."

"But nobody . . ."

"I think this is only the beginning."

Rick said in a calm, practical voice, "When did you last have something to eat?"

"You think I'm pissed!"

"Julia!"

"Oh, I'm sorry, I'm sorry. You're probably quite right. I've been so busy with that confounded duck that I didn't bother about lunch. I brought you in your tray, and I suppose I somehow felt that was my lunch too. Don't pay any attention to me. I'll bath and change. After all, everything's ready except for the sauce."

He said eagerly, anxious to propitiate, "I'll clear up the mess."

"That'd be lovely. After all, it's a nice kind of mess. Common folk spill milk, but we spill brandy. Mark's not coming till seven."

And she gave him a little wave as she ran out of the room. But Rick, now busy in the kitchen, did not see her pause for a moment in front of Sir Richard's portrait, nor did he hear her say very softly, "You and I are going to meet one day. Your girl likes cats and I think she likes young men too, but I like you, Richard, I want to know you, and I swear upon whatever one swears that I am not leaving Fontenoy until we've met and I know the whole story. The sword in the shadow – I'll swear on that sword. You're not the only one to say *Reveniam*."

When Mark arrived rather late – there had been a crisis at the hostel; there was always a crisis at the hostel

– his host and hostess were waiting for him with pleasant, unreproachful calm. Julia looked very pretty and smelt of Paris perfume. Rick, who was more handsome than he expected, had put on a smoking jacket, and there was a small, white cat curled up in front of the electric fire which had been lit to give the place a cosy air, despite the central heating. There was a delightful smell coming from the kitchen, the drinks were poured out with a liberal hand, and Mark, who led such a spartan life without any of its amenities, could hardly believe in the gentle luxury that now surrounded him. It made a nice change from snatched sandwiches, cooling cups of tea, blocked drains and hysterical scenes, all of which had become his life, so much so that he could hardly believe there was any other. Yet, from the moment he came in at the door, wearing his one comparatively decent suit, he had to be aware that despite the warmth of the welcome, the atmosphere was strange and strained.

Julia too was aware of this. She was more flushed than usual and talked a little too much. Only Rick was entirely normal and calm. Both of them were, after all, accustomed to entertaining, and Mark was an easy guest, shamelessly admitting that he was famished, drinking three large whiskies, admiring the house, and only after dinner, where he had two helpings of everything, asking if they had seen any of the celebrated ghosts.

He saw at once that the question embarrassed them. He wished he had not asked it. He was a sensitive and imaginative man, which was one of the reasons why his wife had left him – she declared he was always reading between the lines and often something that was not there – but he did not believe in ghosts, and Julia's extraordinary remark when he had first met her, he had put down almost entirely to drink; she probably was not used to drinking. Moving was always a ghastly business; she had had a couple too many and was simply trying to excuse herself. All that nonsense about summer-houses. He thought that as the weather was reasonably mild, he would ask the Burtons to take him on a little tour of the garden, and then he could have a look at the celebrated summer-house himself.

But the fact remained that Fontenoy was connected with a haunting, and he had heard this from every conceivable source: Mrs Purefoy, the local tradesmen, even the minister from St Matthew's Church. And the moment he stepped inside that hallway with the two strange portraits and that beautiful staircase, he had been aware of something, though he would have found it difficult to define. If he had put it into words at all, he would have said that he felt as if he were not the only guest, that there were other people there. And of course there was no-one there at all except for this handsome, elderly man who apparently wrote novels, and his pleasant little wife who was so marvellous with the hostel children, and who was now talking far too much and was so nervous that she knocked the ashtray over and at one point spilt her glass of scotch.

But there was something else, and this was extremely disturbing, even alarming. It worried him through the mousse, the gorgeous duck – the girl was certainly a marvellous cook – and the profiteroles, which he scoffed like a little boy, having tasted nothing so good for a very long time.

His relationship with Julia, after that first meeting, had been on a friendly and workmanlike basis. In any case in such a place as the hostel there would be neither time nor opportunity for any kind of flirtation, much less a liaison. He worked from morning to night, and Julia, from the moment she arrived, was instantly engrossed, splendid with the children who all adored her, and excellent with the mothers who seemed to take to her at once, despite the language difficulty. She started work immediately, took in the situation within the first ten minutes, and was prepared to do anything, from wiping little Vietnamese bottoms to taking on the cooking, receiving hysterical confidences from homesick mothers and coping with tradesmen whose bill had not yet been paid. Mark could not have prayed for a better helper, could hardly believe that he was so lucky, and on the rare occasions when they were on their own, they simply drank cups of tea. There was one occasion, and one only, when he took her to the local for a beer.

There was not the faintest spark between them. The episode of their first meeting was as forgotten as if it had never taken place. Their friendship was deep and sexless. It is only in films that social workers leap into bed together: in real life there is no time and probably no bed either.

It was therefore horrifyingly disconcerting to find now that not only did he see Julia as both pretty and attractive, but that he was aware of a deep and unmistakable desire to make love to her. He found himself noting the curve of her breast, the elegance of her legs, the movement of her body, and even visualised what she would look like without her clothes on. Mark liked women but was no womaniser: his divorce was due to far more fundamental things and, if he had ever been unfaithful, it was incidental and rare. He supposed that one day he would marry again, if he could ever find a wife who could endure a life of Vietnamese children, not enough money and a husband who was hardly ever at home, but the divorce was still recent and bitter in his mind, and the odd girl-friends he acquired from time to time had frankly been bedmates, with nothing more serious considered on either side. To come out to dinner with these nice people and find that he could hardly look at Julia without passionately wanting to be in bed with her, was not only startling, it was disgusting.

It was not as if she were exceptionally pretty; she certainly was not beautiful. She wore an attractive dress – it was the first time he had seen her out of slacks – she had a nice, if rather plump figure, and she reminded him a little of Julie Andrews who had never attracted him. There was a suburban look to her rather than a glamorous one, she was a good cook but certainly no courtesan, and he could not understand her nervousness which he had never noticed in the hostel, and the quick, anxious way she was talking.

The husband he found amiable and intelligent, perhaps a little of a bore. He was much older than Julia. Later, as the dinner progressed – "Marvellous wine," he said, as indeed it was – he was not quite so sure of the amiability. Rick talked easily and well, was mildly left-wing in politics, anecdotal about his fellow-writers; when they reached the brandy stage they all met on the subject of Mrs Purefoy, and this really got them off the ground: she had once again had sexual relations with Arthur, and as a result undressed in the sitting-room every night so as not to inflame him further.

But the phrase of course aroused other thoughts, and Mark by this time was so distraught and shocked by his own reactions that he decided to go home early. He did not want to go home at all, to his chilly, bare little room when here it was so warm and luxurious, but the whole thing was becoming perfectly ridiculous, and he had never in his life felt so hopelessly out of control. It was at this point that he asked about the ghosts. The urge within him was so strong that he felt he dared not be alone with Julia, and he suspected she was aware of this for she took care to keep her distance, and once or twice he was sure the husband looked at him in a suspicious way as if he too were aware that something strange was going on.

Mark thought, "Perhaps I'm drunk", and, "Perhaps I'm going mad". Certainly he had drunk a great deal but he had eaten a great deal too, and he had always had a good head. It was almost – the thought flashed through his mind – as if he were somehow possessed. The question about ghosts was somehow jerked from his mouth: it was by no means simply idle conversation.

It was Rick who answered the question. "No," he said, "we've seen no ghosts. Don't tell me you're aware of some kind of psychic atmosphere."

Mark was very much aware of an atmosphere, though he would hardly have called it psychic, but answered at once that he was not: the room after all looked cosy and lived-in, with flowers on the table, a large colour television with a remote-control gadget, and the small, white cat still curled up in front of the fire.

He thought a little fresh air might help. He said, "Of course there's no atmosphere. I daresay it's all a story. In fact, I've never been in a place that looks less haunted." He looked at Julia and smiled. "Do you know, I was wondering if I could have a look at the garden and clear some of the brandy fumes from my head. The first time I came here was one of the worst blizzards we've ever known. But it seems mild enough now, and we can see our way from the lighted windows. Have you been able to get anything done to it? I gather it's quite wild." He added, "Mrs Purefoy again. In fact if the word 'ghost' crops up, it's always Mrs Purefoy. I think if she lived a couple of centuries back she'd have been burnt as a witch. I see as little of her as I can, but she tends to pop in with messages for Julia. I wish she wouldn't, she frightens the children."

"She can't bear those Iraniums," said Julia, who seemed to have calmed down and who spoke in her normal husky voice. "It's funny about the children, she has such nice ones of her own. Still, I can't have her frightening our kids. I'll see if I can stop the visits. What does she say about the ghosts? She crosses herself so frequently I'd have thought she'd have scared them off."

"She says you won't stay long," said Mark. He did not know why he repeated this foolish remark, but it seemed forced out of him. "She talks about people called Hepplethwaite – are there really names like that? – who left in a kind of frenzy, after the husband suffered some kind of personality change." Then he said quickly, "I really don't think one ought to listen to anything Mrs Purefoy says. I think she's a bit mad. And Arthur seems such a calm, sensible kind of man. She's just got a mania about Fontenoy. Can't you find yourself another help? It must be a bit off-putting to have someone who crosses herself every time she comes in."

"She's a marvellous worker," said Julia. She refilled Mark's brandy glass. She added reflectively, "I don't think anyone else is very anxious to work here. It's awfully odd, but I must admit that though there are no actual ghosts, there is something a bit peculiar about the place. Even Alan – that's my son – has noticed it. It's not unpleasant, mind you, it's just that sometimes one feels one has sub-tenants."

"Now look," said Rick, "you're talking absolute nonsense. Sub-tenants indeed! I can tell you one thing. I'm working better here than I've ever worked in my life. The new book is a quarter finished. I'd forgotten what it was like to write with such enthusiasm. It's almost like being possessed . . ."

He broke off. Then he said, "Well, if you want to, why don't you two take that walk round the garden? I'll carry all these things into the kitchen." He gave Mark a smile. "You see I am a well-trained husband. Mind you, the garden's still pretty much of a mess. We just haven't had time to get down to it yet. I daresay my son will get busy in the Easter holidays, he likes that kind of thing. And Arthur of course is panting to get at the roses which he says need pruning and mulching – I think that's the word, no idea what it means. I must look it up. He's an extraordinary man, he can do anything. I can't think how he runs his shop; he never seems to be there. Perhaps Mrs Purefoy does it when she's finished with us. But if you like thorns and thistles and weeds and general muddle, by all means have a look at it. My wife says there are some marvellous strawberry beds, and there's a nice little stream at the end, though I don't think there's anything there but mud and some rather slimy vegetation." He paused. He said, "You could take a look at the notorious summer-house."

"Oh, I've heard about that," said Mark. He avoided Julia's eye. He did not say that this was the one thing he particularly wanted to see. He said, "Mrs Purefoy goes on about it no end. She's told me never to go near it, which of course is enough to make anyone rush to it immediately."

"It's hideous," said Julia. "We're having it pulled down."

"We're having it renovated," said Rick.

"I loathe it," said Julia, then, "Come with us, Rick. It'll do you good to have a little fresh air. I'm afraid it was rather a heavy meal."

"It was gorgeous," said Mark.

But Rick refused to come, and to Julia's astonishment actually started loading the dinner things on to the trolley: he had called himself a well-trained husband but this was the first time she had ever known him do a hand's turn. However, she did not argue, only fetched her coat, and presently she and Mark opened the French windows and sauntered out into the garden.

It was surprisingly mild. Julia, who felt confused and a little queasy as if she had eaten too much, though she had hardly touched her dinner, heard the clatter in the kitchen. It sounded as if Rick was actually doing the washing up. He was the least domestic of men as he had told her from the very beginning. "It's not," he said, "that I'm anti-feminist or object on principle, it's just that I'm quite helpless in a kitchen. I seem to break everything I touch, and the only thing I can cook with safety is a boiled egg. And that's never right either, it's either too hard or too soft. Perhaps you could train me. Perhaps you could turn me into a cordon bleu chef."

Julia had laughed at him. Those were the days when she was obsessedly in love: she would have eaten a raw egg if he had offered it to her. She assured him that she was very domestic and an excellent cook: she did not want him in the kitchen and would throw him out immediately if he dared to intrude. Later on, especially when she spent so much time at Fontenoy before the move, she thought occasionally that he might make an effort to fry bacon and egg, but it was only occasionally she felt rebellious, and at this moment could only think it was a pity she had used the best dinner service which, judging from the sounds, was no longer complete. However, it was silly to think that this kind of thing was really important, it was quite chic these days to use plastic plates and if Rick had suddenly decided to become domestic, the best of luck to him.

The garden in the half-light looked depressing. Julia, mainly to cheer herself up, said it would be lovely once Arthur got down to it, and there would be a splendid display of roses once the forest around them had been cleared.

Mark said very little. He was wishing to God he had not made the original suggestion, that he had simply stayed for a coffee and gone back to the hostel. It would have been a quite legitimate excuse: Julia would have understood immediately. The one mother who spoke a little English had been left in charge, but would certainly go to pieces if any crisis arose, and Mark had left her the Burtons' telephone number, telling her to ring at once if anything happened. And here he was, alone with Julia, and the desire within him was so violent that he scarcely knew how to control himself. It was shocking, it was ridiculous, it was incomprehensible, it was obscene. The worst part of it was that he was beginning not to care, even to accept it. In a sense none of it was quite real. He felt as he had once done when much younger, acting in a school play. He was not a good actor, and it was not a good play. He could not even remember the title of it, but he knew he had to play a little clerk in an office. It was not much of a part, and he spent most of his time saying, "Yes, sir, of course, sir, at once, sir," rushing here and there with bundles of files which he always dropped, to provoke dutiful laughter from the parent audience.

He had been bored too. In the end it became so unreal

to him that it was as if he were in the audience, watching himself. He was not bored now, but he was no longer Mark Rossiter, he was someone else and, as they came up to the summer-house, he somehow knew that for Julia it was the same. They were two people in a play and it was about to be played out: the curtain was going up.

The summer-house somehow looked uglier than usual. Mrs Purefoy would have called it Iranium, and the description would have been apt: it wore a bogus eastern air, one would have expected to see some dreadful crippled beggar huddled in the doorway, holding out his bowl.

He looked at Julia. He could not see her clearly, but the passion for her possessed him. The pretty dress had somehow blown about her so that it seemed fuller and longer, the boyish crop was as if it were piled high.

She said, not in her normal husky tones but in a quick, high little voice, "You must not."

He said, "Why not? Tell me, why not? What harm are we doing? He doesn't care. He has his women. You know that. We all know that." And, "Oh God, I love you so much . . ."

And, "Oh Jesus, what the hell am I saying? It's not true, it cannot be true, I don't love you, I don't know you, you are Julia Burton, you have asked me to dinner, your husband writes books, you work in the hostel, this is all preposterous . . ."

"My lady . . ." And he stretched out his hand to run it softly from her wrist to her elbow, then the next moment caught her to him and began to kiss her, at first gently then more and more violently as if he would devour her.

She did not struggle. She only said in a sighing voice,

"Have you no thought for my reputation? For my life? He'd kill me if he found out." Then her voice rose. "Go away immediately or I'll set the dogs on you."

He only stepped inside the summer-house, pulling her after him. Then he released her. They could not see each other's faces. They were in two worlds; the worlds met, yet were miles apart. The ugly little place with its wooden bench and arched ceiling, enclosed them: outside was the wild garden, the pale green of spring flowers already pushing up through the weeds, the early daffodils bowing and becking in the breeze. There was no moon, there were no stars, there was only the distant light from the French windows. The place smelt of dust and mould and age and sweat and perfume as if there were a crowd of people around them. There were distant voices, there was movement and the rustle of silken clothes. The ghosts were there, a myriad of them, their time was done and now they were nothing but socket-faces with great round empty eyes, there was no more love and no more hate, yet their shadows lay dark and heavy upon the little plump girl and the insignificant young man who faced her.

Then the moon suddenly reappeared between the clouds. In the pale light they saw each other. Both moved backwards, and Julia, sick, shivering, icy cold, caught her heel on something in the corner of the summer-house. She stooped to pick it up: the compulsion to know was strong upon her. She could see it well enough in the moonlight. It was a torn and filthy piece of material, a kind of cotton, perhaps cambric. Cambric? She had no idea what cambric was. It had black stains on it. She thought they were blood, but there was no reason to think this: the thing, whatever it was, had been there for a long time, it was probably plain dirt. She held it between her hands, and Mark, always silent, suddenly shuddered.

She swung round towards the entrance. It was still like being in an invisible party. There was no-one there but themselves, yet people thronged round them; she could feel them, hear them, smell them. She looked at Mark with longing and revulsion, a passion for him, a passion to be away. She cried out in a loud voice, "Oh for Christ's sake, get out!" gave him a great shove though he had not so much as moved towards her, then began to run down the path.

He followed her. He kept a distance between them. When Rick appeared from the side path, they both stopped dead.

She could not see his face. She thanked God for it, for the anger came from him like a flame. The moon had gone in again, and they stood there, the three of them motionless.

Rick said to Mark, "I think you had better go home."

Mark did not answer him. He walked silently through the French windows and into the hall. Rick and Julia walked behind him, not speaking a word. He opened the front door and stepped outside. Then for the first time he turned to stare at them. It was as if he were looking at strangers. The tall, elegant man with a great dome-like mass of thick, greying hair, looked so like what a writer ought to be that one felt he must in reality be a chartered accountant. The face would normally be kind; it was lined and lean with deep-set eyes. There was an air of distinction to him that seemed to signify that if he was a bore, he was at least a distinguished bore. This was a man who would at once give a donation to Vietnamese refugees and forget about them the next minute: pictures of dying Cambodian children would make him shudder, and then he would begin working out his next chapter. Mark had met plenty like him in different professions. They were useful to him as generous donors but in his heart he despised them, accepting their gifts as intellectual conscience-money.

And Julia.

He was standing on the path. She stood motionless in the doorway. They were like dummies. It was the first time this monstrous evening that he had looked at her outside the house and garden. He could only believe that he was drunk or raving mad. At this moment he had no wish to make love to her whatsoever. He did not even find her particularly attractive. She was a little too plump and he liked slender women, like his own ex-wife. The boyish hair was too young for her: she must be well into her thirties. The dress was pretty enough and certainly expensive, but there was not much style to it, and her nail varnish did not match the lipstick. She was comely enough, she was certainly intelligent, and she was far and away the best helper he had ever had, but the thought of going to bed with her, though by no means unpleasing, was just silly; she was married, she had a jealous husband, and it was the kind of thing that would be all over Matley Bishop within twenty-four hours.

And yet, for that brief time, he had wanted her more than he had ever wanted a woman in his life.

He did not say good night. How could he? "Thank you so much for such a nice evening." Or, "It really was a marvellous dinner." It would have been ludicrous and obscene. Rick must have seen the embrace. He must have stood outside the summer-house, watching them. Naturally he had thrown Mark out, and who was to blame him? Young men asked to dinner do not normally make passionate love to their host's wife.

He could not even say, "See you at the hostel tomorrow afternoon."

Oh God, oh God! Mark, now a couple of miles away, braked outside the "Bishop's Arms" and in defiance of having drunk whisky, some excellent claret and two brandies, went in and ordered himself a beer. In his inexplicable lunacy he had not only alienated two neighbours, behaved disgracefully and insulted a charming young woman, he had also lost a superlative helper on whom he had come more and more to rely. He saw himself hemmed in once again by well-meaning women who could not get on with the mothers and who could not begin to understand the emotional state of small children crowded together in a filthy boat, who had seen their families murdered and whose shrunken bellies could only absorb small amounts of food at frequent intervals.

Julia had instinctively understood all this, God knows how. She even sent some of the food back to the kitchen, explaining at great length how starved people craved for food they could no longer physically absorb. The mothers doted on her, and Mark had never forgotten the council officer sent to complain (perfectly legitimately) of overcrowding, who had ended by planning with Julia how to fit six children into a room obviously intended for three.

He would never find anyone like her again, and now she was gone simply because for no known reason he had lost his self-control and virtually tried to rape her.

He said aloud, "Christ, what a bloody fool I am!" drove home rather erratically – fortunately, there were few cars on the road at that hour – drank some more beer and fell drunkenly into bed, ignoring the little pile of notes and messages that inevitably awaited him.

Julia and Rick stood in the hall. The portraits looked down on them. Like Mark, she simply did not know what to say or do. Nothing remotely like this had ever occurred before. She really was not – the silly phrase came into her mind – that kind of girl. They had done a great deal of entertaining in their time. For Julia it was part of her job, and Rick, though he seemed reserved and concentrated on his work, liked people, knew how to talk to them and was a friendly, genial host. There had been disasters. There were always disasters. A guest, whose wife had just left him, had turned up totally drunk and in floods of tears. A young couple had brought their three-year-old son with them because the baby-sitter had not come, and Julia had cheerfully put him to bed in the spare room where he howled piercingly and without cease throughout the dinner so that all conversation stopped and his parents had to take him home. It was all part of the game, it did not happen very often, and small, domestic dramas like upsetting an entire casserole on the kitchen floor, which Julia with Alan's help scraped up, put back in the dish and served with charm and dignity, happen to everyone.

This was worse than a spilt casserole. Julia said at last, "I'm going to finish the washing up."

Rick said, "You whore!"

Perhaps it had been said before. *You whore*! The portraits still stared. Sir Richard Vierville wore his customary frown, but Julia could have sworn that his wife was smiling, a soft, sly, cat-like smile that signified a hateful complicity.

That smile was the last straw. Julia lost her temper. She screamed out, "How dare you call me that! All right, so Mark kissed me in that bloody summer-house. I shouldn't have let him. Of course I shouldn't. I don't know why I did. But do you know something, it was rather fun. After all, I'm a great deal older than he is . . ."

"Three years," said Rick.

This disconcerted her into a brief silence. She had no idea how carefully he had worked this out. Then she said more quietly, "Three years is quite a lot, but surely that's irrelevant. Of course I shouldn't have let him, though what the hell I was supposed to do, I do not know. Smack his face? How very Victorian. He'd had a bit too much to drink, life in the hostel is not exactly a riot of sex, you know, he was in the mood, probably been working up to it for months, and there I was, so he just made the most of it. I've no doubt he's furious with himself for being so silly, and tomorrow he'll ring up to apologise. If you hadn't been so melodramatic we could have laughed it off, had another brandy and . . ."

She broke off. Laughing it off and having another brandy seemed, when put into words, as appropriate as putting up an umbrella against a nuclear bomb. She said in a snap, "I want a brandy now."

"You've had too much already."

"That's none of your business. If I want to get pissed, I'll bloody well get pissed."

"What a vulgar little slut you are," said Rick.

"And you," said Julia, "are a crashing old bore."

He received this in silence, but she saw the delicate colour flood into his cheeks. She was horrified. If she could have recalled that abominable sentence she would have done everything in the world to do so. The fourteen years' difference between them had of course been discussed many times, first after the formal proposal and later when Rick chose to assume that she was panting for a life of discos and wild dances, and even begged her to find herself an escort of her own age. Julia had never been one for discos and wild dances and simply laughed. For a long time now the matter had never been mentioned.

But of course the gap was there, and in that shocking phrase – oh, how right he was, she was a vulgar slut and worse – it became a chasm that perhaps they would never be able to cross again. She looked at the old man who was her husband, who seemed now to have aged by a hundred years, and she loved and hated him, wanted to revile him yet longed to put her arms round him and say simply, "I love you, come to bed".

She said at last in a choked, hoarse voice, "I didn't mean that. I'm sorry. But I would like that brandy, Rick, and I think you should have one too and then perhaps we can talk this over in a civilised manner."

"Civilised manner!"

"Why not? Oh come now, is this all so dreadful? Your nice, well-behaved little wife lets a young man kiss her in the summer-house." She swung round to point at the portrait of Lady Juliet. "I bet she did a great deal worse."

"She was a whore too," said Rick, and suddenly took a step forward and slapped her hard across both cheeks. She gave a little shriek of shock and rage and fright, for such a thing had never happened to her before, stepped backwards and trod on Grendel's tail: he had been sitting there, watching them, no doubt picking up the ugly emotions in his feline way, for his eyes were wide and very green.

He gave a squawk and shot forward, not through the cat-door but out of the kitchen door which was a little open, and into the outside lavatory.

Julia cried, "Oh darling, I'm so sorry," and ran after

him. Things were bad enough without brutalising the cat as well. Grendel was no more accustomed to such treatment than she was to a box on the ear. He spat at her as she tried to catch him, and flew into the furthest corner of the lavatory, huddled up so that she could see nothing but the dim whiteness of him and the green light of his eyes. And as she stooped down to pick him up and pet him back into good humour, the door slammed behind her and she heard the key turned.

Rick's voice came from a distance as if he were walking away. "You can stay there," he said. "There's no-one to let you out. I'm going for a walk. I don't know when I'll be back. Good night."

She heard the sound of the kitchen door being closed and the bolt shot. She heard Rick's receding footsteps then the slam of the front door. She stood there with Grendel, purring forgiveness in her arms, and all around was darkness and four windowless walls.

The claustrophobia that had dogged her all her life descended on her like the cap that in the Wild West they put over the heads of men about to be hanged. She could see nothing, she was in the dark and the cold, entirely shut in; for a while she could not even see the lavatory which was of the old wooden kind so that not even a gleam of porcelain illuminated the gloom. Only the warm, furry body, beginning to struggle against her frantic, clutching hands, saved her from complete frenzy.

She cried out, "Rick! Rick! Let me out. You know I go mad if I'm shut up – Rick!" Then she burst out sobbing, dropping the cat, and fumbled for the lavatory: at least this was somewhere where she could sit down, some oasis in this black space that took the breath from her. She could not find it, she stumbled and fell, then her hand at last found the seat to hold on to, but she was so paralysed by panic that she could not get up.

The tears poured down her smarting cheeks. She wailed, "Help, help, oh please, someone help me . . ."

The key turned in the lock. The door slowly opened. Poor Grendel, who had taken more than any cat should have to endure, shot out ahead of her, and Julia, all pride gone, shaking so badly that she could hardly walk, sobbed in a gasping wail, "Rick!"

There was no-one there. Yet the door was open, and so was the kitchen door, with the light still on and a deplorable mess of plates and cutlery overflowing the sink.

There was no-one there, but somebody had opened both doors, somebody had come to her rescue.

And somebody was there.

There was no-one to see, the drawing-room across the hall was empty, but it was as if a hand were underneath her elbow, and Julia, no longer crying, walked almost proudly across the floor, pausing only to look at the two portraits as if to impress them on her memory.

Lady Juliet smiled at her mistily, with her plump cat-face and raised, round breasts. Sir Richard she could not see at all except for his emblem, *L'épée dans l'ombre*. It shone like a star against the blackness, and it comforted her with a deep, sweet comfort so that the terror still hammering within her subsided: she had no longer any reason to be afraid, she was comforted, protected.

She came into the drawing-room. Rick had left all the lights on. The place seemed to her a shambles, and Mrs Purefoy would toss her hair-domed head and remark to the ceiling as she always did, "We were brought up to plump the cushions before we went to bed," then rush round emptying ashtrays and tut-tutting over damp glass rings on the polished tables. Alan, when he experienced this display of temperament for the first time, behaved outrageously, only it made Julia laugh so much that she could not bring out the correct maternal reproaches. Under Mrs Purefoy's very eye he trotted round the room, picked up every cushion, positively hammered it into shape then placed it back with a delicate reverence, standing a little back, head on one side as if to make sure it was in the correct place.

The cushion phase had passed. Mrs Purefoy now accepted that the Burtons were as untidy as everyone else who lived outside her particular heaven. Julia sometimes visualised her paradise as a kind of Ideal Homes Exhibition, where presumably the saved removed their shoes before entering their last resting place: it must be quite incredibly boring. But at least the Burtons were better than the Fosters, who apparently left her all the washing-up as well and had never emptied an ashtray in their lives. However, this time the Burtons would be reckoned the worst of all, with dirty glasses everywhere, brimming ashtrays and cushions fallen to the floor.

And of course none of this mattered. Indeed, none of it was very clear to her. She sank down on the sofa. All weakness and fright had left her. Why should she be afraid? She was no longer alone. There was no-one there, yet the presence of him filled her, his voice, deep, a little harsh, sounded in her ears, she felt the touch of the hand that was not there, could even smell the scent of him, the pommade that gentlemen in those days wore upon their hair.

"Richard," she said, and the tears sprang to her eyes, only they were tears of joy, delight, ecstasy and love.

And again, "Richard. I've so longed for you and I did not even know it. I have dreamed of you, felt you near me, only I believed you despised me, thought me a cheap whore."

"You a whore!"

The voice was clear to hear, with the faint laughter behind it. The voice was in her mind, the sight of him behind her eyes, yet she heard and saw him as if he were at her side, and the face that had once seemed dark and proud was gentle and tender and sad. She held out her hands to him and could have sworn that he took them in his, yet her hands extended in space with nothing to grasp. She knew with the utmost conviction that she was between time, she was in no time, neither 1980 nor 1750, she was in a world that the two hundred years enfolded, protected and loved by someone who was mouldering in St Matthew's churchyard, whose body was dead and whose spirit had bestrode the centuries to be beside her.

The voices rang in her ears, hers and his, yet she did not so much as speak. The warmth of his arms was about her, his breath upon her cheek, and all the love she had never known, a love that bore no relation at all to what she had felt for Rick and innumerable others, enveloped her, was like a mist that brought the tears of happiness to her eyes, a consummation that no sexual ecstasy could attain. She was stripped of all pretence, and when at last she spoke, she could only say, "I love you".

Voices in counterpoint. Voices in silence. An untidy room, circa 1980, remnants of a disastrous dinner party which had enacted scenes that had taken place two hundred years ago, forced out emotions that were not hers, superimposed on her and Rick and Mark by people who were no longer there. Rick was gone.

Perhaps he would never come back. For this moment he did not exist, only a sluttish, wicked girl who married above her and played the devil with a stupid man who got more than he bargained for, whose passion and whose fear were so vast that they enveloped everyone who came into contact with them.

And Sir Richard, betrayed, reviled, slandered and murdered, had stepped out of his frame to rescue and comfort her.

Reveniam.

Voices in counterpoint. Voices within the heart.

"*I loved you the first moment I saw you.*"

"I did not understand. How stupid I was, how incredibly stupid! I was sorry for her. For her!"

An untidy room, circa 1980. No maids in 1980, only Mrs Purefoy who would faint if she found the kitchen full of dirty dishes and the cushions unplumped. An untidy room, with the remnants of an unhappy dinner party, and no-one there except a young woman, a little too plump, lively, intelligent, whose husband had locked her in the lavatory and then walked out.

A room, circa 1980. The Sheraton cabinet – "That's a nice unit," Mrs Purefoy remarked, though she looked with disapproval at the china and ornaments inside it; no taste of course, so untidy, not like the nice things she had at home, the imitation Dresden, the little cat from Southend, the bowl of imitation china flowers her sister had given her for Christmas. A cool yet warm room circa 1750 with furniture to match, no electric fire now, but roaring, crackling, sweet-smelling apple-wood, delicate chairs, an embroidered fire-screen, little occasional tables that the de Viervilles had brought over from Paris a century ago.

And no-one there and everyone there: a tall, dark

man, legs stretched out, hands in pockets, deep-set eyes under the jetty brows, and on his knee a small white cat, purring with contentment, not preening himself as he had done before but leaning back comfortably against an embroidered shirt, eyes half closed as if a strong hand were gently smoothing down his fur.

A small white cat of 1980, sitting on a 1750 knee, stroked by a 1750 hand, whose eyes, half shut, took in two hundred years as if they were nothing.

Julia looked and saw what was not there to see, and for the first time fear shivered through her: the cat's acceptance turned death into life, those slitted eyes saw clearly what was in her heart, and for a second it was as if the world shimmered round her in confusion. Electric fire blended with wood fire, there was electricity and candles, tapestry and modern silk, and outside the noise of motor cars intermingled with the clip-clop of horses' hooves.

Then it no longer mattered. There was no time, it was normal, it was commonplace. The past and future had become a glorious present, and she smiled, extending her hand, knowing it would be clasped in living fingers that were long since dead.

"*Is it all right now*?"

"Yes, oh yes. I don't know why I was so frightened. I suppose it was because he locked me in. I cannot bear being shut up. I have always been like that. Once my mother shut me in a cupboard because I was naughty, and I screamed and screamed. They had to get the doctor; he said I must never be shut up again.

"*How could he do such a thing to you*?"

"Oh poor man, he was so angry. He cannot understand. He will never begin to understand. Do you really blame him? It is a great deal to take in, and he does not have that kind of imagination. It's poor Mark I'm really sorry for. He must be cursing himself. Not only has he disgraced himself by making love to his hostess, but he's now got to look for a new helper. I'd gladly go back, but of course that is quite impossible; I'm afraid the poor little Vietnamese will have to do without me."

"*The poor little . . .? I do not understand what you are saying.*"

"It doesn't matter. It's two hundred years out of time. We are the only people who matter. Do something for me, Richard. Bend your head. Rub your cheek against the cat. And then you can come over and kiss me."

She saw Grendel arch himself with pleasure, raise his head, put out a paw as if to pat a cheek. The next instant he was shot to the floor. He did not jump, he was plainly pushed, and was at once outraged, scurrying to one side as if out of the way of oncoming boots. But Grendel was not one to be easily discouraged. He was spoilt, he had always had affection and attention lavished on him, and a minute later he was back on his favourite knee again, only this time it was on the couch at Julia's side, and it seemed to her as if he were a little suspended in air; he did not touch the couch but reclined there as if on some invisible cushion plumped up by Mrs Purefoy.

She received the kiss that was no kiss at all. She could have sworn that she felt the lips against hers, the encroaching tongue, felt the pressure of his hands on her shoulders. The room was full of him. Her physical vision no longer mattered. She could see and hear and feel; the nothing had become everything.

"*You cannot possibly love him. You love me.*"

"I believe in some strange way I do love him. When I first met him I thought he was the most wonderful person I had ever seen. I'd never met anyone remotely like him. He seemed so wise and so kind . . ."

"*Kind*!"

"But then this place has changed him. As it has changed me. We have all been possessed, we have all altered. I was told this would happen. I did not believe it. I laughed. I'm ashamed that I laughed. But of course it's true. We have in some way been compelled to enact what happened a long time ago. For this moment I have moved into your time. But Rick would never understand that, any more than he understands how much he has changed himself. How could he see that, when Mark made love to me in the summer-house, it was nothing to do with us. But whoever it was, you didn't kill him, did you? I could not bear to think of your killing anyone."

"*Oh, I am no murderer. I believe I have the blackest of reputations, but I have never killed anyone in my life. I drew my sword on him, that's all. He was so afraid, he was trembling like a jelly. He was a poor kind of bastard, though talented enough in his own way. I don't mean Philip. I mean Monsieur Dieudonné. Hardly a suitable name; I never learnt his first one, or if I did, I have forgot. I made him screw the pictures on the wall.*"

"Why did you do that?"

"*Reveniam*!"

"I don't understand."

"*I had to stay. I was waiting for you. When the picture goes, I go.*"

"I still don't understand. Your wife . . ."

"*Oh, Juliet never had any taste except when she married me, and then, poor bitch, she expected all the things she never got. It was she who was the killer. She did her damnedest to kill me and in her way she succeeded. I should indeed have killed her instead of pinking this wretched creature who all but fainted at the sight of his own blood. I had to staunch it with my handkerchief. You saw it there. You can throw it away. It is not my blood. There is nothing left of me but what lies in your own heart. Dieudonné is long since dead, and so is Juliet. So is Juliet.*"

"What happened to her? I hope she came to a bad end."

The echo of a laugh. "*Perhaps. Perhaps she did. She married again. She married a farmer. She had six children. I believe he beat her. He had more sense than me, but she never gave me a child; she said she could not abide children.*"

"Did you want a child?"

"*More than anything in the world.*"

"I at least have Alan, my darling Alan."

"*Your Alan sees me a little.*"

"That's not possible!"

"*Ah, but it is. He resembles your cat, he sees into the past. He does not know it. It is like a mist for him. He believes he is dreaming, but he sees as he sees my sword, though he is deceived by Juliet's beauty, as I was too, and takes it for granted I am a monster. I think his vision is growing clearer.*"

"I don't like it. It's not good for him."

"*I'll do him no harm. He is a remarkable boy. You are fortunate to have such a son. I wish you could have mine.*"

"Oh, how I wish I could!"

"*I think it's time you knew about Juliet. And also about your husband . . .*"

"My husband! But I know everything about my husband."

"*You know nothing, my dearest dear. Nothing at all. And he has decided to make his confession.*"

"I just do not know what you are talking about."

"*There is a great deal you do not yet know. I see things too. But though he has not seen me, he has seen Juliet, and now you are going to read what he has written. He'll not be back till the morning. You will see me as Juliet wished the world to see me. That is one reason why he is so angry, why he has treated you so abominably. He has written this down as she wished him to do, and in his heart he knows it is wrong, he knows he is writing lies. It was after all so easy. A loosened girth . . .*"

"What do you mean?"

"*So easy an accident. Only it did not kill, and then she chose the final revenge, she determined to keep me alive. It was the cruellest revenge imaginable. It was fortunate for me – But never mind. Read. It is all written down. You will see all the love and devotion of a faithful little wife. Read it, Julia. Read it now. And then . . .*"

"Oh God," said Julia with a sudden sob. "And then – What then? He'll want to leave here. They all want to leave."

"*Yes.*"

"I'm not leaving, Richard."

"*You may have no choice.*"

"I'm not leaving. If Rick leaves, he goes without me. Must I really read this now? Yes. Yes, I must. I know. But how could he know? How could he write it all down?"

"*It is Juliet who has written it. Read it. You have heard my story. Hear hers.*"

Julia rose to her feet. She was aware of his presence but he was no longer beside her. She cried out in sudden passion, "You won't go? Promise me you won't go."

"*I'll not leave you till the end of time.*"

She went into Rick's study. She nearly took a drink in

with her, but decided she neither wanted nor needed it. She was trembling with love and a strange kind of happiness. It was the middle of the night but she was as refreshed as if wakened from a deep sleep. She sat down in Rick's swivel chair. A pile of typed sheets lay on the table. It was all in complete disorder for Rick, in everything else a neat and tidy man, invariably left his desk in disarray, not even troubling to cover up the typewriter.

Only the books were in order, the anthropological books that had produced Marcus Tremayne. The statuettes that so offended Mrs Purefoy were where they had always been, the pictures on the wall, mostly photographs, straight, dusted, with the right distance between them. There was, Julia saw, her own photo on the desk, taken three years ago when they were on holiday, smiling, sunburnt, happy. But everywhere else was a mess of biros, notebooks, boxes of paper-clips, typing and carbon paper. No-one was allowed to touch this, and Mrs Purefoy moved round it almost with reverence: Julia had caught her once or twice dabbing at a small bare space with her duster and looking very guilty when she realised she had been seen.

She pushed the typewriter back, and set the small pile of typescript in front of her; she began to read.

Oh, I am so bored. So bored! They all tell me I'm a lucky girl. Why am I a lucky girl? I am very pretty, there is no reason, dear Diary, why I should not say that. I know I'm pretty; I'm far prettier than any of the other girls in Matley Bishop. I am seventeen and men adore me. And this is as it should be, I adore being adored, and so far I have had five proposals of marriage, which does not include Sir Charles; he did not propose marriage and had no intention of doing so as I very well knew from the first. Sometimes – oh, Papa, you would kill your daughter for such wicked words – but sometimes I wish I had accepted his offer, for instead of living in the schoolhouse with horrid little boys surrounding me and you, poor Papa, still mourning after Mama, though I sometimes think you did not truly love her, I should be in Park Lane with dozens of servants to do my bidding, fine clothes, as much money as I could spend, and every night the playhouse or a ball or some wonderful party. Why, I might even have met the King, though they say he is fat and ugly and has a dreadful German accent.

But I was a good girl. I said no. I shall never really understand why I did this, except that for the first time I saw Sir Richard Vierville and made up my mind *instanter* to marry him.

I believe, Papa, you would wish to use your ferule on your daughter as you do on your naughty boys. You always said to me, even when I was a little girl, "Juliet, if you would use the intelligence the good Lord gave you, instead of thinking all the time of young men and love and marriage and suchlike, you could do a great deal for yourself. Why, you might even become a writer, though God knows, it is no profession for a lady, and I would not wish you to follow in the footsteps of Mrs Aphra Behn, or write such lewd and wicked stuff as those ladies who dream of nothing but corpses and ghosts and murder. But of course you do nothing of the kind, for all the schooling I so diligently gave you, and indeed, it sometimes seems to me that if I had whipped you more you would be the better for it, forget for a while the pretty hair you are so inordinately proud of, and the young idiots who for no good reason seem to fall on their knees before you . . ."

No, Papa. Dear foolish Papa who could no more use his rod on me than cut my throat. Not that I would endure it – I will never permit anyone to strike me, and if my husband, when I marry, ever presumes to do so, I shall kill him, I swear it. I will not be struck. Mama once gave me a great box on the ears for which I never forgave her, though I was nine years old at the time. Do you remember, Papa, how she fell down the stairs and broke her leg; she had to stay in bed for more than a month. That was my doing, though it is something I'll never admit to a soul. I tied a thin piece of string across the stairs, and she caught her heel in it and fell the length of them. It was her fault. She had no right to hit me. I do not know if she suspected, but she never hit me again. In any case, Papa, why should I not think of such things? Of course I am proud of my pretty hair, and of course I am amused by all the young men who follow after me.

There is a great deal you do not know, Papa, and one is of your young Latin tutor who offered only last month to marry me, and wished me to run away with him. His teeth stick out, and he has no money, so there was not the least danger, but I enjoyed it all the same and very much. We had to elope of course for he knew you would never agree. And I said yes to everything, for it amused me to do so, and I believe he even bought a little cottage for us which used up all his savings. We had it all planned for last Tuesday: I was to leave the pantry window open and at two in the morning, when you were all asleep, I would climb out with my little portmanteau and start my new life as Mrs Winterbottom. As if I would ever marry a man called Winterbottom! I do not know how long he waited, for of course I was fast asleep, all snug in my own bed, but if you are astonished, Papa, that you are now without a Latin tutor – the new one, I see, is at least fifty and long beyond such frivolities as marriage – you will understand that your little daughter's virtue was at stake, and you should congratulate me on my good sense rather than reproach me.

I saw Sir Richard long before he saw me. Of course I had heard all about him. Mistress Purefoy saw to that. She is a wicked-tongued old bitch, and when I marry Sir Richard, which I am resolved to do, she is going to have a most dreadful shock, for among other things I will not have her in my house. She is a mischief-maker with an idle tongue; I have seldom heard her say one good word for anyone, and I do know for certain that she believes I lay with Sir Charles. Indeed, she has already told half the town.

Did I? No, Papa, I did not. I so nearly did, but then you do not read my Diary. Indeed, you do not know of its existence, which is just as well, for you are a naughty, inquisitive old man, and those long, interfering fingers of yours would be instantly at its clasp if you had the least idea where it was. But as you can never find it I can tell you where it is, and it is you who told me what to do. "If you want to hide something," you once said, "the only thing to do is to put it in the obvious place. If you conceal it somewhere mysterious and secret, that is where any intelligent person will at once look. But lay it down on a table or on the window-sill, and no one will think that worth the examining." I did not quite do that, Papa, but I have put it in your library among those old textbooks you no longer use. It is leather-bound so it does not show. I have never known you even go near it, which is a pity for you, for you would have heard most interesting things of Sir Charles who was so determined to make me his mistress, and you would have learnt about poor, silly little Tom Winterbottom, Mr Crabtree who is not so suited for a minister as one might imagine, Will who taught history, Jamie with that dreadful Scotch accent who is so mad about the Stuarts, and of course Monsieur Dubois who was so concerned with my petticoats that he forgot the boys he was supposed to teach French to.

And many others. Including Jack the farmer who swears that one day he will marry me. As if I would marry a farmer! Oh, he is handsome, only he frightens me a little, he is so fierce and determined. I always keep out of his way and dodge him when I see him coming.

Ask Mistress Purefoy about them. She knows everything. Oh, how I wish I could burn her as a witch! I can see her now, tied to a stake, with the flames licking her horrid feet. How she would yell, and how I would laugh. Only I would duck her first, and when she was sizzling away, I would read out to her all the nasty things she has said about me.

But Sir Richard . . . I often saw him out riding. When I first set eyes on him, Papa, I was sixteen, and thinking a deal of marriage and wondering why all the men I met were so prodigious uninteresting. I did not find Sir Richard uninteresting, from the very beginning. He rides hard, he does so most days, and his horse, Aramis, with the white star on his forehead, is, it seemed to me, more of a companion to him than any woman.

Though of course there are plenty of women. I do not need Mistress Purefoy to tell me that. "Whores," she calls them, "painted whores, stinking of damnation." I would not mind stinking of such damnation for it must cost a guinea an ounce. I have smelt it sometimes, it is wonderful, and when I marry Sir Richard, I shall have my damnation made specially for me, as all the fine ladies do, and it will probably cost more than one guinea.

How do I see these ladies? Oh, I have sharp eyes. And I am little. I put on my grey cloak and nobody notices me; I see the ladies roll up in their fine carriages, to end no doubt in Sir Richard's bed.

Oh God, oh God, how I wish I were in his bed. With his arms about me and his mouth on mine, and other things, other things. Papa, you do not know your daughter, but you taught me to read; there is a little poem I remember and it goes something like this, though I do not know who wrote it.

> Oh western wind, when wilt thou blow
> That the small rain down doth rain,
> Christ, that my love were in my arms,
> And I in my bed again.

I look at the ladies and I hate them, with their painted faces, their fine clothes and shrill voices. When I marry him, there will be no more ladies. They will come to Fontenoy and I will fill their bellies with rich food, but that is all, otherwise their bellies will remain empty and so will every other part of them.

And my belly will remain empty too. I do not want children. I do not like children. They are horrid, ill-smelling little creatures who scream and whine and want attention. I prefer to have a cat. I like cats. I think I am like a cat myself. But I shall never have a child, though this reminds me of something rather horrid that I should prefer to forget, yet which remains with me. I met Jack, the farmer, again. He stood in my path. He is a big man, as big as Sir Richard, and I could not pass him. He speaks with the local accent. He terrifies me.

He said as he had done before, "One day, missie, you

and I will wed, you will bear me children and do all the work that a good farmer's wife should."

I said, "Let me pass, please."

"The day will come," he said, "when you will not pass, any more than you will speak to me in such a fashion. I have tamed wilder things than you, Miss Juliet, and in the end I will have my way. I always do."

The thought of marrying such a monster frightened me so much that I burst into tears. Then he laughed and, as I pushed by him, suddenly caught hold of me and kissed me. I slapped his face. He said, "You'll pay for that. You'll pay for that a hundred times."

But he let me go and he did not try to stop me as I ran past him.

The thought of bearing his children is something so monstrous that I cannot endure the thought of it, yet it recurs in my dreams. Mistress Purefoy – oh, how I hate that woman! – has five, and much good may it do her. She is always breeding. When she don't have a noisesome little brat at that skinny thing she calls a breast, she is all pot-bellied with the next one. I called her a witch, but bitch is the better word, she is always on heat.

But we do have our witch, papa, though you say she is just a poor old woman and no-one has the right to persecute her. Last week I went down to see her in her filthy little cottage on the fringe of the town.

"Mother," I said, for so everyone calls her, affrighted that if they do not, she will put a curse on them, "Mother," I said, "tell me my fortune."

And I crossed her palm with a guinea, though her hand was so dirty I did not like to touch it. I waited there, thinking to hear some silly tale about a handsome man, a deal of money and travels abroad, the kind of fustian these old dames always relate.

She gave me a very strange look. She had beautiful eyes. I thought that when she was young, a hundred years ago, she must have been a good-looker, not so beautiful as me but still well enough to make some young man take her into his bed. He would have to wash her first. I had to stand near the door, for the filthy smell of her made me sick.

"You will marry twice," she said. "For the first you will make your own fortune, though you will break his: for the second it is you who will be broken; you will pay doubly, trebly, for all you have done."

"What can you mean?" I was startled, yes, and afraid too. I did not like what she said. I could see now why people tried to propitiate her, for indeed, she seemed far more of a witch than Mistress Purefoy who is just a silly, disagreeable, ill-bred woman.

"You will get your heart's desire," she said.

This was more what I wanted to hear, but I had to laugh all the same, for it was just what I predicted. Only her next words stopped my laughter, and I do believe the colour left my cheeks for I suddenly felt very cold and my head began to swim.

"And you will lose it," she said. "You are proud and selfish and silly, and you would spite the entire world to get your own way."

"Mother!"

"You could kill, little lady, you are so small and so pretty and your heart is like a stone."

Then I was furious. No-one has ever spoken to me like this before. I stamped my foot at her and I shouted, "I'll have you whipped at the cart's-tail, I swear it, and your cottage burnt to the ground. How dare you speak to me in such a fashion?"

She only answered calmly – she had a strange, deep

voice, and it was the voice of a lady; there was no trace of an accent – "You would do anything to harm me or anyone who stands in your way, but I shall be dead before you can touch me." Then she cried out, her voice soaring up, "Oh, leave him. Let him be. He'll be no good to you, and you will break and ruin him. He seems strong and hard and fierce, but his heart is soft, he is a good man, and between the two of you there will be no happiness, no peace, no love; he will end as half a man, while you will become nothing of a woman."

I said – I could hear my own voice trembling and high – "I'll see you hanged for this," and I turned to go, only as I did so, there was a little thud and the coin I had given her, the golden guinea, fell at my feet.

"It is Judas money," she said. "It is accursed. Take it. I would not touch it if I was starving."

She died that night. The neighbours found her in the morning. I was sorry she died. I wanted to see her hang. I was going to call on Judge Mannering. I knew he would listen to me, for after all he was always kissing me when his wife's back was turned. But the old crone died, and I tried to forget about her, only somehow her words remained with me like vomit in my throat.

But these things are all nonsense, and when I saw Sir Richard riding out on Aramis, I no longer cared.

He did not see me, and I took care he should not, for I was wearing my everyday clothes, my hair was blown by the wind, and I wanted him to see me for the first time when I was at my most beautiful.

He is the best-looking man I have ever seen in my life. He is quite old, of course, but that does not matter, and I am sick to death of young men who have nothing to talk about and who only think of fondling and kissing and the like. Besides, men and women tire of each other, and though I could not believe I would ever tire of him, I would be left a rich woman and marry again.

The old witch said I would marry twice.

He is well over six foot. I myself am five foot two. I have always liked tall men. I could only look at those magnificent shoulders and the wonderful long, lean strength of him, and marvel that so wonderful a man should exist, a man moreover whom I was going to marry, whom I knew with absolute certainty I was going to marry. The dark eyes, the thick jetty brows, and the wavy black hair – like many countrymen he wore no wig except when he had company – made me think of things that made me blush: I was grateful that no one could read my wicked thoughts.

He had dismounted. Aramis was cropping the grass. Sir Richard was leaning against a tree, hands in his pockets. I believed his thoughts were miles away and I crept a little nearer, when he swung round with such sudden speed that I had no time to hide, and spoke to me.

"So, it's the schoolmaster's little daughter, is it?" he said.

I was bitterly ashamed of my appearance. The grey kerseymere I was wearing was two years old, one of my gloves had a hole in it, and my hair, which is naturally curly and one of my best features, was half covered by a scarf, with the rest of it blown about my face. I was sure my nose was red with the cold. At that moment I made a resolution that never again would I walk out in my old clothes, I would always wear something new and smart, never mind if it was only Mistress Purefoy I was meeting.

But it was too late now, and I was determined not to be set down by any gentleman, even if it was Sir Richard

Vierville. I dropped him a curtsey and said as calmly as I could, "I am Juliet Smith, Sir Richard, and certainly my father is headmaster at the Matley Bishop school. But I see you would prefer to be alone, so I apologise for disturbing you."

And I made as if to go, only he called me back. He had a beautiful voice, deep and strong. I thought of the thin, young, reedy voices of Tom and Will and Jamie – oh, that Scotch twang! – and wondered how I could ever have endured so much as talking to them. I suppose I thought they were better than nothing, but at that moment I knew I would rather remain a spinster all my days than converse and flirt with such stupid boys.

"Wait a moment," he said. "I have not done with you yet. Tell me, Miss Juliet Smith, do you ride?"

"Naturally," I answered, though I had never ridden in my life, and was terrified of horses: they have such horrid yellow teeth, and I am always sure they will trample me to death if I come near them.

I suspected he did not believe me. His lips twitched into a smile. After all, he attended the local hunt and I had never been there in my life: besides, schoolmasters' daughters do not do such things; they are for fine ladies with a great deal of money.

"Then," he said, "we will ride together. I am tired of my own company and we can converse on the way. You have, I presume, no objection to riding side-saddle in front of me? As an accomplished horsewoman you might possibly find it insulting."

I had every objection in the world, first to his derisive manner, for I did not miss the mockery in his tone, and secondly to the appalling idea of mounting a horse that to me at that moment looked like an Arab stallion.

He added, "Aramis is a gentle beast, well accustomed

to ladies."

It was at this moment that I made up my mind. It sometimes pays to be honest. Besides, it can be disarming. I could see that he was fooling me to his utmost and that I was about to make the most prodigious exhibition of myself. I had not the faintest idea how to mount a horse, I did not know how to sit side-saddle, I would certainly fall off unless he held me with both his hands, and the sight of Aramis, still peacefully cropping the grass, made me sick and faint with terror.

I said, "You are funning me, sir. And of course I deserve it. I have never ridden a horse in my life. I am terrified of them. I shall certainly fall off within the first five minutes, and I am convinced your horse will bite me if I so much as approach him."

And I raised my face to his. There were tears in my eyes. They were perfectly genuine. I have always been able to cry at will. It saved me many a scolding when I was young, though sometimes I think my mother saw through me.

He half smiled, then came towards me. He took my hands in his. I cannot describe the ecstasy I felt at this contact, only I hoped he did not see the hole in my glove. "You make me ashamed of myself," he said. "Why should you know anything about horses? It's my fault for making fun of you, and it's you who must try to forgive me. I live too much on my own. I have forgot the decencies of good manners. Miss Juliet, I will teach you not to be afraid. You will ride with me, you will not fall off, you will not be bitten, and I swear you will enjoy it so much that you will want to do it again and again. Indeed, I might present you with a mount from my own stables, and then you will become notorious throughout Matley Bishop."

I could not prevent myself from laughing. When he offered me his handkerchief I wiped my eyes very delicately. I said in a timorous voice – my voice is a little high but it has its advantages; it can sound childish and pathetic – "It is I who am ashamed. My father would never forgive me for telling such lies."

Poor Papa! He has put up with my lying for a great many years now. But I think Sir Richard imagined I was feared of being whipped, for he said at once, "Your father will never know. If that is the worst lie you have ever told, I daresay it could be forgiven. Now, Miss Juliet. We will start the first lesson. Don't be afraid. I swear to look after you. You will come to no harm."

I came up to him, and suddenly he caught at my scarf and with one tug pulled it from my head. We both watched it blow away in the wind. He said, "You have beautiful hair. It is a sin to cover it up. Now, my little madam. Put your hand on Aramis's neck."

I was genuinely afraid. This time there was no play-acting, and the tears that started to my eyes were real tears, of pure terror. But I took off my glove (the one with the hole in it) and laid my hand on Aramis's neck. It was soft and silky to the touch, not alarming at all, and he paid me no attention, simply went on munching the grass.

"Is that so frightening?" asked Sir Richard.

"No!"

"Then now you shall give him some sugar."

"Oh but . . ."

"Here it is. You hold it so on the palm of your hand."

"Please, sir, I couldn't . . ."

"Are you such a coward, Miss Juliet?"

Aramis had raised his head and was looking at me hopefully. Perhaps the word "sugar" was something he understood. He had a kind, gentle face with a white streak down his nose, but I could only see the yellow teeth, and I was shaking so that I could not keep my hand steady. Then Sir Richard's hand came under mine, and I managed to hold out the stick of sugar in my palm. Aramis took it so gently that I suddenly lost all fear and patted his neck again, even rubbing my cheek against it.

I have never been afraid of horses again.

"You are a good girl," said Sir Richard calmly, "and now you are going to mount him, only as you are so little and this is your first time, I shall lift you up. That is the stirrup you would normally put your foot on. This is the girth that keeps the saddle in place."

"What happens if it comes loose?"

"Then," said Sir Richard, "I would have a very nasty fall, but my groom would never permit such a thing to happen. Come. I am going to lift you. Are you not terrified?"

"No."

"Are you perhaps looking forward to it?"

"Yes, sir."

He looked at me for a second in silence. I thought he was going to kiss me. I prayed, oh God how I prayed, that he would kiss me. But he did not, only picked me up as if I were a child, and there I was, sitting on Aramis's back, my feet dangling down one side, and there was not a vestige of fear in my heart, only such happiness and elation as I have never known.

"You weigh as much as a feather," he said, then set his foot in the stirrup and the next instant was behind me, one hand round my waist.

I will never forget that ride. I was so happy, so happy! We hardly talked, but his hand gripped me tightly and I could feel the strong beating of his heart. There was only one moment when I felt a little chilled, and that was the sight of Jack the farmer, with two dogs at his heels: he was away in the distance and he turned to look at us. I do not know why he frightened me so, but I exclaimed, "I do not like that man. I always seem to be meeting him. Who is he and what does he do?"

Sir Richard answered in some surprise, "He works on my estate. He is an invaluable worker and I would not part with him. They say he drinks heavily and has a fierce temper, but that is no concern of mine, he has a remarkable way with animals and he would willingly work all night if need be. Why do you not like him? You are unlikely to meet him, he lives by himself, and mostly he is out tending my sheep and cattle." There was a trace of laughter in his voice. "You are quite safe. I believe he does not like women."

Then he said suddenly, "They say you are a great flirt, Miss Juliet."

I answered pertly, "By 'they', sir, you perhaps mean Mistress Purefoy."

He said gravely, "It is possible. But I hear it from other quarters too. Are you a flirt, Miss Juliet?"

I said, "I am just on seventeen, sir. I am a woman. I am a human being. I am not, I think, ill-favoured. What would you expect of me? If a young man smiles at me, I am surely permitted to smile back."

He said after a long pause, "If a young man smiles at you, my dear, and you smile back and I am there, I believe I should black his eyes. And perhaps yours into the bargain."

I was too taken aback to say anything, but I have never felt as I did then. I can confide in you, my Diary, so I will confess that if he had asked me to lie with him that instant, I would have jumped down and done so. I was possessed of such a passion for him that I had to keep my face averted. I was terrified he would feel my shivering, as indeed he must have done, but I could not speak to cover up my feelings; I could think of nothing to say.

All I did say after a long, long time, was, "Will you be at the hunt ball, Sir Richard, next week?"

"Will you, ma'am?"

"Yes, sir."

"Then we will meet there."

And that was all.

That was our courtship. For I knew it was a courtship, I knew then for certain that I would marry him. And we did not speak another word until we came back to the schoolhouse, where he lifted me off and rode away without so much as a goodbye.

Papa must have been watching from his study window. It was holiday time: there were no gawping boys to snigger at me. He came out to meet me. He said in a bewildered voice, "That was Sir Richard Vierville."

"Yes, Papa."

"Come into the study. I want to talk to you."

"Papa . . ."

"Juliet, you're not listening to me. I told you to come into my study."

"I'm coming, Papa. Only – only – Papa, I must have a new ball-gown."

He gave me a strange look, almost of despair. But he did not answer me directly, only said for the third time, "Come into the study."

I followed him in. I must have looked as if I had been in a shipwreck. My scarf was lost – I do not know where Sir Richard threw it, but I never saw it again – my hair was in wild disorder, my cheeks scarlet, and the hands which had at first clung on to Aramis, would have disgraced Papa's worst pupil. Also my dress was torn, and I could see his eyes moving down to the rent in my skirt, though it was caused by Aramis's stirrup as I was lifted up.

I sat down with a sigh. I knew I was in for a lecture. When Papa poured out two glasses of wine, I knew it was serious. Poor Papa, he so hated scolding me: the wine was more to put courage in himself than in me. But I said nothing. I have always believed that in such situations it is best to remain silent. I simply looked about me at things I had seen a thousand times before: the endless rows of books with the special shelf at the end behind glass. It was there that Papa kept his rarest and most valuable tomes, including several pieces of what I think he called *incunabula*. The Lord knows what that means, and when I looked at them I could not make head nor tail of them, but it seemed they were worth a lot of money. I said once to Papa that we would never be poor with such things to sell, and he answered that he would rather starve than part with such treasures. But then I myself have never cared for reading, except occasionally romances when I have nothing better to do, and if I had had my way I would have cleared all this dusty rubbish away and bought myself a dozen new gowns in its place. Papa had always made sure that I received a good education – I have never understood why, for learning is useless in a woman – but at least it meant I could write and spell better than most of my friends, and hold my own in conversations where, to be honest, I did not understand the half of what was being said.

He said sternly, "Juliet, where did you meet Sir Richard Vierville?"

I made innocent eyes at him over my glass. "In the woods, Papa. He was out on one of his excursions. He offered me a ride on his horse, Aramis. Did I do wrong to accept? He behaved like a perfect gentleman."

And so indeed he did: Papa was not to know how much I had longed to behave like a most imperfect lady.

"Why is your dress torn?"

His voice was so stern that I was quite frightened, and this made me blush. It was after all as innocent as the day, and I was behaving as if I had been guilty of some gross impropriety. I said as calmly as I could, though the glass in my hand was shaking, "I caught my skirt on the horse's stirrup."

I could see he did not believe me. How absurd we all are! If I had told some arrant lie, he would have believed me at once. But he only said, "Your hair is very disordered. Where is your scarf?"

"It blew off in the wind, Papa."

"And why did you not pick it up? It was a present from your Auntie Bella. It was a good silk. I could not afford to buy you such things."

It had always been an ugly scarf, and I never could abide my Aunt Bella who thought I was fast and was constantly telling me so. But I could not think of an answer, so I did what I always do in such circumstances: I began to cry.

He did not, as I had expected, run to put his arms round me, but he looked distressed, and his voice, when he spoke again, was not so harsh. He said, "I do not like you riding with Sir Richard. We arc not in his class."

"Papa!"

"We are not, Juliet. And he has, though I regret to say this, a bad reputation. I do not wish a daughter of mine to consort with him. What persuaded you to such foolishness? You have never ridden a horse in your life."

I said, sobbing, "There was no harm in it. He was very kind. He never spoke one ungenteel word to me. He could not have been more gentlemanly."

"That is as may be. But I do not wish you to speak to him again. Is that understood, Juliet?"

"Yes, Papa."

"*Yes, Papa, I have every intention of speaking to him again. I have every intention of marrying him; I hope that is understood too.*"

"I mean what I say, Juliet."

"Yes, Papa."

"He comes from good stock, he is a gentleman, but his ways are not ours. He is, moreover, forty, and the women he consorts with are not of a kind I would wish you to know. You would be lost in such a society. They talk bawdry, they commit such sins as you do not know about, they are licentious and lewd. Moreover, daughter, they would eat you alive: to them you would be like a lamb for the slaughter."

"*Oh no, I would not, Papa! I have teeth and claws too, and I am not frightened of fine ladies, nor of pretty gentlemen who would expect to lie with me after five minutes' conversation. You never met Sir Charles, Papa. I could now be his whore in a grand London house, and here I am in your study, being lectured like one of your pupils. I wonder you do not threaten me with the rod.*"

"Yes, Papa."

He said abruptly – I could see he was ashamed, he hated having to scold me – "What's all this nonsense about a new gown?"

"It's for the hunt ball, papa. I always go. You surely have no objection."

"And which of your numerous beaux is escorting you?"

"Jamie, Papa."

He said, with a hint of a smile, "I thought you could not abide his accent?"

"He is a good dancer. He once taught me something called a reel."

And I thought privately that I must inform Jamie of the honour done him. I did not think he would object. Indeed, he was always asking me to go out with him.

My father said, "But you cannot need a new gown. You seem to think I'm made of money. What about that blue affair with – oh, I never know how you ladies talk of such things – but there was a bow and some lace . . ."

"Oh Papa, I wore that last year!"

"No-one will remember."

"Oh yes, they will. It's the kind of thing that's always remembered."

He said wearily, "I am not a rich man, Julia. I am just a schoolmaster. Have you forgot?"

But he loved me and his conscience was plaguing him, so in the end he gave in. I ran off to Mrs Woodthorpe, who is our town dressmaker, and together we planned a gown all in white and silver, the last word in fashion, yet entirely simple and without adornment. I knew there was no lady in Matley Bishop could outshine me, whether she was one of Sir Richard's whores or not. Only it was very expensive, and when I told Papa, I was frightened that he would refuse. But he said nothing, only looked at me, then walked over to the glass-fronted shelf and took out two volumes.

He must have seen my aghast expression. He laughed a little bitterly. "You can say," he said, "that Chaucer has dressed you."

He never mentioned the matter again.

Julia skimmed over the next few pages. It was two in the morning. There was no sign of Rick, and this seemed to her so strange that at one point she came out of the study and looked in through the bedroom door to see if he had returned and simply gone to bed. He might even be drunk. He was a most temperate man and she had never seen him drunk in his life, but the whole set-up was so crazy that nothing would surprise her. And on the way back she poured herself out a large drink, for there was a great deal of the manuscript still to come, and she had by this time taken such an acute dislike to Juliet, who seemed to her selfish, spoilt and cruel, that she felt she needed fortifying.

The unbelievable thing was that Rick could have written this at all, and what Marcus Tremayne would have thought of it was beyond imagination, but then of course *he* had not really written it: was he aware in any way of the small, predatory hand that had directed him?

The next two chapters were very boring, gushing excitement over the hunt ball, a great deal about the new dress which made Julia, now huddled into a rather worn chain-store dressing-gown, feel acutely envious, and a vast amount of girlish gossip. There were even references to the unhappy Jamie with his "Scotch twang": the poor fellow was plainly a dead bore.

Julia, glancing cursorily through this, thought about Chaucer and was consumed with rage. The poor, silly old father had obviously sold two volumes of immense value to pay for that white and silver dress, and the wretched girl did not even seem impressed. However, she read the detailed description of the gown – it really did sound lovely – the admiring comments of friends, and one acid remark from Mistress Purefoy, who did not seem to have changed at all in two hundred years. Perhaps the two families regularly intermarried. "I do think," she told young Juliet, who must have made a great face at being so spoken to, "it is the most wickedest extravagance to spend so much money on a gown that will probably only be worn once."

The description of the ball was more interesting. Obviously everyone who was anyone at all attended, and though Lord X and Sir John Y meant nothing to Julia, she could visualise the setting with the long staircase, the presiding Master of the Hunt and his wife, and all the fine ladies and gentlemen ascending as their names were called out. Juliet, she was sure, must have behaved with perfect aplomb, rather like Eliza in *Pygmalion*, but she had a definite impression of poor Jamie, sweating in his party clothes, appalled by all the grandeur around him and perhaps tripping over the top step.

There seemed as yet to be no sign of Sir Richard, and Julia for the first time felt some sympathy for Juliet, now surrounded by eager young men. She must have been incredibly beautiful and the portrait did her little justice. It would be dreadful if all this had been for nothing, just an idle flirtation, Sir Richard simply amusing himself in the fashion of his class and time. He must, after all, be a man well accustomed to the ways of women, and he would sense quickly enough that a marriage ring was not essential to bring Juliet to his bed.

She began to read with more concentration.

My card was full ten minutes after my arrival. I did not give a rap for Jamie, who looked like a stable-boy and behaved little better – (perhaps he had stumbled over that step after all, poor lad) – but I allowed him the first minuet and, as a great favour, one more later on. I told Papa he could dance, but this is not true: all he can do is that silly thing he calls a reel, hopping about and shooting out his arms, quite ridiculous, especially as to do it properly one has to wear a skirt. A skirt! On a man! But there was no lack of partners and I could see that Lord Francis was greatly taken with me, while the Colonel from the local regiment was a little too free with his compliments and I had to give him a set-down. It does not pay to make oneself cheap, and he was much more respectful afterwards.

And then Sir Richard Vierville arrived.

Julia stopped with a little gasp. She detested Juliet. She had no time for husband-grabbers, and all this young madam really wanted was a place in society, a handsome man and as much money as she could spend. Yet she was a woman too, and it must have been quite a moment, perhaps in sudden dead silence, when this tall, good-looking gentleman strode up the stairs and, after a perfunctory greeting to his host and hostess, went straight towards the lovely young girl in her white and silver gown, hemmed in by young men, about to embark on the first dance.

Juliet's card was, as she had said, full. A pretty girl is a pretty girl, even if she is only a schoolmaster's daughter, and Mrs Woodthorpe's gown must have been stunning. Juliet at least had good taste. No doubt the other ladies wore jewels and furbelows and bright-coloured taffetas and silks: that plain white and silver dress must have stood out like a lily among the weeds. And it was to her that Sir Richard came, brushing aside her admirers who backed away from him, for all that most of them were his equals, even superior in rank. What poor Jamie with his foursome reel thought was not recorded, but doubtless he returned to his native land a sadder and wiser boy, to marry some nice, decent girl who could dance the reel with him and cook him his porridge.

Sir Richard stood, towering over her. He did not speak a word to the people around him. It was as if they were the only two in the room.

"I looked at him proudly," wrote little Juliet, "I did not simper or smile, though I believe I blushed: I could not control the colour in my cheeks."

She looked down at the card in her gloved hand. Julia had seen one of these dance cards, long and white with flowers painted at the top, and numbers for the partners. There was not one blank space.

"Give me that card," said Sir Richard.

She handed it to him in silence.

He tore the card into three pieces and dropped them on the floor. He looked at her, then held out his hands. She moved without a word into his arms.

They danced together the whole evening. Jamie must have had a miserable time, utterly out of his class and without a sliver of the necessary cheek that just might have helped him tide it over. He probably slipped out as soon as he could. He certainly did not take Juliet home.

I rode in his carriage. It is the first time I have ever done so, but it will not be the last. I only had a lace shawl with me for I had no money to buy anything more and I was not going to wear an ugly cape, but he seemed to have anticipated this, for he had a fur wrap with him that he laid about my shoulders.

"You will keep that," he said, then he smiled. He has a surprisingly sweet smile for so violent a man. "I have no doubt you will be a most extravagant wife, so I am starting well in advance."

I looked at him. A great many men have asked me to marry them, and a great many more have suggested other things, but this was not a proposal, it was more like a declaration of war. There was a deal I wished to say. I wanted to draw back, to tell him roundly that he had no right to take me so for granted, but I did none of these things, only laid my hand on his, and presently his arms came round me, and I leaned against his shoulder, loving him, loving him, oh God, loving him so much that I felt as if I were breaking into tiny pieces.

Yes, she did love him in her own way. Or did she? Did she perhaps love his looks, his undoubted charm, his breeding, his money or the fact that he was far and away the best catch of the district? Whether it was love, passion or ambition, six weeks later Sir Richard Vierville married Miss Juliet Smith in St Matthew's Church where in the brief space of five years he was to be buried. The whole of the county was at the wedding, bewildered, furious, envious, dazed, according to their temperaments. The couple spent their honeymoon in Venice and came back to live at Fontenoy.

Juliet wrote interminably of the wedding, but did not mention the honeymoon, except to say that they rode in a gondola with a handsome Venetian singing love songs to them. She did not seem to Julia to be a girl much afflicted with reticence, gentility or reserve, but perhaps in her age certain things could not be mentioned, even in a private diary. A modern young miss of her temperament would no doubt have described the honeymoon night blow by blow, but little Juliet did not refer to it at all, except to say that she was very happy. On the subject of the wedding, however, she was such a bore that Julia marvelled that Rick could bear to set it down, even though it was as it were dictated to him. It must, of course, have been an unparalleled occasion for the little schoolmaster's daughter to be married with everyone there: there was even a minor royal princeling down from London. But Julia was not interested in diamond necklaces and French silks, though Sir Richard's new wife spared her nothing, describing every outfit in the utmost detail, especially her own superb wedding dress, and revelled especially – this one could understand – in the school choir singing Handel after the ceremonial walk down the aisle.

Julia skimmed through all this, greatly improving her knowledge of eighteenth century fashions, and reflected briefly on her own wedding which had taken place in a register office in the town where she was born, with some thirty guests, mostly family, and a fork lunch afterwards. The honeymoon had been in Arles, where Rick was setting his next Marcus Tremayne book, and Julia's main memory was of sitting beside an empty grave in the Alyscamps, while Rick worked out his dramatic denouement.

Lady Juliet would not have liked that at all.

When did the rot set in? Julia imagined it was fairly early. There is, of course, a period in every marriage, however heaven-made, when dirty socks override glamour and romance becomes intermingled with rice pudding. Even in 1750, when all the work was done by servants, the principle must have remained the same. Julia herself, though she was married to a man she loved dearly and who seemed in so many ways superior to herself, passed through a phase when she would have liked a little more attention from a husband who spent all day at his typewriter and who took long, solitary walks in the evening. But she was too much in love to take this seriously, and she discovered that Rick rather enjoyed her being autocratic. "We are having dinner out tonight," she would say, or, "Next week I want to see the new Pinter play." And of course there was always the excitement of books being accepted, typing to do, proofs, publishers' parties, and finally there was Alan, whom they both adored, and who turned a lively, if occasionally surface marriage into a real family thing.

There was no Alan for Sir Richard and Juliet, no little girl, no sign of a baby. She had said from the very beginning that she did not like children, but Julia thought this was a little mean. She could at least have had one, and there would be no lack of nurses and servants to look after it. She was certainly not barren, as her second marriage proved, and Julia, who had an inquiring mind, wondered vaguely how she managed to avoid children: there was after all no pill in the eighteenth century, and no-one seemed to know anything about contraception.

There was no baby, but what there was was boredom. There was also something else: a young man called Philip. Juliet never mentioned his second name. There was to be another man and much more important, later on, but Philip provided the first rift. He was not a nobleman, he had no pedigree, indeed, he was what Jamie would have called a factor. He managed the Vierville estates which were extensive and stretched throughout half the county. Juliet had probably never considered such things, which were entirely outside her province, but Sir Richard's solitary rides were not as purposeless as she had imagined: there were crops and orchards and sheep and cattle, and a big estate of tied cottages, which had now been taken over by the council and used as old people's homes. Jack the farmer lived here, but Juliet never saw him: she probably took pains to avoid him, and as lady of the manor would in any case never come into contact with him.

Philip was in charge of all the estate management and strode in and out of Fontenoy most days. No doubt his eye lit instantly on the beautiful new lady, and no doubt the lady, already bored, responded. And no doubt there was one hell of a row, and Master Philip was sent packing. Only Juliet was cunning and a little in love: there are always side entrances and pleasant, useful rendezvous in fields and lanes. By this time Lady Juliet, who had once been so frightened of horses, had a pretty dappled mare of her own, not to mention some delightful riding habits, and she often set off on a little jaunt while her husband sat at home, dealing with accounts and coaching the new factor who was middle-aged and plain, and would never have considered making a pass at his employer's wife.

"Oh Richard," said Julia aloud, "what an ass, my darling, my dear darling, you were. You marry a wife twenty-three years younger than yourself, you never seem to take her out, you do not give the parties she really had some right to expect, you don't even take her up to London. You just leave her mooching around, and then you're surprised when the inevitable happens. You must admit it was largely your fault."

And the deep voice inside her: "*Yes, I know that now. It would have been different if we had had children. Yet, despite everything she did not have the right to kill me.*"

The honeymoon was indeed over. Juliet was now shamelessly grumbling, angry and aggrieved.

When I talk to him he does not even listen. He treats me like his dogs, except that they get more attention.

When I protest he laughs and ruffles my hair as if I were a child, then he will suddenly decide to take me to his bed, and he knows I like being made love to, but it does not in any way affect the situation. Tonight I made a grand scene. I put on my best gown – he is not mean, I must grant him that; he gives me everything I ask for – and it was very beautiful, and I wore the family rubies and drank a great deal of wine with my dinner so as to give myself courage. I did not tell him that I had met Philip that afternoon. We lay in the field together. We did nothing wrong, but that is only because I am a good wife. I do not promise the next time . . .

I stormed up to him. He was drinking his brandy and doing his damned accounts. He did not even tell me how pretty I was. He stared up at me, and this was the last straw. I began to scream at him. I cried out, "I am so bored. Why can't I go to London? Why don't your friends ever come down here? I'd like to go to the play. I'd like to have a ball here, a big, wonderful, grand ball, with music and people and laughter, wine to drink, rich food to eat, to go on and on and on . . ."

Julia had heard that voice before. She laid the typescript down and covered her face with her hands. The world was whirring round her like a clock gone mad. It was three in the morning, four, five, six. It was 1980, it was 1750, and the high young voice rang in her ears, blotting out the modern world around her.

It was a little girl's voice. One would have expected Juliet to have a husky voice, sexy, low, seductive, and this high young voice was unexpected, suggested an innocence that was not there, and a vulnerability that was.

Ghosts. Ghosts. Come. Tell me.

"You will never see Philip again."

"What do you mean?"

Terror now; after all he was a big man. She was very small, she was the schoolmaster's daughter, and Sir Richard was of Norman origin. The little girl caught eating stolen sweets, due for a spanking, searching wildly for excuses, lies, anything to stave off disaster. Then tears, floods and floods of tears. "I want to see Philip again. He amuses me. He's kind to me. He tells me how beautiful I am. When do you ever tell me I'm beautiful? You're an old man, you're too old to notice me. You'd best be careful, Richard. I'm not going to put up with this much longer. Why should I? You treat me like a piece of furniture. If I choose to take a lover, you cannot prevent me . . ."

He rose to his feet. I was terrified. I felt like fainting. He stood right over me. He spoke very quietly. He said, "If you ever speak to me like that again, I shall beat you. I mean that, Juliet. I will not tolerate such language. And you will not see Philip again."

"You've killed him!"

Then he laughed. It was ugly laughter. I thought I would die with the fear and ugliness of it. He said, "Killed him? Do you think you're worth a murder? I've sent him home, up north. He was a very frightened young man. He will never come down here again. He knows what will happen to him if he does. Your beauty is worth nothing compared to his own precious skin, and if he comes here again, there'll be little left of that. I saw you this afternoon. Have you lain with him? Answer me. I intend to know. Have you lain with him?"

"No!"

"Is that true? Yes, I believe it is. It is as well for you.

Go to bed. I'm sick of the sight of you. As you apparently are of an old man . . ."

Then I caught at his hands, crying, "No, I didn't mean it. Don't, don't, don't! Can't you see I'm so unhappy I do not know what I am saying? Oh please, please be kind to me. I'm so miserable, and nowadays you never smile or make a joke or even love me . . ."

I stopped. Sometimes it is as if one speaks without knowing what one is saying. I said without tears, my voice calm, "If you ever strike me, Richard, I'll kill you. I swear it."

He looked at me. Then he began to smile in his old way; he put his arms round me and drew me against his chest. "There's my girl," he said. "I did not mean to be so rough with you. Perhaps I am so old that I've forgotten what it is like to be young. You shall have your party. Is it not your birthday in a month's time? We'll ask all the fine ladies and gentlemen you can think of, you shall have your music and everything else you wish, and the most beautiful new gown imaginable. Indeed, next week I will take you up to London to have it made. We'll forget about Philip and think of ourselves. Come to bed, my darling. Do I never tell you I love you? Then I'll tell you now. I love you. I love you with all my heart. You are the most beautiful creature I have ever met. Have you forgiven me, Juliet? Can you forgive me?"

Of course I forgave him, and we went to our bed and he was very loving, but my own words haunted me, and I knew that I had set something in motion that was beyond my control. I did not understand it, but it frightened me, and for some strange reason I was haunted by the memory of Jack the farmer who had sworn to marry me. It was perfectly ridiculous because I never saw him nor was like to do so, but somehow he was there in my dreams. None of this was to do with Philip. I did not give a rap for Philip. If Richard had thrashed him half to death, I would not have cared. I liked him to make love to me, and he was young and handsome, but I was glad to be rid of him: he was certainly not worth my marriage.

I did not know that I would soon meet someone who was.

Julia Burton, whose sympathies during this had been largely with her near-namesake, shook her fist at Sir Richard who really had behaved with the utmost imbecility, then found that in the boring descriptions of preparations for the grand ball – Juliet was always at her most tiresome when writing of social gatherings – there emerged a Monsieur Dieudonné, the artist who had been commissioned to do two paintings of my lord and his lady.

It was, she supposed, the custom among the gentry of the period to have their portraits painted. In the old days when she sometimes visited stately homes – it was not Rick's amusement; other people's lives bored him – she remembered that there were family portraits everywhere, going down the centuries: my lord in full military uniform, my lady in some wonderful evening gown. Sometimes there were family groups with impossibly cute children, and Julia's mind, which tended to function in a mundane manner, could somehow hear the hissing of outraged nannies: "Miss Ermyntrude, if you don't keep still, it'll be bread and water for a week," and little Miss E, with the air of an angel in paradise, stood there gazing fondly at her mama.

Certainly Juliet was excited and delighted. "We are going to be painted," she wrote, "by a French artist called Dieudonné. Good God, what a name, I cannot begin to pronounce it."

Why the portraits were to be done on wood, she did not explain. It was certainly unusual, and Juliet at one point lamented the absence of some wonderful gilt frame, but on this Sir Richard was adamant: wood it must be, and the portraits must be screwed into the walls as well. When Juliet remonstrated, he answered merely, "*Reveniam*!" which could have made no sense to her at all, even if she knew what the word meant, and indeed, if it did make sense, it revealed a strange knowledge of the future.

Juliet was not much concerned with her husband's sitting until the day she came in to see how it was going, and met Monsieur Dieudonné face to face for the first time. Painters, it seemed, were regarded as little better than superior servants. Monsieur Dieudonné did not dine with the family but had meals brought to his rooms. Her only view of him so far had been when he walked round the garden, which he did regularly every morning and evening, always ending up in the summer-house, which seemed to fascinate him. Juliet had never cared much for the summer-house which, she said, was full of earwigs and smelt horrid, but the artist seemed to like it, and sometimes, watching him from the window, she saw him sketching it.

"I hope," she told her husband, "he don't expect to paint me there," but Sir Richard only laughed and said she was to pose in the drawing-room by the French windows, in her white dress, with the blue and gold curtains as a backcloth.

Her first real sight of Monsieur Dieudonné was cataclysmic, and Julia, reading her ecstasies, was chilled and shocked. She knew now how the story would end, and the girlish outpourings, expressed in Juliet's usual over-emotional style, terrified her, for they presaged death, and nobody but herself, two hundred years later, could possibly know it.

This was no Philip. Whether she had ever, to use her own words, lain with Philip was unimportant. Julia thought she certainly had: one could not imagine Juliet lying quietly by his side, admiring the view. But he was simply a young man, and she was married to what she would consider an old husband: Philip would provide amusement and physical pleasure, an insignificant, amorous intrigue of the kind she needed. Philip was lucky to be still alive, but Sir Richard was no fool except with his wife. He must have understood that this was nothing but a silly boy who had fallen under the spell of a grand lady of fashion, with no idea of the danger he was running. Philip was well away now. He would certainly never come back; he was probably courting some more suitable girl whom he would eventually marry.

Monsieur Dieudonné was different. He was thirty-five and apparently ravishingly handsome, well over six foot, with enormous, flashing dark eyes, black moustache and beard, and of course that wonderful accent that has always wrecked British hearts, and which no doubt he intensified for the occasion. He was also a painter of some renown, for he had done portraits of members of the royal family and quite a few well-known noblemen.

He would, of course, see Juliet as ripe for the picking. She was after all very beautiful. Julia, reading about this in appalled fascination, surmised that the pair of them did not wait very long: certainly once the second portrait was begun, they had been in bed together or perhaps engulfed in passion on the settee.

How on earth, she thought, after reading pages of passionate splurge, did he ever get the picture done? And what about the servants, never mind Mrs Purefoy who, like her descendant, must have known about it from the very beginning. There is something unmistakable about two people passionately in love, and the lowest scullery maid would notice flushed cheeks, shining eyes, dishevelled clothes and hair. Sir Richard would presumably be riding round his estates, but it must all have been very precarious, even though Juliet enjoyed the danger and Monsieur Dieudonné was used to this kind of situation which was entirely in the French comedy tradition.

"He is so beautiful!" Juliet wrote, "Those eyes, they are like fire, they burn into me. And he has such beautiful white, long-fingered hands. That voice, that accent, it all drives me mad. I did not know one could feel such passion, and he makes love in such a way that I can hardly bear it. I dream of nothing else; I did not believe one could experience such ecstasy."

Juliet, in modern times, would have made a fortune with "bodice-rippers". If only the end of it had not been so appalling, Julia would have laughed: as it was, the taint of death lay over the idiocy and she could only shudder, half wishing it was done. But she understood now the cream-fed look on the portrait. Monsieur Dieudonné had been painting his lady fresh from the arms of her lover; her body was still quivering with the glory of it, her face alight with gratified desire. She must have sat there for the portrait to be finished, still trembling and aglow: it was a miracle it was ever finished at all.

It was also a miracle that Monsieur Dieudonné, who seemed to have grossly overrated the stupidity of the cuckolded husband, was not finished altogether.

Julia, wading through "wonderful, beautiful, sweet caresses, I shall never love another man again," and so on, saw, as Juliet never appeared to consider, that this could not go on.

The end came when the portrait was at last done. Julia suspected that Sir Richard waited until this point. It was not possible that he was any longer in love, and it would suit his cynical nature to feel that if he was to be saddled with a whoring wife, he might at least have his money's worth. He must, she was sure, have known about it from the very beginning.

It was Monsieur Dieudonné's last day. "He tells me we will meet again soon," wrote Juliet, so genuinely in love that she forgot her normal practical good-sense. "We have already arranged a rendezvous. How happy I am that Richard is out this evening; he is visiting a sick friend and will not be home till after midnight."

But reckless as she undeniably was, she was not foolish enough to take Monsieur Dieudonné into her room. It was a fine evening, and after they had dined apart, for the sake of the servants, they slipped into the garden together, to make their way to the summer-house, which must have seemed the most suitable place of assignation.

Julia, who for some reason visualised Monsieur Dieudonné as a kind of waiter – it must be the moustache and memories of *Fawlty Towers* – would have laughed, only at the reference to the summer-house she suddenly laid the typescript down. For a second she felt faint. The voices rang in her head.

"*Have you no thought for my reputation? For my life? He'd kill me if he found out.*" And then with the laughter rising in her throat – she had never realised there was laughter – "*Go away immediately, or I'll set the dogs on you.*"

It was all play-acting. Julia had taken it seriously but Juliet had been to bed with him at least a dozen times already: somehow this derision angered her. To deceive your husband was one thing: to make a mockery of it was another. She had seen it from the wrong angle: here was a young woman fighting, perhaps not too seriously, for her virtue, longing to give in, not quite daring, then almost capitulating. "*You must not. You must not*..."

And it had all been a joke. Both of them laughing, wild with desire, not love, not love, simply the four-letter word that the century called "lust", falling into each other's arms, his hands already at her skirts, pulling at her bodice, everything forgotten in the moonlight, the scent of flowers, the soft summer breeze . . .

"I trust I am not disturbing you."

Sir Richard stood there, very upright, very still. He was a tall man, he seemed like a giant. His face was expressionless. He simply looked at his wife who was half naked and Monsieur Dieudonné, green-white with terror, with his breeches down, hardly able to stand upright.

Juliet wrote simply, "I did not know what to do or say."

"I bet you didn't," thought Julia, "Oh, I bet you didn't." What was there to do or say? She did not read any more: somehow it was as if she too were immersed in this gross lack of decency and dignity. And anything Juliet could have written would have been a stutter, a frantic attempt to explain the obvious, all smothered in sheer blind terror. Her craven lover, unused to such British stark simplicity, dropped his lady as if she were a hot coal and turned to run for his life: a hand clamped down on his collar, twisting him, squirming, shrieking for mercy, round and round, and dashed his head three times against the summer-house wall so that at last he collapsed to the floor.

Juliet, who had managed to dress herself, cowered against the wall, crying bitterly, wailing, "Don't, don't!"

She did not write this but Julia saw her fumbling at the fastenings of her dress, and heard her. She only wrote in the diary, "I believed he would kill us both. He drew his sword."

L'épée dans l'ombre.

This was the moment for Monsieur Dieudonné to display his Gallic heroism, become a d'Artagnan, draw his own sword, prepare to defend his love and himself. He was after all a big man and younger than Sir Richard. He did not. He rubbed frantically at his cracked head, wept, continued to entreat for mercy in his native tongue, and when Sir Richard deliberately pricked his chest with his sword, spurting his blood over Juliet's disarranged white dress, fell into a dead faint, while husband and wife looked at each other over his body.

Then Juliet wrote again.

He calmly replaced his sword in its scabbard. He pulled a handkerchief from his pocket. "Wipe the blood off yourself," he said, "and get back into the house. I'll deal with – with this *ordure*, and then I'll deal with you."

"What are you going to do to him?"

"Kick him into the gutter where he belongs."

I said, "He might die."

He gave me a long, strange look. He said, "Would you really care?"

I stumbled back into the house, letting the handkerchief fall to the floor as I fled. Richard did not pick it up.

I don't know what happened in the summer-house. I never saw Dieudonné again. I do not care. He is hateful. He is a coward. He never even attempted to defend me. He left me alone to deal with my husband.

She recounted what did happen in so clipped and strange a style that it was almost as if someone else had taken over. Perhaps sheer terror robbed her of melodrama. She faced her husband in the drawing-room. She was in a lamentable state, half-undressed, bloodstained, one slipper gone. She was so frightened that in her own words she behaved like a child: she wet herself a little, was bitterly ashamed but could do nothing but stand there, trembling, whimpering and crying.

When Sir Richard came to stand in front of her, she could not raise her eyes to him.

He said very little. He only said, "I have known for a long time that you are a whore. I will not turn you out of my house, Juliet, but I will never speak to you again and from tonight we will sleep apart. Did you not say you would kill me if I struck you? I swore I'd beat you if you provoked me again, so I am waiting for my death. Here is my warrant."

And he struck her with the flat of his hand across the face and shoulders and breast, and went on striking her until she nearly fell. Then he caught hold of her and stopped.

She whispered in a voice choked with tears, "I will kill you, I swear it. Oh I will, I will – I'll never forgive you!"

"You will never forgive me!" Then he turned away as if he could not stand the sight of her. He looked exhausted and twenty years older. He said in a despairing voice, "Oh get out. Get out. I cannot endure the sight of you." And then, as she tottered away, dazed from the beating, almost out of her mind with fear and rage and humiliation, he poured out a brandy and shoved it into her hand. "You'd best make yourself drunk," he said. "It's what I shall do. Would you not take the bottle with you?" Then in a different voice, choked and rough, "You could have spared me this, Juliet. I may not have been the best of husbands, but I believe I deserved better than to be displaced and betrayed by a snivelling, cowardly little gigolo in my own home, who makes a laughing-stock of me, a creature moreover who did not so much as attempt to defend you."

There was a great gap here. Apparently Rick changed the ribbon. The next sentence came out brief and black and bold.

Today Richard had the most dreadful accident. They say he will never walk again.

That was all. There was no mention of Monsieur Dieudonné. There was, however, a newspaper cutting from something called the *Bishop Recorder* which gave full details of the accident. As for Monsieur Dieudonné, he no doubt survived perfectly well: the Dieudonnés of this world usually do. He could paint after all, that was undeniable, and despite everything, the two portraits were screwed onto the wall in the hallway. It sounded as if Sir Richard had simply scratched him with the point of his sword to frighten him, then thrown him out of the house with his belongings presumably hurled after him. No doubt he scuttled away to the nearest inn and eventually went back to Paris, to make some more fine paintings and probably some more fine wives.

Julia did not think again of Monsieur Dieudonné. She felt cold and sick, and the whisky she sipped at made no difference: the shock of it all was so terrible that the room was undulating round her. She had already known about it of course, but Juliet's two bleak sentences gave it an almost unbearable horror. It took her a long time before she could summon up the strength to scan the yellowed newspaper cutting.

The accident happened a week after the quarrel. What went on during that week Juliet did not say. It was plain however that the break was irrevocable. Sir Richard would never forgive such behaviour, and there must have been a great many others besides Philip and Monsieur Dieudonné, though perhaps at the beginning Juliet showed a little more discretion. She did not seem to be fastidious in her choice of men. Her appetite had been whetted by that first easy conquest, and after him there must have been plenty of handsome grooms, farmer's boys, together with the occasional visitor. There would have been a number of amenable males at the birthday party, and in any society at any time it is instantly known if the hostess possesses an easy virtue. Monsieur Dieudonné must simply have been the last straw, but in the eighteenth century his class-rating would be low, especially as he was a foreigner, and a far more amiable husband would not have been pleased to find his wife and portrait-painter locked in a passionate embrace in the summer-house.

On the day of the accident Sir Richard set out on one of his rides round the estate. "An excellent landlord," wrote the *Recorder*, and Julia was sure this was true. She knew him now and loved him, but in any case he was the sort of man to concern himself with his tenants and workers. The brusque manner concealed a kind heart.

He was apparently riding out to see a farm-worker who lived in one of the tied cottages: he had been gored by a bull and was seriously ill. The *Recorder* spoke a great deal of his family of a wife and three children, and obviously Sir Richard was prepared to make provision for the unfortunate man who seemed like to die, and the family he would leave behind him.

It was on his way back to Fontenoy that it happened. The girth slipped, apparently loosely fastened, and Sir Richard fell, breaking his back as he did so. He was paralysed from the waist down. The rest of his life must be spent in a wheelchair. His arms were still powerful, but the legs were totally useless: for the remainder of his days – Juliet called him old but he was after all still a reasonably young man – he would have to be entirely dependent on others.

The newspaper extolled his virtues in the fashion of its kind. He had never been a particularly popular man, and his extraordinary marriage could hardly have added to his reputation. But nobody had ever accused him of cruelty or injustice, his tenants adored him, and many a neighbour in trouble had cause to be grateful to him. His main faults seemed to be the chauvinism that gave his house its name, and his solitary nature: a sad disadvantage in one who must have been Matley Bishop's most eligible bachelor.

The cutting finished abruptly as if it had been torn, and then there was added a sudden extraordinary outburst from Juliet. Julia, who had been wondering why the girth loosened and whether, unspeakable as it seemed, it had been done deliberately, read this in sick revulsion:

"He will never walk again, my darling, my husband, my love. Oh how I will love him, how I will care for him.

He shall lack for nothing, I will always be there to attend to his smallest needs. I will always be at his side, I will be the most devoted wife imaginable."

The deep voice inside her spoke.

"*It was her revenge. It was the most complete revenge imaginable. During the whole day she never left me alone. She was always there. I could see the joy in her eyes. She had me at last at her mercy. I was never permitted one second's privacy. Everyone believed her the most wonderful wife imaginable. Wherever I turned she was there. Wherever I was, she was beside me, watching, smiling. Only at nights was I permitted to be alone, for she had other company, including the boy who so generously loosened the girth that was meant to kill me. But this was worse than death. She had promised to kill me if I struck her: this was a living death and she enjoyed every moment of it. If she had not been foolish enough to taunt me with my own sword and left it within reach of my hands, I might have lived this living hell for another twenty years.*"

The sword lay with his clothes in the dressing-room. Juliet, as always at his side, was wheeling the chair, and picked up the sword that he would never use again. "*Reveniam*," she quoted from it, smiling, "Now what does that mean, Richard? I have forgot." Then, with the tears springing to her eyes, "But forgive me. You will never be able to use this again. How cruel of me to remind you . . ."

Someone called her. For a few minutes she was out of the room. Sir Richard, using his still powerful arms, managed to reach out for the sword. Then he deliberately hacked at his wrist, with such violence that the sharp blade almost severed his hand. When Juliet, filled with a sudden premonition, came running back, he was already dead in a pool of his own blood spurting forth from the cut artery. His head had fallen back against the chair. His face was grey-white but there was a smile on his lips. The blood was so profuse that as she backed, half-fainting with the shock, she skidded in it and had to cling on to a chair.

Julia bowed her face into her hands and wept. The voice spoke with a hint of laughter. "*Do not weep for me, Julia. It is over, it has been over for more than two hundred years. And now you too must deal with a husband, only be kinder than she was. He is a fool and a coward, and I find it hard to forgive him for so treating you, but he is human too, and he needs your kindness more than he has ever needed anything in his life.*"

Julia heard the front door open and shut. It was four in the morning. Rick stood in the doorway.

He looked dreadful. He looked as she had never seen him. He had always been an exceptionally well-groomed man. Even in the casuals he affected when working, he was elegant. Julia had never seen him with a spot on him: his shirt might be open-necked but it cost thirty pounds, the slacks were impeccably creased, his hair always brushed, and he was never unshaven. It was one of the things she had admired in him. She herself when cooking or cleaning looked crumpled and disordered, but never Rick, though he seemed to pay little attention to himself and was devoid of vanity.

Now he looked dirty and shabby and was certainly drunk. The grey hair fell across his cheeks, the pullover was stained and torn, and there was an unmistakable smear of lipstick on the collar of his shirt.

She rose to her feet as he came in. She made no attempt to excuse herself for reading his typescript which she now pushed back across the desk. She looked at him in silence.

He said, "I'm sorry," then collapsed into the nearest chair as if his legs would no longer support him.

Julia in moments of intense emotion always became practical: it was for her a kind of exorcism. She had never been the screaming kind. She said in a rough, brusque voice, "I expect you're hungry. I'll make you a sandwich."

"I want a whisky," he said.

Julia could see that he had already had several whiskies too many, but then she had had a couple herself while reading the typescript, and in view of what she suspected was coming, it might be a good thing if they were both a little drunk. She filled two glasses, automatically fetching in the ice that Rick liked, then sat down again, looking at him without further comment.

"I didn't mean to hit you," he said.

She looked at him in surprise. She had forgotten all about it. She said, "It doesn't matter. But you shouldn't have locked me in. That was unnecessary and cruel."

He stared at her. "Locked you in?"

"You locked me in the outside lavatory. Don't you remember?"

She thought he probably did not, but for the first time with a faint show of interest, he said, "How did you get out?"

"Oh," said Julia, "the lock doesn't fasten very well." And as she said this she knew that she would get Arthur to remove it altogether first thing next morning.

Then she said, "You've got lipstick on your collar."

He hung his head. He looked ashamed to death. He reminded her of a time when Alan, aged five, robbed his own piggy-bank. It was perfectly easy for an intelligent child, involving nothing more than a pointed kitchen knife, but then Alan was not as easily set down as his father, and though he too hung his head, Julia saw the glimmer of a wicked smile and was compelled to burst out laughing, even though the stolen coins had all to be returned.

There was no smile on Rick's face. He was silent for a while then his eyes moved to the typescript. He began to speak in a loud voice. He said, "Quite a story, isn't it? She was not a very nice girl, taunting him like that. He slashed his wrist, you know. Have you come to that bit? It must have been his great moment of triumph. There was nothing she could do. I expect she was terrified people would think her responsible. Well, she was, wasn't she? I don't suppose for one moment that loose girth was an accident. She tried to bury the sword in the summer-house. The doctor said it was really a mercy. But it was not her mercy. She did not know the meaning of the word."

Julia repeated, "You've got lipstick on your collar."

He stood up. He took a great gulp of the whisky and it went down the wrong way so that he was seized with a fit of coughing. She waited in silence. When he had recovered, he burst out, "You may as well know what you have married. I can't help it. It's a kind of compulsion. It's like a twilight world that I have to enter. You always believed I took those long walks to think out my plots. It wasn't that at all. I do love you, Julia, I never thought I would marry, and I knew I hadn't the right to marry you! I was too contaminated, but I wanted you so much and I thought it would cure me . . ."

Julia said in a gasp, "Are you telling me you pick up whores in the street, any woman, just like that?"

"Just like that," said Rick. His face was sullen and

sad, yet with an odd flicker of triumph.

"And you come back to me!"

He said with a kind of monstrous pride, "I always have a bath first."

At this, for the first time in her life, Julia burst into peals of hysterical laughter, knocking her glass over the typescript, shaking from side to side, the tears pouring down her cheeks and the great shrieks of joyless mirth pealing from her. Only when Rick, muttering, "For God's sake!" came over to her, putting his hands on her arms, did she suddenly recover, shoving him away, the laughter switched off, her face wild and pale and frantic with bewildered disbelief.

He said, "I never meant you to know. I can't explain why I do it. I don't want to. It happens. I know everyone believed me to be the perfect bachelor, a man women liked but who would never marry them. I knew I hadn't the right to marry, especially someone like you. But you were so sweet, so lovely. And for a long time it seemed to work. I just didn't want anyone else. I thought that part of my life was over and done with. And then one night just after Alan was conceived, I felt the urge come upon me again. I couldn't stop myself. I went out, and after that it was just as it always had been."

"So tonight," said Julia, "you hit me, you locked me in the lavatory and you fucked one of your whores. I hope the local girls come up to the standard of the London ones. But it's a pity you didn't bother to wash the lipstick off your collar. I'm so sorry to swear, by the way. I know how genteel you are."

She was entirely calm again. As she spoke she tidied the typescript, wiping off the spilt whisky with a piece of blotting-paper. She put the paperweight on it as she always did. Her face was still pale, but there was no trace of hysteria. Only as she straightened up, retying the girdle of her dressing-gown, did she ask, "Why? What do you get from them?"

He answered simply, "Marcus Tremayne."

"What!"

"I hate them. I can't tell you how much I hate them. They're old and dirty and disgusting; they . . ."

"Doesn't that apply to you too?"

"I suppose it does. But they only want money. They regard me as an old queer, and suggest the kind of thing that poor, deprived old queers need. It wouldn't matter to them if I fell down dead, provided it was well away from their room. But I need them. I couldn't write without them. It doesn't matter to me what they look like, if they say disgusting things. When I come back, I can write again."

"Giving me the pox in the process . . ."

"No. Oh no, don't say that. Please."

Julia exclaimed, "But you could never write properly about women . . ."

"Women!" he said. "They're not women."

"They are, you know."

His face was twisted with disgust. "I could never put anything like that in my books. But I need them. I don't know why. I only know I do, and now perhaps I can write again, and this . . ." he jabbed his finger down on the typescript. "This can be burnt. It's trash, pornographic trash."

"You typed it, Rick."

"I didn't write it. I shall never finish it. How could I? She was one of them. She was the kind of woman I hate and despise. She made me write it. We should never have come here. This is a bad place. I'm going to bed."

Julia called after him as he made a slightly unsteady

progress towards the door. "Rick," she said.

She thought he was hardly aware of her, and for herself he was a complete stranger. He said roughly, "What is it now? Are you going to tell me about that young man of yours? I don't care. I have no right to care. Do you love him? You look as if you're in love."

"I have never loved him," said Julia wearily. "I only wanted to ask you the end of the story."

"What story?"

"The story you've been writing. The story of this house. What happened to Juliet? I understand she married again."

"Juliet?" He began to laugh. It was one of the ugliest laughs Julia had ever heard. "Oh, Juliet married, all right. She lost her looks, you know. There wasn't much pity or compassion in her, but the sight of her husband swimming in his own blood was a bit much even for her. They say – I don't know – that she had a slight stroke from the shock of it, and suddenly became an old woman."

"But she was only twenty – twenty-four or five!"

"Well, it must have been quite a spectacle. And he was smiling, you know. That must have been the final touch. Besides, there was nothing much left for her, and the boy who did the damage with the girth was so horrified that he talked. He didn't actually say he'd done it, he wouldn't dare, but it was plain enough. No-one would speak to her, and her father had died two years before. And there was no money, Sir Richard left it all to a distant relative, only Fontenoy, and the servants wouldn't stay with her. They say – I mean, I really don't know, but that Mrs Purefoy – they say she wandered away quite lost and desolate, and there was a farmer found her, he took her in . . ."

"Oh my God!"

"Well, I suppose it was better than nothing. What else was she to do? She married him. His name was Jack. She had six children by him. The sixth one killed her. I gather he wasn't very kind to her; he beat her and made her do all the farm work."

Julia, who had gone a little white, said almost in a whisper, "I wonder she didn't kill him too."

"I don't think she had enough spirit left in her," said Rick. "Does it matter? She was as wicked a bitch as I have ever heard of. She deserved everything that came to her."

Julia said, the words coming out of their own volition, "Poor Juliet."

"*Poor Juliet.*"

The deep voice sounded in her ears, but Rick only said with the utmost scorn, "Good God, you're surely not sorry for her? She should have been hanged. She was lucky to find anyone to marry her."

Julia thought of the lovely girl who had made such a fine marriage, who must have believed herself the happiest person in the world. She could never have even contemplated such an ending. She was indeed wicked, she had whored and plotted and murdered, yet the tears came to her eyes in sorrow for such a fearful retribution.

She heard Rick say suddenly, "I wish I was dead," and did not even turn her head. She heard him going upstairs. She looked around her but was no longer aware of Sir Richard's presence. Only it was now five in the morning, and the lights suddenly dimmed. Perhaps this always happened only normally she would be asleep at such an hour and not notice. She was too utterly exhausted to care. She walked up thc beautiful staircase but paused for a moment by the portraits. In the dim light they seemed devoid of character, Sir Richard fierce, dark, unsmiling, and Juliet cream-fed, over-plump, delighted with herself.

It was still not possible to believe that it had all ended in catastrophe.

It was very cold. Julia glanced in at the half-open bedroom door. Rick was already asleep, a half finished glass of whisky on the table at his side. Julia walked over to Alan's room, slipped off her dressing-gown and climbed into bed. She could not have endured at that moment to lie at Rick's side, but was pleased when Grendel, who always slept on Alan's bed, came purring up to her, delighted by the company: she cuddled him to her, burying her hands in the soft fur.

She fell almost instantly asleep. Too much had happened for it to seem anything but an exhausted dream. Only after a while, as she tossed and turned, asleep yet with her mind full of horrors, it was as if strong arms enfolded her, and a sweetness, a love, a passion that she had never experienced in her life, overcame her: a sexual joy and deliverance that was so magnificent that all the frightfulness of the evening was obliterated in sheer delight, happiness and ecstasy. When at last she awoke she was so happy, so overcome with the joy of it, that she could no longer feel anything but love for the entire world.

She got out of bed. She walked into her own room. She looked at her husband, now stirring wretchedly in his sleep as if the night had been ugly for him, and found that all her hate and disgust had vanished, leaving nothing but pity, even a kind of love.

He woke up suddenly. He looked at her, the flush deep on his cheeks. He said, "I suppose you are going to leave me. You'll never believe this, indeed, you'll never believe me again, but I do love you, Julia. Could you try to forgive me, or is it absolutely impossible?"

She did not answer this, only said, "Poor Rick," and gently touched his cheek. It was eight o'clock. She had slept perhaps for two hours. She felt refreshed as if she had slept the whole night and, as she took her bath, she poured in an extravagant amount of lotion, and sang, so full of joy and happiness that she wanted to embrace the whole world. When Rick, looking more his normal self but still too ashamed to meet her eye, came into the kitchen, she smiled at him, gave him his breakfast, then turned to answer the front door when Mrs Purefoy arrived, as always, on the dot of nine.

She saw with amazement that Mrs Purefoy had changed her hair-style. Julia still knew nothing of the strange sect she belonged to, but she had believed something so exclusive to be above fashion, and was astonished, almost to the point of giggling, to see that Mrs Purefoy had, as Alan would have put it, gone mod. She had frizzed her hair into a monstrous Afro which, surrounding as it did a thin, minute face, gave her the unmistakable likeness of a lavatory brush. It did not suit her at all, it made her look ludicrous, but then Mrs Purefoy was human like everyone else; perhaps this kind of thing turned Arthur on, perhaps there would now be another little Purefoy to celebrate.

She said, "You look very exotic, Mrs Purefoy," then broke off. Mrs Purefoy still stood in the entrance. She did not cross herself as she always did. She only turned her head from side to side, almost as if sniffing the atmosphere. It was absurd and strange, yet sinister: the cold sweat began to crawl on Julia's face. She remained silent, staring at this odd little creature who seemed to be seeing things that were not there.

Mrs Purefoy said at last, "I'll not be working for you any more, Mrs Burton."

"But Mrs Purefoy . . ."

"I'll be going home now," said Mrs Purefoy, turning towards the gate. She added in a conversational voice, "It's more warmer today. It looks as if spring has really come."

"Mrs Purefoy," said Julia in her firmest voice, "you can't go like this without giving me some explanation. What on earth has happened? Have I offended you in some way? If I have, I'm terribly sorry, I can only assure you it was quite unintentional." Then she said in a bewildered way, "Is it the money? If you feel you want a rise . . ."

Even Mrs Purefoy, who had probably always gone her own way without considering that any explanation was needed, could not ignore this. She stopped. She turned the pale eyes full on Julia. The hair really was a dreadful mistake – how long would it take to grow out? – but there was no denying the power in her.

She said, "Don't get me wrong, Mrs Burton. You've always treated me right, you've paid me very fair, I've nothing to grumble at. Only I couldn't work here no more. Since yesterday there's been things happening that didn't ought to happen. I knew it the moment you opened the door. It's like some sort of black shadow. I couldn't stay here for one single second, not one. It's more worse than I've ever known it; it would be as much as my life is worth to set foot inside the threshold. There's blood here, Mrs Burton, I can smell it. I don't know what you has done, but you've wakened them all up; this is no longer a place for any God-fearing person, and if you takes my advice you'll leave straight away, that's what I'm telling you, leave straight away before something awful happens."

Julia found herself trembling uncontrollably, for indeed, it was true. She had wakened them all up, the ghosts were astir, the house was alive with its past: love and hate and murder and suicide walked beside her. She forgot the glory of last night, the only picture in her mind was of a smiling man, dying in his blood. She was on the verge of tears. Mrs Purefoy with her absurd hair-do somehow represented sanity: she could not bear her to go.

She cried out, "Oh Mrs Purefoy, please don't go," then the shameful words burst from her, "I'm frightened!"

"You take my advice," said Mrs Purefoy. She turned again and marched steadfastly to the gate, a staunch little figure with the negroid hair-do, the kind of thing the wicked Iraniums wore, totally incongruous above that prim, pointed little face. "You go, Mrs Burton, and take your husband with you. This is a wicked house, and there's things moving here as should not be. You go back to London. If you don't, you'll regret it, mark my words."

Mr Thomas heard about Mrs Purefoy with his morning coffee. "She's gone and left them," his little secretary told him. "It's all round Matley Bishop." She recounted what had happened, much embellished in the telling. How she knew nobody could say, but then everyone knew everything in Matley Bishop, and it appeared that Mrs Purefoy had looked in the open doorway and fallen into a dead faint at the horrible atmosphere that overwhelmed her.

Mr Thomas did not believe a word of this: it was impossible to think of Mrs Purefoy falling into a dead faint, but he said drearily, "Here we go again. They seemed such sensible people. I thought they might somehow break the jinx." Then he exclaimed, "I wish to God Fontenoy would burn down," and followed this up by saying in a loud, insistent voice, "Kindly buy me a bottle of scotch."

"But Mr Thomas . . ."

"Did you hear what I said? Take it out of the petty cash. I want a bottle of scotch. Now, Before Mrs Burton arrives."

Julia arrived an hour later. She had rung up to say she was coming, and she could tell from Mr Thomas's voice that he had already heard all about it. He was by now three scotches to the bad. He was not a drinking man, and the main effect it had on him was temper, but he saw to his relief that Mrs Burton was not hysterical, indeed she seemed reasonable and calm.

She said without preamble, "You are perfectly right."

Mr Thomas offered her a drink. She accepted it as if she hardly knew what she was doing. She looked, he thought, very beautiful, and this astonished him for he remembered her as a very English looking girl, rather like Julie Andrews, agreeable and pleasant but totally without glamour.

Perhaps it was the effect of the unaccustomed whisky.

She went on, "The house is definitely haunted. Not even the most hardened sceptic could deny it. But I'm not leaving, you know."

He said in a bewildered voice, "I understood – Mrs Purefoy . . ."

"Oh her! I can manage without Mrs Purefoy, thank you. But I knew you'd expect me to be going, so I thought I'd better come round to reassure you. I've no intention of going at all. My son is coming up this weekend, and we are inviting all the ghosts for a welcoming Easter party."

He said weakly, "Have you actually seen a ghost?"

"No. Not exactly. But I know they are there. I don't think," said Julia, "they'll hurt us. Mind you, I talk like this, but there is just a possibility we may not stay. It depends entirely on what happens. It might become impossible. But at the moment I have every intention of staying, and I can assure you of one thing: the ghosts, as you call them, are in no way malevolent. The only harm they can do us is through ourselves."

Mr Thomas did not know what to say to this. Before, it had been very different. Mrs Foster had been completely hysterical, so much so that she had had to lie down, and the other tenant had shouted at him and been so abusive that he had been on the verge of calling the police. This calm, beautiful young woman who talked about ghosts as if they were the most natural thing in the world, nonplussed him, and her next remark was so extraordinary that he began to wonder if he were going out of his mind.

"I think," she said, "I'm pregnant."

As Mr Thomas said to his wife much later, it was not the kind of thing one expected in an estate agent's office. People of course were always odd, and there were stories he could tell that were hardly believable, but mostly they concerned money, the incredible shifts clients went to to avoid paying, and so on. No-one so far had told him she was pregnant, which was, after all, none of his business, and surely a personal matter one kept for one's family and intimate friends.

He was so disconcerted that his next remark was jerked out of him.

"Not, I hope," he said, "by one of the ghosts?"

"That," said Julia, "is quite possible."

Mr Thomas left the office soon after her departure. He said he did not feel well. Fortunately, Mrs Burton was as startled by her own remark as he was, muttered something about shopping and was out of the door almost immediately. He could see that she had never meant to say this. He wondered why on earth she had. But though he was in no way an imaginative man he would never forget the look of her as she walked out of the office: there was a pride and beauty and – the word slid into his mind – fulfilment to her that was quite startling.

III

1980

Alan arrived on Thursday evening with a friend called Colin. Colin seemed a nice, ordinary little boy, more interested in boxing than ghosts: this presumably was the link between them. If he had heard the story, he had in no way been impressed by it, and Julia was thankful to see him, for somehow he brought everything back to normal. It was hard to dwell on ghosts when two young boys were sparring away, bloodying each other's noses. There was of course no Mrs Purefoy, and the employment agency in Matley Bishop was terribly sorry but had no-one available, but Julia was young and healthy, she no longer went to the hostel, and the housework was a Godsend: it kept her occupied and out of Rick's way.

She was furious with herself for what she had said to Mr Thomas. It was most unfair on the poor man who had surely suffered enough from Fontenoy already. Besides it was quite absurd. How could she be pregnant and why was she so absolutely convinced she was? Her period was not due for another two weeks and even that was hardly proof. Rick seldom came near her. They had to share the same bed, because the spare room and Alan's room were both occupied, but they lay side by side like strangers. They hardly spoke. Rick indeed looked so ill that even Alan noticed: he asked his mother what was the matter and she replied vaguely that he had been overworking.

He was certainly not working now. There was no sound of the typewriter and she saw when she was tidying up that the typescript had vanished. She had hoped he might now start a new Marcus Tremayne: if whores provided his inspiration he should be well on the way. But this was something she struggled to push out of her mind. The idea of Rick, so fastidious, bathing twice a day, never wearing anything faintly rumpled or stained, consorting with some cheap little street-girl was inconceivable. Of course, despite her efforts, she thought of little else. She could not forget those evening walks that she had always assumed were solitary rambles, knowing now that they all ended up in some grimy little room. She tried to behave as if nothing had happened, but the slightest contact made her recoil, and she thought that when Alan had gone back to school she would move into the spare room: it was no longer possible to share their bed.

She heard nothing of Mark but Alan, who did not ask her why she was no longer working there, went down to the hostel with Colin, taking with him all the toys he had declared he would not part with. Teddy-bears, the celebrated rocking-horse, an old football and three boxes of Lego, all went to the Iraniums, and Mark was apparently delighted.

The boys were mostly out, for the weather was good. Julia used to pack them vast parcels of sandwiches and fruit and not see them again until supper-time. But she sensed that Alan was waiting in his own good time to talk to her, and she was a little alarmed by him for he seemed to have grown too thin, and there was a drawn, pale look to his normally robust face that made her glance unhappily at him from time to time. Sir Richard had said that he, like Grendel, could see a little through the shadow of the past, and she could only pray that this was not so. Certainly for the most part he and Colin behaved very much like other boys: scuffling, fighting, arguing and giggling. Perhaps Alan's appearance was partly due to his age, for he was now nearly thirteen.

In the meantime she had a long talk with Arthur, who seemed quite unaffected by his wife's second-sight, and who turned up with cheerful regularity.

He remarked to Julia, "What do you think of the wife's new hair-do?" Mrs Purefoy must have a Christian name, but Julia had never heard him use it.

She said a little awkwardly that it was very nice. "It's all the fashion nowadays," she said.

"I think it's terrible," said Arthur, caught Julia's eye and they both burst out laughing.

"How long does it take to grow out?" he asked.

"Oh, months, I think."

"I look forward to having my own wife again," said Arthur. Then, "I see you're growing your own."

"I thought I was a bit old for the boyish crop," said Julia. And it was true, her hair which was silky and thick now covered her ears, and looked so attractive that even Alan noticed it with approval.

Then she had a serious talk with Arthur about the outside lavatory and the summer-house. The bolt she had already had removed: another must be put inside, together with a window and electric light. "I want this done as soon as possible," said Julia very firmly, and Arthur promised it would be finished in a couple of days. "And then," she said, "the summer-house."

She looked away from him. A faint colour came into her cheeks. "I want it pulled down," she said.

Arthur showed no surprise. She had never seen Arthur show any surprise. Even the sight of his wife's new Afro hair-do probably provoked no reaction. "Right down?" he said.

"Right down."

"To the ground?"

"To the ground."

"Okay, Mrs Burton. Your wish is my command."

"And then you can build a new one in its place. Something not too modern because it wouldn't go with the house, but I want it open and airy, somewhere we can sit in the evenings and with a nice little balcony. White. Definitely white. And we'll go romantic and have ramblers and flowers and things. Do you think you can do that?"

Arthur thought he could do that. Only for the first time he looked directly at Julia who knew then that Mrs Purefoy had discussed everything with him. "The wife knows," he said, "and I think it would be better when you've pulled it down to grow plants there and just leave it, but if that's what you want – I see exactly what you mean, anyway. It's like your boy selling that sword of his, the one with the blood on it that always seems to come back."

"Arthur, what do you mean?"

"Didn't he tell you now? Perhaps he thought it would frighten you. I must say, it gave me a bit of an odd turn myself. We cleaned it together and it was as bright as a new pin, and then a few days later there was the blood marks all over it. We tried again but it was no good. It's as if it's got into the steel. Anyway, your boy's going to sell it and give the money to them Iraniums. He asked me what I thought it was worth. I told him to take it to the Matley Museum. I don't know nothing about such things but I bet it's worth a bomb."

"Alan," said Julia at teatime – Colin who seemed possessed of inexhaustible energy was kicking a football round the garden – "What's all this about the sword?"

He went very red. "I suppose Arthur's been talking. I was going to tell you, Mummy, honest, I was, but I could see you were a bit upset so I thought it had better wait. I haven't done anything wrong, have I? You did give it to me. I thought I could do what I liked with it. I haven't actually sold it yet. I wouldn't have done that without asking you first. But I rang the Museum. They were very excited. After all, it's local history. They couldn't say much until they'd seen it, but probably it was worth at least a couple of thousand pounds. Mark could do with that for his kids. He says he never has enough money for them."

Julia said quietly, "I'm not sure if you have the legal right to sell it. It's part of the house. It belongs to the family."

"There isn't any family. If there was, they'd have the house, wouldn't they?"

"They may have wanted to get rid of it," said Julia, and she sighed as she said this. "It's understandable. And I agree that Fontenoy was up for sale with presumably everything that was in it, including those two portraits, but of course nobody could get those off so they just had to stay. But nobody, not even Mr Thomas, seems to have heard of the sword until we found it in the summer-house, and I'm sure it is valuable, with all those jewels in the hilt. I suspect it's worth more than two thousand. There may be some distant relative in Australia or something like that. I think we ought at least to ask Mr Thomas, though he's so fed up with Fontenoy that he'll probably say, "Have it". Where is the thing? I see it's no longer in your room. Don't you like it any more? You were so excited about it when we found it."

Alan said in a choked voice, "It frightens me."

"Why?"

He said after a pause, "It's that blood. It is blood, Mummy. And it won't come off."

Julia only said, "Where have you put it?"

"In the cupboard. Where my toys were."

"Let's have another look at it. If it interests you," said Julia without looking at him, "it frightens me too."

Alan did not answer this, only left the room. He returned a couple of minutes later with the sword. Julia took it. Then she went so white that Alan believed she was going to faint, and rushed to put his arm round her. It was at this moment that the lights dimmed. She felt Alan's hand grip her shoulder. He did not move. She looked down at the sword and could only see blood – black stains everywhere.

She said with a shaky laugh, "Those damned lights – Anyone would think they did it on purpose." Then with all the energy she could summon, "We're both being hysterical. It's only an old sword. Everyone wore a sword in those days. There's nothing to be scared of, and it's probably rust, not blood."

But it was no use, and she knew she convinced Alan no more than herself. She could only see a man in a wheelchair with one hand half severed, the blood pumping from it: the whole room was full of blood, the world was full of blood, and a terrified, white little face staring down at the ruin she had caused, her feet skidding in the red pool that trickled across the floor.

Then the lights went on again. There was just herself and Alan and an old, stained sword. Julia was very pale, but she managed to smile, laying the sword down on the table as she did so. "The trouble with us," she said, "is we've too much imagination."

"He killed himself with it, didn't he?" said Alan.

"Oh good God, I don't know. What on earth makes you think that?"

"I know he did. He cut his wrist. There'd be blood all over the place."

"Alan . . ."

"He had no choice. I think – I think he was in a wheelchair."

Julia said as firmly and calmly as she could, though she was shaking from head to foot, "Darling, I don't know what you're talking about. I – I suppose this thing has killed people. After all, it's what it's for. Like a gun. But you don't really know what happened, and we're just going to forget about it. Only I'm glad you've taken it down. I never really liked you having it in your room." Then she said, "Alan, you know your father was writing that book."

"Yes."

"Did you ever see it?"

"No, Mummy."

She believed him. Alan never told lies. Sir Richard was right. "Your Alan sees me a little. I think his vision is growing clearer." It was wrong, it was dreadfully wrong. He was beginning to see things he should not see. She said, "Oh, we'll forget about that relative in Australia. If he exists at all, he 's probably some hairy old sheep-farmer who wouldn't know a sword from a ploughshare and is only interested in kangaroos. Take it to the Museum. They'll probably buy it themselves. Never mind what they offer you, just take it and hand it over to Mark. It'll buy the Iraniums lots of lovely rice and curry. If this sword has killed people, it can now help to feed the starving. It's a kind of poetic justice. I think Sir Richard would like it too."

Colin, bored with the football, was shouting out for Alan to come and join him. Alan neither moved nor answered. He said, "Mummy . . ."

"Yes, love?"

"Please, could we leave here?"

"Alan! I thought you were so happy here."

He said in a strained little voice, "I am in a way. It's a lovely place. It's home to me. Only – only – Mummy, I'm not going bananas or anything, really I'm not, but I see funny things in the shadows. I feel as if I'm never really alone. It makes me frightened. Sometimes I wake up in the night and there are people there. I can't see them, but I know they're there all the same. They're not always nice people. If we go I shall miss it terribly, it's like nothing I've ever known, but sometimes I just can't bear it. It's like that sword with all the blood on it, and I don't like those portraits on the wall either; I am beginning to feel as if they own me. You talked about Rochester once. You said Sir Richard was like him. I don't think he was that sort of man at all. I think he was a kind, good man who got tied up with all the wrong people. And I can't bear that Juliet any more. She was a horrid, beastly girl, she was cruel and selfish, she didn't care about anybody but herself. Only neither of them will leave me alone. I almost feel as if I'm haunted. Oh Mummy, let's go back to boring old London. This is a beautiful house, but it's so sad and sometimes it's really frightening. I'm getting to the stage where I dread coming here for holidays, though I know that when we leave I shall miss it like hell."

Julia was so overcome that she could only say his name over and over again, "Alan, Alan, Alan."

Colin's amiable, cheeky face peered round the door.

Alan said quickly, "Okay, I'm coming. I have to ask my mother something. I'll be there in a sec."

Colin said, "They're pulling down the summer-house."

"You see," Alan said to Julia, "You see. You don't really like it either."

"I love it with all my heart," said Julia. She handed the sword back to him. He took it very gingerly. "You and Colin can take it to the Museum tomorrow. If they don't want it, they'll tell you what to do. Perhaps Christie's would be interested. All right, Alan. Don't worry any more. I couldn't bear you to be unhappy here, so I'll see what can be done. I don't think we'll ever be quite rid of Fontenoy, but perhaps the time has come to go. If," she said, her voice changing, "I'm not mistaken, I think the house will take charge of everything for us. Perhaps it wants us to go. In any case, I'm sure the choice is no longer ours. Perhaps it never has been. Only there's one thing I can tell you, darling. You won't be harmed. Please take my word for it." Then more briskly, "Where's your father? I haven't seen him since lunch-time, and he doesn't seem to be typing."

Alan said in a surprised voice, "He's decorating."

"Decorating? Dad? Oh nonsense! He wouldn't know one end of a paint-brush from another."

"He is, you know. Come and have a look."

Julia followed him out on to the porch. She could see that Arthur had already demolished the summer-house, which lay in ruins about him. Rick was perched on a ladder, painting the side of the house, by the kitchen and outside lavatory. She stared in utter amazement. He was the least domestic of men, incapable of hammering in a nail: if he had attempted to mend a fuse, all the lights of Matley Bishop would be extinguished. He also suffered from poor balance so that even looking over a staircase could bring on vertigo. And here he was, high on a ladder, slapping white undercoat on the wall: the sight scared her so much that she dared not even call out his name.

Arthur's voice came over her shoulder. "The wall could surely do with a lick of paint, Mrs Burton, but I offered to do it for him and he just laughed and said he'd do it himself, it was thera – Oh, I'm not an educated chap, can't remember the word."

"Therapeutic!"

"That's it. Therapeutic. The wife would know all about that, but then she's a reader, she knows all the long words. So I just left him to it and went on with the summer-house. It's down now, Mrs Burton. Would you like to come and have a look?"

Julia followed Arthur with some reluctance. The place still filled her with a kind of panic. Rick glanced down and waved his brush at her. He seemed to be in high spirits. He was doing the painting rather badly, and she saw that Arthur would probably have to apply the second coat. She came up to what was left of the summer-house, now simply a mass of planks and stones and tiles. She was possessed of the feeling that there might be something terrible buried beneath the debris, perhaps the skeleton of Monsieur Dieudonné – after all no-one actually knew what had happened to him – but there was nothing there at all, only woodlice, ants and spiders, all of which Arthur, plainly no friend of Friends of the Earth, stamped on cheerfully.

"Right old mess it was too," he said. "You were quite right, Mrs Burton. Given a high wind, it would probably have fallen down of its own accord. The supports were all rotten and worm-eaten. Now I've done a little plan . . ."

Julia did not say that she might not be there to see it. She wondered what Mr Thomas would think of all this, but suspected that he was so utterly fed-up with Fontenoy that he would hardly care if it were razed to the ground.

Arthur's idea of a summer-house was not hers. It looked more like an ice-cream parlour, especially as he suggested painting the inner walls pink. She managed to dissuade him from this without hurting his feelings, and presently with the aid of paper and pencil evolved a cosy little affair, in no way original or artistic but eminently suitable for sitting in, on summer evenings, and with a bench going all the way round.

"There's a nice rambler," said Arthur, "that I could get cheap for you – know the chap in Matley – and we'd have boxes on the outer wall. Geraniums perhaps or those bright blue things I've forgot the name of. It'll look real pretty. That was a good idea of yours, Mrs Burton. It'll cheer up the garden no end, and now I've tidied away some of those blinking weeds, you'll be surprised how nice it'll be. Especially . . ." His eyes moved up to Rick who was splashing more paint on himself than on the wall. His mouth creased into a grin. "All spick and span, aren't we? And a nice crop of strawberries coming too. You might even have some fish in that stream. Oh, nobody'll recognise Fontenoy by the time we're finished with it, and I'll bet you anything you like the wife will be back shortly, if only to see what's going on. She does go on so about ghosts, but with everything so bright and new and clean, she'll forget all about them."

The weekend passed quietly enough, though Rick

was withdrawn and taciturn, spending the evenings reading in his study. There was no sound of typing. Julia prayed that he was researching a new Marcus Tremayne. The two boys went to Matley Bishop Museum on the Saturday and left the sword there for the experts to examine.

"They were very excited about it," said Alan. "I think they want to buy it for themselves." Then he said quickly, "Mummy, would you mind if I spent next week with Colin before I go back to school? It would mean going this afternoon. His mother has asked me down, and it's his birthday; there's going to be a party. It sounds rather smashing."

"Of course I don't mind. I think it's a very good idea." Then Julia said, "You still really want to leave here, don't you?"

He hesitated. She saw suddenly that he had grown up. It jolted her a little. The hands, over-large on the thin wrists were a man's hands, no longer the soft baby hands that remain with children for such an unexpected length of time. He would be tall like his father with long thighs, and the shoulders, though bony, were widening out. But the face was still a child's face, disturbed, anxious, longing for comfort, a comfort she could not give him.

He said, "I can't really explain. Only Dad's so strange, one minute he's slapping paint all over the place, and then he comes off the ladder and you talk to him, and he somehow acts as if he's seeing something that isn't there, he doesn't listen to a word you're saying. Grendel's gone funny too, purring away when he's on his own, and sometimes I could swear he's rubbing himself against someone, only there's nobody there. It's weird and I don't like it. I'm beginning to have funny dreams, and there's always blood in them."

He began to giggle nervously. "Perhaps I ought to go to a shrink."

Julia was horrified, and prayed that the horror did not show in her face. She thanked God for Colin. She said firmly, "I think you should definitely go to that birthday party and spend the whole week with Colin's family. It'll do you far more good than any shrink, as you call it, and you'll probably find when you come back that all this has passed. I think it's that sword that's done it. I'm thankful the Museum is taking it. Anyway, when you're back, we'll talk the whole thing over. By the way . . ." Her voice changed and the colour came into her cheeks. "Would you mind terribly if I had another baby? There'll be a frightful difference in age and all that, I know, but I wondered."

Alan looked completely taken aback. When he spoke, in an oddly old, wise voice, he said the last thing she had expected. "Well, of course I wouldn't mind, but would it really be sensible? I mean, the chances of something going wrong with the child when you're old . . ."

"Oh, come on now!" exclaimed Julia with considerable irritation. "I'm only thirty-four, damn it. I had you when I was twenty-one. You make me sound at least fifty."

Then he laughed, looking like himself again. "It would be rather fun," he said, "provided I don't have to change nappies and things like that." And as he turned to go back into the garden, he said over his shoulder, "Does Dad know?"

Julia threw a book at him, this being the nearest thing to hand, then suddenly sat down. The question had far more importance than Alan could possibly have realised. *Does Dad know*? She had had no sex with Rick for a long time now, and this pregnancy that she talked of with such calmness was an illusion, based on a dream. A ghost could surely not beget a child, and she had no right to mention the matter to anybody at all, much less Alan. Yet the conviction that the child was there was so strong, so overwhelming that she simply could not bring herself to deny it. The disgraceful thought was stirring in her mind that somehow Rick, for all his whores and extraordinary behaviour, must be persuaded to make love to her, even though the idea of it sickened her.

There was such a thing as an hysterical pregnancy. Mary Tudor, if she remembered rightly, carried it to such lengths that her belly swelled and she showed signs of giving birth. But Julia did not feel hysterical, and the awareness of a child within her was such that she would have sworn to it on a Bible oath.

Then she made up her mind to do something that really she should have done days ago. She left Arthur hammering happily away, waved to Rick who was again at his painting – she wished the ladder would not sway so – and set off for the hostel to have a talk with Mark Rossiter. She looked in on Alan before she left, to say goodbye. He was packing, which meant hurling everything into a suitcase, leaving behind half the things he needed and taking a great deal he would never use. She made no comment. Colin's mother was presumably used to young boys and would no doubt provide spare underpants, socks and pyjamas. The only thing she did was to fold a new silk shirt that would certainly be needed for the party, and place it on top of what looked like skiing boots. She said goodbye very happily. She was only too thankful that he was going away, and Colin was just the right companion for him, a jolly, extrovert little boy who had never heard of ghosts in his life, who liked sport, boxing and television, and would find the story of Fontenoy a load of balls. She had heard him use the phrase when he did not know she was within earshot. Rick would have a fit. In a way he was an odd friend for Alan to choose, but the two seemed to get on very well, and there would be plenty of other children at the party, girls, games, dancing and masses of food: for that week Alan would forget his fears, doubts and anxieties.

It was a dreadful thing to say of one's own beloved son, but Julia had never been more relieved to see the back of him. Sir Richard was right: he had the sight, he was seeing and sensing far too much. Somehow when he was there the house seemed more haunted than ever, as if he were transmuting to her the vision of his inner eye.

She drove down to the hostel. It looked exactly the same: shabby, down-at-heel, dilapidated. Only the children playing outside seemed happier, less lost and forlorn. They did not seem to recognise her, no-one ran up to greet her except Mark, who was in the front garden when she arrived and instantly came towards her. He was smaller and younger than she remembered, and there was, thank God, not a flicker of emotion between them, but she found herself glad to see him and, when he took her hands, holding them lightly for a moment, she suddenly leaned forward and kissed his cheek.

She saw the colour flame into his face. She laughed. "That's really an apology. You don't mind my coming, do you?"

"I've been praying you would," he said. "I wanted to ring you but I just didn't dare. I really am glad to see you, Julia. Come in. We'll have a drink to celebrate. I don't usually drink while I'm working here, but I think this is something of an occasion, and I do have a bottle of scotch."

"Do you have anyone to help you?" asked Julia, adding, "Apart from the scotch."

Mark jerked his head in the direction of the playground. Julia could see a middle-aged woman there, holding a child with either hand. "She's very nice," he said. "She's not a patch on you, but the kids like her, and she's kind. I miss you every minute of the day, Julia, but I expect it's better like this."

They sat in his room by the window. It was a small, bare room, its only furniture a bed, one table, two chairs and a filing cabinet. There were not even curtains to the window. Once Julia had longed to make the place more comfortable. Now she understood why it was so plain: it was a kind of conscience, it satisfied some need in him to make up for the cruel inequalities and injustices of the world. In some ways he was raffish, even unscrupulous; he had broken his marriage, he wandered no doubt from woman to woman, but the horrors of the boat-people, the sufferings of his children, the incomprehensible wickedness of humanity, weighed him down so that to put up curtains, fill a vase with flowers, have a carpet on the floor, would be a senseless self-indulgence that negated everything he was trying to do.

He said at last – she saw that his eyes were always on the playground below – "I'll never really be able to explain what happened. It was completely crazy. I can only think I was blind drunk."

"It wasn't your fault," said Julia.

Then he did look at her. "But why? I just don't understand. It's not the kind of thing – Look, please forgive me, I'm not meaning to insult you and you're a very attractive girl, but I mean . . ." He broke off, flushing again. "Oh God. Whatever I say just makes it worse. I can only say that I'm not in the habit of leaping into bed with my host's wife, even if she was Mata Hari in person . . ."

"And I'm not Mata Hari. Look," said Julia, "I can't really explain it to you, you'd just think me mad if I did, but will you accept in defiance of all reason that Fontenoy is haunted; truly it is, and it somehow drags people into its past, makes them behave as they behaved two hundred years ago. What you did was nothing to do with you at all. Oh Mark. What's the use? You really do think I'm crazy. Sometimes I think I am too. But it's like this: Something very terrible happened in the house, and it's left its shadow so that everyone who comes within that shadow is knocked out of character. It's not only you. It's as if we've all been dragged back in time. My husband is just no longer the person I married, though I suppose he might always have been like that and I didn't recognise it. Even my little boy is affected. He's very sensitive and I think a little psychic; he sees something of what has gone on, though I can only pray he doesn't fully understand it. He wants to get away. He's beginning to be scared. I don't really want to go, but I think for the sake of all our sanity that we'll just have to leave and get back to London. It's not really a haunting. It's a taking-over. We've all been taken over. We're all different people. Don't you find me changed?"

He said slowly, "You're very beautiful."

"Oh," said Julia, "I suppose that's something. The only people who aren't affected are types like Arthur who doesn't seem to notice anything, but then he lives here, he's probably used to it. You were taken over, Mark, whether you like it or not. You became a French painter called Dieudonné."

"Now look . . .!"

"I told you you wouldn't believe me. And I behaved like a whore."

"Julia!"

"Well, I did, didn't I? Perhaps I am a whore. But it wasn't really me." Then she began to laugh a little hysterically. "You think I'm nuts, don't you? I'm beginning to think so too. But please believe one thing. None of this was your fault, it didn't mean anything, and if you hadn't come to dinner that night, nothing would ever have happened, and I'd still be working here."

Mark said at last, "I don't understand one word you've been saying, but I know one thing. I'll never go out to dinner at Fontenoy again. Not," he added hastily, "that I'm likely to be asked. Are you really leaving us?"

"I'm beginning to see," said Julia, "that I have no choice. Richard said – Never mind. But I'm afraid it's not ended yet. I'm sorry to sound such a coward, but I'm scared."

"Would you like me to drive you home?"

"Oh no. That would only make things worse. I never thought," said Julia, draining down her whisky, " – No thanks, I don't want any more – I never thought I was a scary person, but I've got the heebies good and proper. I think I'd better go." She jumped to her feet as she spoke, shaking her head as he held the bottle out. "Really no. Mark, I've such a feeling of disaster. I don't know what's the matter with me. Oh God, I'm so thankful Alan is away. He's spending the week with a schoolfriend, a nice, common, sensible sort of kid who'd laugh his head off at the thought of ghosts. I wish I could laugh . . ."

"Look," said Mark, "why don't you come and have supper with me? We could go to our usual little caf'. It would be like old times. I don't suppose your husband would mind. And I'd like to introduce you to Tina. That's my new assistant."

"I don't want to meet Tina, and I'm sorry, Mark, I couldn't choke down a mouthful. I must go home."

"But the children would love to see you. They still talk about you, you know."

Julia only said, her voice rising, "I must go home."

He caught at her arm as she moved towards the door, but the face she turned on him was so wild and distraught that he instantly released her. He exclaimed, "What on earth is the matter? You seemed all right a few minutes ago. At least let me drive you. You're in no state to drive. You might have an accident."

"An accident!" Her voice shrilled up then quietened immediately. "I'm sorry. I'm being hysterical. But I must go, I must go now."

"At least," he said, running after her for she was almost running herself, "give me a ring. You've got me worried now. Will you promise to ring as soon as you're home? I'm sure nothing has happened. You've just worked yourself up with all these tales of ghosts and hauntings. I do wish you'd at least let me come with you."

But she was already in the car and had started up the engine. Her face was very pale. He said, "Goodbye," but he thought she did not even hear him. The car disappeared round the bend of the road. She was driving much too fast. All this was quite unlike Julia, who could cope so calmly with a sick child or an hysterical mother, who had once told him that the worse the catastrophe the calmer she became. If she had lived during the war she would have been essentially one to shepherd people out of bombed buildings, comfort the injured and bereaved, behave with composure in the worst of blitzes.

And now she was driving at what seemed to be seventy miles an hour onto a busy main road.

Tina came up to him, saying, "Anything the matter? Mrs Burton seemed to be in quite a state."

She spoke with a certain amount of satisfaction. She was a woman of forty-five, a trained social worker, and ever since her arrival had heard how marvellous Julia was. She was secretly delighted to see that Mark and Julia had plainly had a row: she had seen Julia running towards her car and, like Mark, had noticed her wild driving.

But Mark did not even answer her. Julia's palpable terror had communicated itself to him, and instead of going into the playground he returned to his room, drinking more whisky and waiting almost with panic for the telephone to ring.

The front door of Fontenoy was wide open. The panic seething within Julia that had twice nearly involved her in a crash, turned now to a fatalistic calm. She came into the house quietly enough and looked at Arthur and Mrs Purefoy who were standing there, waiting for her.

She looked from one to the other. Arthur, always so jolly, looked pale and grim, while Mrs Purefoy's little face under the ridiculous mop of curls, was almost eclipsed.

She said in a steady voice, "It's Mr Burton, isn't it?"

"I'm afraid it is, Mrs Burton. There's been an accident."

This was Mrs Purefoy, speaking in the assured way of one attuned to disaster, but it was Arthur who led her to the nearest chair and poured her out a drink.

Julia said, "How bad?"

Mrs. Purefoy began, "Oh very bad indeed, terrible, terrible . . ." but Arthur who seemed mysteriously to have taken control, said quickly, "He's not dead, Mrs Burton, nor like to be. But they've taken him to hospital. Matley Bishop General. He fell off the ladder. One of the struts was cracked. It could have happened to anyone. Only he fell awkward like, and it's his back."

The house gathered about them, spotlighting them in the shadows of two hundred years ago. A terrified yet triumphant little face, the servants huddled together, the groom shaking convulsively, and the grim quartet in their hunting pink carrying the stretcher, with Sir Richard lying there motionless yet fully conscious, his hands folded at his chest.

"It's his back."

The surgeon, hastily summoned, not knowing how to put it, not daring to look into that young face, speaking at last with the brutal directness of one who did not know what to say.

"I'm afraid he'll never walk again."

Julia said in the same quiet, conversational voice, "Is his back broken?"

The house enfolded them. It was the whole world, 1750, 1980, the only world. This time Mrs Purefoy did not speak. Arthur answered, and Julia loved Arthur because he spoke directly without dramatics.

"They don't know, Mrs Burton. It's possible."

"In which case he will never walk again?"

So many things to say: Modern surgery. Stoke Mandeville. Miraculous transplants. These days they can cure almost anything. Arthur only said, "If it's his back, Mrs Burton, he probably won't. But they don't know.

They can't say till they've examined him. They want you to stay here and they'll ring you the moment they know."

"Stay here!" Julia jumped to her feet. At that moment all calm left her. Her voice came out in a shriek. "What do you think I am? My husband desperately ill, and I'm just to sit here, waiting for the bloody phone to go? You'll drive me down now, Arthur. This instant. I couldn't stay here one second more. Oh for God's sake, don't just stand there, the pair of you. Get me to the hospital. I – I just can't do it myself. I think I'd collapse. My car's outside. Drive me there at once."

"Look, Mrs Burton." It was hard to associate this quiet, strong man with the jovial creature who did all the odd jobs and built new summer-houses. Julia could no longer think coherently at all. Afterwards she understood why Mrs Purefoy, whom one seldom associated with the gentler emotions, loved and obeyed him. He said, "You can't do nothing by going now. He's in the operating theatre. They specially asked for you to stay here. The second they know they'll ring you and send a car for you. You'd only be in their way. You wouldn't do any good. You stay here, and the wife will cook you some supper."

"Do you really believe I could touch a thing?" Then Julia said faintly, "I'd like a cup of tea."

Mrs Purefoy, acknowledging a nod from her husband, at once vanished into the kitchen. Arthur came up to Julia and put an arm round her shoulders. "I think it might be all right, Mrs Burton. I saw him move one leg. He couldn't do that if his back was broke. You'll hear soon. We'll stay with you."

"I'm sorry," said Julia, "but truly, I'd rather be on my own."

Then he did hesitate. She could see that from his point of view this was simply not done. He said, "You didn't ought to be here all by yourself. Isn't there someone you could ring? That chap at the hostel. I'm sure he . . ."

"I must be on my own," said Julia.

They left very reluctantly. She was grateful to them but thankful when they were at last gone. But of course she was not on her own. They all hemmed her in, crowding round her, touching her, mouthing at her. She sat there in a shivering huddle, a pot of tea on the table beside her, a small plateful of delicately sliced bread and butter and – this was Arthur, more worldly than his wife – a glass and a bottle of whisky. She touched none of it, though she craved for something hot and sweet. She was too choked to swallow, too frightened, too oppressed by the people surrounding her. In desperation she pushed at the murderous slut who had set out to kill her man, then it seemed to her that the slut was herself, and she burst into a panic of tears. All about her were vast, accusing eyes, voices saying, "Murderess!" And all she could do was listen for the telephone bell that never rang.

Then she heard the car outside. And then she heard the footsteps: trudge, drag, pause, trudge, drag, pause.

She had never before experienced such pure, unadulterated fear. It was a fear that melted the body like wax, froze the blood in her veins. She was paralysed with terror. Her face was ashen, her dry mouth could not produce a sound.

Trudge, drag, pause. Trudge, drag, pause.

Once she had read a story called *The Monkey's Paw*. A woman was given three wishes: her son through one of them was killed and hideously mutilated in some machine, and she wished for him to return. Only he returned as he had died, chopped into pieces, and she heard him coming heavily up the stairs, dragging his feet, and knew that the sight of him would be so frightful she would never survive it. There was one wish left to her and she frantically wished him back in his grave again.

Julia had read the story when young, and it had frightened her almost to death. She could still hear those slow steps mounting the stairs – trudge, drag, pause – then the door would open and the sliced corpse would be standing there.

The door did open. She nearly fainted. The room swam round her.

Rick stood in the doorway, an ambulance man on either side of him. He had a bandage round his head, and a crutch under each arm. He looked white and ill, but he was at least upright and moving. Julia, managing to push her faintness away, leapt to her feet to help him, then saw the hate and anger on his face: she recoiled, her hand going to her mouth.

And at this moment the lights dimmed.

One of the ambulance boys spoke. He must have been in his early twenties. He said, "What's the matter with your electricity?"

Julia, hardly able to get the words out, whispered, "It does that from time to time. How is he?"

"He insisted on coming home. We wanted to keep him in for another couple of days. But he'll be all right, and I expect with you looking after him he'll get better much quicker. It's not nearly as serious as we thought. He put his back out and pulled a muscle in the right leg. The back's in again, but of course it's painful, though he must keep moving. Get your doctor in tomorrow, and we'd like to see him back in a few days' time. The hospital will be ringing you to make an appointment. Let's give you a chair-lift up the stairs, Mr Burton. Bit dangerous, this electricity, isn't it? Does it often happen?"

"Only occasionally," said Julia. "It'll be on again in a moment. Can I help?"

"I can manage on my own," said Rick.

The ambulance man was looking at the staircase. He said doubtfully, "It really would be better, sir, if – I mean, you don't want to fall again, do you?"

"Thank you, I shall be perfectly all right."

"Well, at least the light's on again." For the electricity had returned, as bright as ever. The two boys left at last, looking doubtfully at Julia. They asked her if she had a neighbour who could give her a hand. She assured them she had, and indeed both Arthur and Mark would come running round if she rang them. When at last the ambulance drove away she poured Rick out a drink and took his arm to help him to the nearest chair. She tried to ignore the look of hate on his face, though it brought the sickness up in her throat. She wondered frantically how she could get him up to his room, for he moved with the greatest difficulty and was obviously in pain, but managed to say in a shaking voice, "Oh darling, what in God's name happened?"

He said in the rough, harsh voice she had heard before, "You didn't quite pull it off, did you?"

Julia said faintly, "What do you mean?"

"I suppose you thought I wouldn't be in any state to notice. I imagine you thought I'd be dead. Pity, isn't it? But I did notice. The rung was sawn almost in half."

She was angry enough to lose some of her terror. She cried out, "That is simply not true. It was cracked. Arthur said so."

"That's what it was meant to look like. That's what most people would think. How fortunate that Arthur left all his tools in the summer-house. Saws and blow-lamps are so useful, aren't they? Did you enjoy your afternoon with your lover? I saw you driving off."

"Rick," said Julia in despair, "what has happened to you?"

For one brief moment a look of bewilderment flashed across his face as if he too did not understand, as if he were shocked by himself. But the next instant the same cruel, malicious expression returned.

He said, "I thought it wouldn't be long before you saw him again. You were together quite a long time, weren't you? I daresay it was he who told you how to break the ladder. What a pity he couldn't do it himself, he might have made a better job of it."

Julia said nothing. It was like the worst kind of nightmare. She could hardly believe it was happening.

He waited, as if for her reply. Then he said, "I'll tell you one thing. You were badly out of luck. I should have broken my back. They said so at the hospital. Indeed they thought I had, and of course then I would never have walked again. Do you remember how we once discussed it? Outside that church, after we'd clinched the deal on Fontenoy. We laughed, didn't we? You would have had to look after me, Julia. I wonder how you would have managed it. I expect you would have walked out. You are not the self-sacrificing martyr type. Fortunately – or is that the right word? – I didn't fall across the ladder. I somehow landed straight on the ground, and all I've done is to put my back out. It's in again now. They've strapped me to make sure. The doctors said I was remarkably lucky." Then he said in savage bitterness, "I wonder if I was, I wonder if I was."

Julia rose to her feet. She felt cold and lightheaded, but perfectly calm. She wondered if this was how he appeared to his whores, the casual pick-ups he met on those solitary promenades. She looked at the man she had been married to for fifteen years. She remembered as if he were a stranger the amusing, witty person with his fine, impressive head of grey hair – it went grey when he was fifteen, he told her – the gentle face, the humour that was sharp without being barbed, who had from the very first concentrated his attention on her, with whom she had fallen instantly in love.

The grey hair was still wavy and thick. The handsome face was in essence the same. But the eyes that had been so loving, were filled with hate, the wincing as he stretched out a hand for his drink was more a wincing away from herself than pain.

She spoke very clearly. At the back of her mind was the thought, "Thank God Alan is away. Oh, thank God, Alan is away". She saw that Sir Richard had taken over, not the Richard who loved her, but the man brought back from the hunting field, who would never walk again. She was no longer Julia, she was Juliet, Juliet who believed him dead and was appalled to see that, though hideously disabled, he was still alive. They were enacting a scene that had taken place over two hundred years ago. It was Richard's hate for Juliet that struck at her: in her husband's fevered eyes she was a wicked, unscrupulous girl who had revenged herself in destruction, and indeed she had destroyed him, only she was not rid of him nor he of her: they were lumbered with each other to the end of their days.

There was only one solution, one hope.

She said, "Rick. We must leave here, and as soon as possible."

"I have not the least intention of leaving!"

"Then I will leave you," said Julia. The words were forced from her, words that she hardly knew she was speaking. "We are living in hate, Rick. It is not our hate. We have been taken over. It all happened two centuries ago, but they are still down there in the hall, Richard and Juliet, fastened into the wall, and while they are there, what happened will never be forgotten. The terrible accident is being replayed between us. It has nothing to do with us. I never tried to kill you. You must know that. I am not capable of such a thing, and I love you, I love you as you once were: if only you could see things clearly you would know that you love me. You talk of my lover – Mark isn't my lover. He never was and never will be. He doesn't even like me particularly except as a helper with his children, only he too was taken over, by this artist, this Monsieur Dieudonné. I went to see him this afternoon simply to reassure him; I think he thought he was drunk or mad. Oh Rick, I am dreadfully sorry this happened, but you must know I'd never try to kill anyone, much less you. It was simply a terrible accident, and you haven't even hurt yourself very badly."

He said sullenly, "I could have broken my back."

"Oh my God," said Julia, and began to cry. She did not want to cry, but she was so tired and it all seemed so hopeless.

He only said, "She cried too. They all thought it was the heartbroken little wife crying because her husband was so badly hurt. But of course it wasn't that at all. She was crying because he was still alive. That is why you are crying. I should be dead, shouldn't I, Julia? But I'm not, my dear. I'm very much alive and have every intention of staying so. Besides, I know now it's not Mark you're in love with. You've fallen in love with a ghost. You no longer want a living man. You're in love with Sir Richard Vierville. That's true, isn't it? Why don't you answer me?"

"Because it's all so absurd," said Julia. She had stopped crying almost instantly. She turned a little away. "Sir Richard has been dead for over two hundred years. Are you going to sue him as co-respondent?"

But she looked through the doorway, where the two portraits faced each other, and the love that consumed her for the dark, fierce-looking man, Rochester as she had once called him, was so all-devouring that she knew that while he was there there could be no peace for her, no happiness, even with the child she was so sure she had conceived, growing within her.

Fontenoy was his and while she was there, she was his also. Perhaps if she could tear the portraits away – But they were tightly screwed in; it would bring the wall down.

She said again, more quietly. "I mean what I say, Rick. If you don't leave Fontenoy, you stay here without me."

He shouted at her with a fury that astounded her, "You can't leave me."

Then she realised how ill he was, he probably had a fever, through sheer shock if nothing else. The words pricked the hair on her head, but she was filled with a kind of weary shame: whatever he said to her, he was in no state to quarrel and she had no right to provoke him. She said as gently as she could, "Look, love. You must be exhausted and in a lot of pain. Let's talk this over tomorrow, and in the meantime we are going somehow to get you up to bed. Then I'll make you something nice to eat and you'll have another drink, and tomorrow we'll both be calmer. It's been quite a day for me too, you know. Shall we try those stairs? If the worst comes to the worst, I could ring Arthur . . ."

He said, "You are leaving me. For a ghost . . ."

She said coaxingly, "No. I didn't mean it. Come on, Rick. What do you want me to do? If you could lean on me . . ."

And she thought with terror of that circular staircase, too wide for him to hold on to both sides, with deep steps and a carpet that left the slippery edges uncovered. And a terrible thought like a snake writhed into her mind: so easy for him to slip, no-one could blame her, he was tall and she just over five foot; he would crash down to the bottom and this time the second shock . . .

"Oh Christ, Oh Christ, what am I thinking? This place stinks of death and I am becoming like Juliet, I am dreaming of murder."

He seemed quite unaware of her thoughts. He said in a snarl, "If I could tear that bastard from the wall and chop him into little bits . . ."

"Well, you can't," said Julia. She was in control of herself again, she was Julia Burton who had to get a badly crippled man in great pain up a wide staircase that at that moment seemed as high as Mount Everest.

Rick said, "He's there now. I know it. That bloody cat knows it."

And indeed Grendel was preening himself and purring: Julia, who loved all animals, hated him passionately and was filled with an urge to kick him out of the room. Suddenly she felt too exhausted to cope with anything more. She said weakly, "Oh never mind the cat. Come on, Rick. I don't know how we'll manage, but we must try. I think if you put your arm round my neck and I held your waist . . ."

It was as if he had lost spirit. He said helplessly, "I should have let those two boys chair me up. I can't manage, Julia. I just can't."

Julia did not answer him immediately. He looked white and frail and very old, but she was aware less of compassion than of resentment and fury. She said calmly enough, "You're quite right. It would be lunatic to try. I don't think I could manage it myself. The staircase is too wide. You stay down here. I'll make up a bed on the couch. We've got the downstairs loo. You'll be perfectly comfortable and tomorrow morning Arthur will be here and we'll get you upstairs quite easily."

He made no further protest. He watched her in silence as she put sheets and blankets on the couch, and when she held out her hand to help him up from the chair, he took it without a word and accepted the crutches from her. Only when she wanted to help him to the lavatory, which now had a neat inside bolt fitted on by Arthur, did he shake his head, saying he could manage on his own. And no, he had had supper in the hospital. She could pour him out another drink, and he was quite capable with the aid of the crutches of crossing the room.

Julia waited for a moment, after opening the lavatory door for him, then said good night. She did not kiss him. With her own evil thoughts still terrifying her, she was appalled at the thought that he would fall, and she stood in the hall for a long time, listening to the trudge, drag, pause of his steps, thankful for the flushing of the lavatory and the sound of the door closing, only beginning to move again at the sounds of someone settling himself on the couch and pulling the bedclothes round him.

She paused between the two portraits. She did not

look at Juliet. She never wanted to see Juliet again. She only gazed at Sir Richard as if it were for the last time. It was simply a portrait that stared forbiddingly up at her, but the love that stirred within her was so strong that it almost broke her. She whispered, "We have to go," and the tears trickled down her cheeks as she said this: she could not have prevented them if Rick had appeared behind her.

And now she was again aware of his presence, and it seemed to her that the child quickened inside her, for all it was still a nothing, perhaps did not even exist.

She whispered again, "We should never have come here, but thank God we did. You have changed us both beyond recognition. You have made us live your lives. For our own salvation we have to go because we have moved out of our world. No-one can live out of his world. We have to get back. I don't know how. I shall never forget you. I don't know how I'll live without you. I can only pray there is a child, your child. But I wish, oh how I wish, you could stop hating. I love you so much, and the hate is foolish now; it is all over."

And she said, "Goodbye, Richard," and went slowly up the stairs.

She did not undress. Sleep was something from another world. She flung the window wide open and sat there, smoking, staring out across the garden. It was a beautiful night with a full moon. She could see the battered remains of the summer-house. Arthur would clear it all up for the new tenants. Arthur was a tidy man who plumped up cushions and always swept up the last speck of dust. The new summer-house, all pretty and rose-ramblered, would be up soon. She knew somehow that the ghosts were laid. The new people would be happy here, such a charming house, so old world, such good condition. Mr Thomas would be happy too. How lovely for him to sell Fontenoy at last to tenants who would stay.

Mrs Purefoy would have to stop crossing herself.

The new tenants would change the place. They may even modernise the lovely staircase and put a gate at the top so that their children did not tumble down. By the time they have finished, it will be a house like other houses, and the lights will no longer dim at five o'clock.

Would there not be a flicker? A faint echo from the past? An outstretched hand, the shadow of a stretcher with its grim burden, a gleam of blood on the floor?

Julia, exhausted beyond sleep and beyond absurdity, visualised Fontenoy turned into a bijou residence, with nice little paintings on the wall, sensible units in the kitchen, pretty chintz curtains in the drawing room, a chute in the kitchen and a three-piece suite.

It might never happen, yet the thought of it hurt her, and she continued to stare out at the moonlit garden: in the far distance she could see the little stream and the strawberry beds.

Here Juliet had stolen out to meet her lover. If it was not Monsieur Dieudonné – what on earth did happen to him? – it would be the groom or some handsome farm-boy or a half-drunken guest who found it amusing to cuckold the dark, handsome husband.

What did she really feel when they brought Sir Richard home on his stretcher, never to walk again yet still alive? And what could she have felt to find him smiling and dead, her slippered feet skidding in the blood still pumping from him, the reddened sword lying on the floor?

She had once loved him, once desired him.

They said her looks went. She married Jack after all.

She had six children, and he beat her. The sixth child killed her.

Poor Juliet.

No, no, no – Yes. Poor Juliet.

And what about Rick? Quiet, charming Rick, with his books that were never in the top rank but which sold well enough. Rick, urbane, hospitable, distinguished-looking, creeping out at nights into his twilight world to sleep with cheap whores, returning to play again the role of gentleman and loving husband.

And Alan – Fontenoy had laid its hands on Alan too: perhaps he too would never be the same again.

Julia, still smoking her life away, it was as if she could not stop, remembered vividly that first sight of Fontenoy, how both she and Rick had felt immediately that this was the house for them. It seemed fated: hands had drawn them in, they had both been overcome with love and desire for this beautiful place that seemed so welcoming, so happy.

She became aware of movement in the garden below. She stubbed out her cigarette and leaned out of the window. To her shocked amazement she saw it was Rick, hobbling along with the utmost difficulty on his crutches, making for the ruined summer-house. She was on the verge of calling out to him, then it struck her that the sudden sound of her voice might make him lose his precarious balance for the path, now littered with fragments of wood, nails and Arthur's bits and pieces, was still treacherous. Normally, he would have tidied up but the accident had taken up all his attention, and he was obviously leaving it till tomorrow. She wondered what on earth Rick could be doing: there he was, dragging himself along – trudge, drag, pause – and in the clear moonlight she could see that his face was white and taut with pain.

At the summer-house he paused. The pillars were still standing, the only part of it left, ready for the new building, and Arthur's box of tools lay beside them. Rick managed to stoop down, clinging onto a pillar, and the movement must have jarred his strapped back atrociously, for he let out a moan of pain.

She could not see what he took out, but it was something fairly large. He hobbled back towards the house. He was still dressed. He had only pretended to go to bed. The brief journey took him nearly a quarter of an hour, and Julia, her hands gripping the window-ledge so tightly that her knuckles were white, saw that twice he nearly fell. But she neither moved nor spoke, and presently heard the French windows close, then steps dragging their way through the drawing-room to the hall.

Then she gave a little cry, jumped to her feet and ran towards the bedroom door, flinging it open.

Rick was standing in the hall between the pictures. It was a blow-torch he was holding in his hand. When Julia, now at the top of the stairs, called out his name, he did not seem to hear her, only held the flame first to Sir Richard Vierville's portrait, then to that of Juliet.

There was a roar of flame as Julia leapt down the stairs. The pictures were made of wood, dried through two centuries, and the paintings were oils. They went up like tinder and, as Julia cleared the last three steps in a great, frantic leap, the flames ran along the wall and caught at the stairs. If she had not made that last jump she would have been immersed in fire.

She did not say a word. She caught at Rick and somehow dragged him back into the drawing-room. She pushed him down on the couch, then rang the fire brigade. She could hear the roaring of the flames, smell the stench of burning oil and blackening wood. She still did not speak. She and Rick looked at each other and then, though he was on the verge of collapse, she pulled him to his feet again and with a strength she did not know she possessed, half-carried him towards the garden. He still held the blow-torch in his hand, and this she seized from him, hurling it away in the direction of the summer-house.

The fire engine arrived within a few minutes. Its headquarters were in Matley Bishop, and there were never many calls, except occasionally in the winter months, due to faulty heaters and over-abundant wood fires. They did not waste time. Two of the men carried Rick who had almost fainted, and brought him round to the front, with Julia walking beside him. The rest of them coped with the fire which they managed to control in half-an-hour. The hall was a blackened ruin with no trace left of the pictures, the beautiful balustrade twisted and ruined and though the bedroom itself had more or less escaped, the door had fallen in and the carpet was stinking with fire and black with soot.

The men, looking as if they had just come from the pithead, did not seem surprised. One of them said, "I always knew this would happen one day. Those pictures were death traps. I see you smoke, Mrs Burton. You must have dropped a fag-end. Oil on wood and dry as dust – What else could you expect? Thank God you were awake. We'll get your husband back to the hospital, and then . . . Do you have someone to put you up for the night? You can't stay here. Apart from anything else, there's no front door left."

"I'll go to the hospital with my husband," said Julia quietly. "It's all right. I'll drive him there. The car's okay."

She talked for a while with the men, apologising for not being able to offer them a cup of tea; they had turned off the gas and electricity. They assured her there was no danger of the fire breaking out again. She was perfectly calm. Indeed, her calmness disturbed them, one of them offered to get her some brandy which she refused for herself, though she took out a glass for Rick. Another said he thought he could climb up into her bedroom and get her coat and handbag. She refused, saying she was not cold and Rick had money in his pocket. She watched them lift Rick into the car, and repeated that she was quite capable of driving.

She watched the fire engine go, then turned to look at Fontenoy, as if for the last time.

The front door, as the man had said, was gone. Fontenoy was wide open to intruders, but the owners had gone for ever. The portraits were in ashes, and the whole wall so blackened and pitted with great shards hanging from it that one would not have known anything had been there. The staircase was a shambles: Arthur would have to use the ladder to get in at the bedroom window. Julia, still feeling as if she were not quite there, too stunned to feel any emotion at all, glanced back at the car to see that Rick had apparently fallen asleep. She walked through the drawing-room. The flames had spread there: it was reasonably intact but filthy beyond measure. She had not until now realised the defiling degradation of a fire. The stench was disgusting so that she coughed and choked, then flung open the garden windows.

Any burglar could walk in and take what he wanted. It did not seem to matter.

She came out into the moonlit garden. From the back Fontenoy looked much as it had always done. She picked up the blow-torch and laid it in the box with Arthur's tools. No-one would examine it for fingerprints. No-one would believe that tenants who had been here only for a few months and who had made the place so beautiful, could deliberately destroy it, much less a man so badly hurt that he could hardly walk.

She looked down at the ladder that still lay where it had fallen. She stared at the broken strut. She could see that it was badly worn: there was no clean cut, it had simply rotted away. She was filled with a wild relief: somewhere in her heart had lain the strange delusion that it was she who had done it, hacked at it, pushed into murder by the beautiful little Juliet so determined to kill her husband. It was simply that the ladder was old, had stood for too long in the damp and cold. Arthur, she hoped, would bring his own ladder with him. Probably Mrs Purefoy would make certain that he did: Mrs Purefoy would never trust anything in Fontenoy.

Mrs Purefoy would be in her element clearing up. She would not have to cross herself any more. The ghosts were gone. She would know that the moment she crossed the threshold. She would doubtless work for the new tenants who would laugh at the silly rumours and stories of what had happened two hundred years ago.

Oddly enough, Mrs Purefoy was perhaps the one person who would understand.

There was a policeman on duty in the front garden. The fire brigade must have summoned him. He saluted Julia, saying, "What rotten luck, Mrs Burton. I'm so sorry. But I'll be here, I'll see nobody gets in."

"It can't be helped," said Julia. "It might have been worse."

He said, "It's a funny house. They say all sorts of things went on here."

"I think," she said, "it'll be all right now. Thank you for coming. Good night."

She looked back at the house once more before she climbed into the car. She whispered, "Goodbye, Richard." Then she clasped her hands across her belly, and smiled. "Reveniam!"

Epilogue

1980

Rick gave her a sleepy smile as she settled herself in the driving seat. She asked if his back was very bad, and he said, yes, it was, but the hospital would give him something for it. He was very white and drawn, but she saw to her bewilderment that he seemed quite unaware of what he had done. She did not remind him. He looked very much as he always did, except that the kind, intellectual face was puckered with pain. When he spoke, it was in his normal voice.

He said, "Of course we should never have left London. I don't know what possessed us, except that you were so taken with the house. Do you know, Julia, I think we could probably get a flat in the same block. We were good tenants after all, and I'm sure in the circumstances the landlords will do everything they can. You could ring them tomorrow. We could go into a hotel in the meantime. I don't suppose you fancy going back to Fontenoy any more than I do."

"*Look, Rick. You must look. It's absolutely gorgeous.*"

And, "*It's lovely, it's perfect, but I want to go away now.*"

"*It's too late.*"

She only said, "Poor Mr Thomas."

"Who's he?"

"Oh you remember. The house agent."

"Well, he'll just have to find new tenants. It shouldn't be too difficult."

"And this time," said Julia, "they'll stay."

They were driving through Matley Bishop, still and silent in the dark. The hospital was a few miles out.

Rick said drowsily, "I don't know what you're talking about." Then in a sudden sharp voice, "My God, the cat!"

Julia laughed. "Don't be silly. Do you think I'd forget poor Grendel? He's in his basket. In the back."

"That's all right then. There's one thing, we've been here such a short time that at least we don't have to say a lot of goodbyes. That young man you worked for. I've forgotten his name."

"Mark. Mark Rossiter. I must ring him tomorrow."

"Of course. My memory must be going. But then it's been quite an evening. I wonder how that fire started."

She looked at him sharply. Surely he was making fun of her. But his face was totally innocent: he plainly meant exactly what he said. Those frantic moments would be eternally forgotten. Then he said, "By the way – I suppose I shouldn't say this in the circumstances – but I have a marvellous idea for a new Marcus Tremayne. Set in a country house. I know it's a bit corny, but it'll be owned by a celebrated explorer who has brought back an African statue with a sinister history. Once this damned back is better, I'll get cracking. Stupid of me to fall off the ladder, wasn't it?"

"Accidents will happen," said Julia, seeing with thankfulness that the hospital was visible in the distance: she did not feel she could continue with this conversation much longer, and suddenly she was desperately tired.

Rick's voice became a little querulous. "We are insured, aren't we?"

"Yes, of course we are."

"I don't know where we're going to stay. I feel a hotel will be all right for a week or two, but I have to work, and I don't know where I'll put my books . . ."

Julia was driving into the hospital grounds. She said as reassuringly as she could, "Look, love, stop worrying. We'll rent a temporary flat or something. Leave it to me. I'll manage."

He said after a pause, "What about Alan?"

Yes, what about Alan? Julia parked outside the hospital. She saw the night porter in the doorway. Alan. Alan, like Mrs Purefoy, had somehow known. But he was young, he would forget, and if something remained at the back of his memory it would be obscured by time. She was happy for Alan. She suspected deep within her that Fontenoy might have destroyed him.

"Alan will be all right," she said.

As the porter came towards them Rick said with a sudden, almost sly smile, "If you really want another baby, Julia, it's okay by me. I think I'd rather like it."

She stared at him. "Do you mean that?"

"Of course I do. We'll have to do something about it, won't we?" He put his hand on hers. It was very cold. "I do love you, you know."

She said, "Yes, I believe you do." And she thought that in her own strange way she loved him too, the kindly man who walked the streets at night, who had nearly killed her and from whose mind was expunged for ever the story of love and hate and terror and death.

All that was left was a house, a pretty, seventeenth century house, with a sword in the shadow, going for thirty thousand pounds.

And a new baby.

Suddenly she smiled. The porter opened the car door. She told him what had happened. He went back to collect a wheelchair. And presently he wheeled Rick into the hospital, and Julia walked beside him.